Chilli Heat

'Nadia, I'm sorry ...' I begin, and then the words stop coming and I just stare at her, thinking about how all this must look.

She waves one hand airily, sits down on a nearby recliner and starts to take off her clothes.

I gesture back at Charles, where he's sitting finishing up his drink. He raises a hand at Nadia.

'Nadia, this is Charles Hoffmann,' I say. 'He's staying in the hotel on business.'

She nods and stands up in her bikini. 'Pleased to meet you,' she mutters, or something like it, and then she holds her nose and leaps forwards into the water without testing the temperature first.

Charles and I exchange looks, our Rajasthan trip in jeopardy unless I can do something to thaw the ice. I've taken enough liberties already; there's no way I can swan off up north with Charles for a couple of days of wild sex and leave Nadia in the lurch. For a while, as Nadia notches up the lengths, he remains where he is, seemingly contemplative, and then he gets up, walks slowly alongside the pool to where I'm standing watching my daughter.

'I was going to try to talk to her,' he says. 'But she looks like a tough cookie. I think I'll fade away into the background, let you guys sort things out.' He takes my hand, discreetly. 'I want you to come with me,' he says. 'I want you. Let's talk in the morning. My flight leaves just after midday so we can play it by ear.'

Chilli Heat
Carrie Williams

BL

Black Lace books contain sexual fantasies.
In real life, always practise safe sex.

First published in 2008 by
Black Lace
Thames Wharf Studios
Rainville Rd
London W6 9HA

Copyright © Carrie Williams 2008

The right of Carrie Williams to be identified as the Author of the Work has been
asserted in accordance with the Copyright, Designs and Patents Act 1988.

A catalogue record for this book is available from the British Library.

www.black-lace-books.com

Typeset by Palimpsest Book Production Limited, Grangemouth, Stirlingshire, FK3 8KG
Printed and bound in Great Britain by CPI Bookmarque, Croydon, CR0 4TD

Distributed in the USA by Macmillan, 175 Fifth Avenue,
New York, NY 10010, USA

ISBN 978 0 352 34178 5

The Random House Group Limited supports The Forest Stewardship Council [FSC],
the leading international forest certification organisation. All our titles that are
printed on Greenpeace approved FSC certified paper carry the FSC logo
Our paper procurement policy can be found at www.rbooks.co.uk/environment

13 5 7 9 10 8 6 4 2

To Nuala, eternal inspiration

Prologue

It's sizzling outside, but the room is cool. I lie on the bed, listening to the regular clunk of the fan as it moves the air around the small space, and I try to sleep, worn out by the night's activities. But before long I hear the squeak of the door on its hinges, and I know that one of them is back. In spite of my exhaustion, a throb starts up between my legs, and I become wet in seconds, spilling out onto the sheet like an overripe fruit. I can't, it seems, get enough. This is like a disease.

I don't – can't – open my eyes, although my ears are keen to the footsteps as they move across the room, to the flap of flip-flops against the stone floor. Who is it? I'm thinking, and of course I hope that it's him. Little has been denied me, save what I want the most – him, to myself, just for a time at least.

A hand grazes my bare hip, alights on it. I start, shudder with longing. The other hand moves between my legs, slides easily between the lips of my sex. Two fingers slip inside; the thumb stays on my clit, brushing at it, quickening, driving me half mad with the tantalising lightness of its caress. I arch my back as if in greeting, in welcome, in salutation. Already I can feel my climax building, threatening to overwhelm me.

I'm stretched back over the bed, head over the side of it, hair trailing down to the floor, displayed like an offering. Unable, it seems, to act, to reciprocate, only to take, give myself over, abandon myself to this force . . . And then a mouth closes around one of my nipples, and teeth take the soft flesh and clamp down, till I cry out in surprise and joy. My eyes flash open, and I blink several times in the early afternoon sunlight filtering through the gauze curtains. Then I watch as he sits up and back on his haunches, takes his cock in his hand and proffers it to me like a gift. I smile, delirious, as he comes towards me; it's now, only now, that I can react, reaching down and peeling myself open for him.

And then suddenly he's inside, and pleasure is coursing through me like the most powerful drug imaginable. But as I twist my head from side to side, wailing in ecstasy, I catch sight of her standing over by the door, watching us, a curious half-smile on her face. A half-smile of victory – that's what I know it to be. And suddenly I understand, without any doubt, that I'll never have him to myself.

She peels off her bikini top and, with her hand down her bottoms, rubbing at her snatch, she walks towards us, eyes strangely bright, greedy for us.

1

I stir as we begin our approach to Mumbai, when the captain comes over the Tannoy to announce that the seatbelt sign is about to come on. I turn my face to the window and see nothing at first beyond my own reflection, my face still scrunched up and my hair mussed from sleep. Then I lean nearer to the window. Though we can't be that close to the city yet, lights glimmer far below us, in isolated clusters, and I feel my excitement mount.

I turn to my companion, and for a moment I feel surprise as well as a degree of disappointment, before it all comes back to me. I hadn't planned to bring my mum along with me on my gap year, but when my best friend Katie dropped out at short notice and Mum suggested taking her place, I didn't have an excuse ready. And besides, India is not the type of place an eighteen-year-old girl wants to travel around alone. With no other likely candidates presenting themselves, I had the stark choice between bringing my mum and cancelling the trip altogether. This trip I've been planning, saving for, dreaming about for so long. No, not coming to India was out of the question.

My mum's name is Valerie, and she's fine, she really is. Just not my ideal travelling companion. She's led a pretty staid life, after marrying young and starting a family. Since then she's been the dutiful doctor's wife, never straying far from my father's side, bringing up my brothers and me, uncomplaining in her self-sacrifice. Or perhaps she never saw it as a sacrifice.

Perhaps we girls just automatically expect more of our lives these days.

So it came as a real shock when Mum and Dad split up. There was no drama, no fighting or scenes – just an announcement, seemingly out of the blue, that they were going their own ways. Neither of them, to my knowledge, had had an affair, and throughout the whole divorce proceedings and afterwards they have remained on speaking terms. It would appear that they simply fell out of love. Or perhaps they hadn't been in love for a long time, and with me, the youngest, preparing to fly the nest, had admitted to one another that there was nothing to hold them together any longer.

Mum has never really travelled, except for our annual holidays in Tenerife or Spain, which don't count. And even when we were abroad, she was content to lie and fry by the pool with the latest Dick Francis novel in her hand. Dad went back to India several times over the 25 years of their marriage, mainly to visit his family there, but she never accompanied him, said she 'didn't fancy it'. Which made it all the more surprising that she offered to come along with me on this trip, all the more surprising that she's sitting next to me now.

I smile at her, a little too cheerily perhaps. 'Not getting cold feet?' I say.

She laughs. 'No chance,' she says. 'Are you?'

I shake my head and look quickly back out of the window.

It's getting late, and Mum insists on splashing out on a taxi into the centre. She's not risking one of the lethal-looking buses, she says; she saw one of the drivers swigging something from a hip flask. I let her, telling myself there'll be plenty of time for roughing it. I've booked us a hotel to ease us into our stay, but a budget one at that: the Aqua on Marine Drive. The taxi driver knows it and we're there within about twenty minutes, all our attempts at conversation en route drowned out by the *bhangra* that he turns up loud and sings along to. He's tone deaf, and soon I feel a headache coming on.

As we step into the hotel foyer, out of the light spray blowing in off the Arabian Sea, I'm satisfied with my choice. But when I get close to the reception desk, mouth already open to speak, I feel a tug at the sleeve of my jacket.

'Nadia, we are *not* staying here,' says Mum, and I turn to see her eyes full of threat. She's serious. I look around again: it's not that bad, all things considered. A little institutional, certainly – it looks like it might have been converted from an old hospital. And very basically furnished. But I don't see any cockroaches, or not yet. For the price, it seems just fine. And we are only staying two or three nights, while we get our bearings and formulate an itinerary.

Before I can argue back, however, Mum has turned on her heels and is disappearing out of the door. I run after her, cursing Katie and her stupid glandular fever. It wasn't meant to be like this. I catch up with Mum just as she's stepping from the pavement and hailing a taxi.

2

I should have asked at the hotel before hailing that damn taxi. Then I would have known there were some five-stars within just a few minutes' walk of the dreaded Hotel Aqua. As it was I felt a bit of a fool jumping into a taxi only to climb straight back out, with the driver laughing at me, convinced I was deranged. But I was in such a huff with my daughter. I know this is her trip, in many ways, and that I am only a fellow passenger – perhaps a nanny, of sorts, or maybe even a body-guard – but sometimes she just goes too far. There was no way I was going to stay in that cesspit of a hotel she'd earmarked for us. Something she'd found on the internet, no doubt.

We end up at the Intercontinental ten doors down, which is much more my cup of tea, although the prices are a little eye-opening. Still, Ravi was more than generous when it came to the terms of our divorce, and if I bung it on my credit card I won't have to think about it for a while. And it has been a long trip. I could do with a good night's sleep on a comfortable bed.

But before that, it's time for a nightcap. Nadia and I leave the staff to take care of our bags and head straight to the Czar vodka lounge, where I offer to buy her a cocktail. Anything to take that frown off her face. I can tell, however, as we enter, that coming here is causing her mood to deteriorate further still. She's a grungy kid, into Courtney Love and strange indie films and God knows what else, and the ornate drapes and live piano music just aren't her scene. And sure enough, she's barely over the threshold before she cries off with a headache, blaming the loud music in the cab.

I settle on one of the squashy seats and peruse the scene. The place is not so busy. Aside from the handsome young waiters in their smart uniforms, I can make out only a handful of other guests: two white couples, both sitting silently over tall iced glasses and little bowls of nibbles, and a solitary man hidden away behind a newspaper. I note his well-polished shoes and the gold glinting on his fingers; he's a businessman here alone, I decide.

All at once one of the waiters is inclining towards me, asking what I'd like to drink, and I smile and say that I could murder a martini. It feels strange, being here in a bar all by myself. I can't think of the last time I might have done such a thing. I'm not sure if I ever have done such a thing. But it also feels good. There a kind of fizzing in my veins, a pleasurable buzzing in my head. I think I might stay here a while.

My drink arrives and, as I sip it and let the alcohol relax me, I think of Ravi and of how surprised, perhaps even shocked, he'd be to see me somewhere like this, alone. I wonder what he's doing right now. He's probably not long home from work – as a surgeon in casualty his hours have always been long. Perhaps he's unwinding, as he often did, over a glass of whisky, as he waited for me to serve dinner. Only I won't be serving dinner tonight, of course. I'm halfway around the world, and no longer his wife. I still have trouble getting my head round that one: that I'm no longer Ravi's wife. That I'm no longer anyone's wife. It was my role for so long, my raison d'être. Sure, it was I who decided I didn't want to go on in that role, but it doesn't mean I don't miss it, the security of it, the reassurance of having a label, even if it wasn't a very exciting one.

I'm on my second martini, and feeling more than a little tipsy – I know I'm quite drunk because I'm holding up my glass and making a silent toast to Ravi and our 25 years of marriage – when the man behind the newspaper folds it, tucks it under his arm, and, rising to his feet, heads towards me. His eyes are trained on me, and for a moment his direct gaze leads me to think that I must know him. I study his salt-and-pepper hair, neatly cropped, and his pale-blue eyes, and I decide that no, I don't know him, but I'd like to.

He evidently feels the same, for he stops in front of me and waves an expensively clad arm towards the empty seat beside me. 'Would you mind?' he says, and I think I hear New York in his voice, although I'm not well travelled and my scant knowledge of accents is derived only from TV shows.

'Not at all. Please, help yourself.' There's an assurance in my voice that comes more from the alcohol than from any self-confidence. It's a long time since a man has paid me any attention, and although I can't say I'm not enjoying it, I've forgotten how to act. Inside, I feel like a schoolgirl again.

'Charles,' he says, extending a hand. I shake it, and his grasp is firm, authoritative. It tells of a man who knows what he wants. And at this moment, it looks like what he wants might be me. I feel a pulse shoot up inside me. He's undeniably attractive – what you might call suave, debonair. His clothes are well cut and elegant, and he smells of some exotic, faintly spicy, but manly fragrance. What catches my attention most of all, however, is his skin: for a man who must be in his mid-fifties, it has remarkable radiance and elasticity. I wouldn't swear on it, but I'd guess he is no stranger to professional facials.

'I'm Valerie,' I manage at last.

'Ah, a Brit,' he says. 'And what brings you to Mumbai, Valerie?'

'I wanted a change of scene,' I say. I don't know why I don't tell him I'm travelling with my teenage daughter, but I quite like the sense of mystery that being vague brings.

It seems to work, for a light comes on in those piercing blue eyes. 'A change of scene,' he says with a wry smile. 'And what line of work are you in, Val? You don't mind if I call you Val?'

I shake my head vehemently. In fact, I've always hated my name being shortened to Val and refused to answer to it, but I don't want to discourage the intimacy this man is trying to create. Like I said, it's a long time since I've been paid any attention of this kind and I'm not going to blow it.

'I'm in fashion,' I say, glancing coolly across the room, as if it's the most normal thing in the world, as if it's almost tedious for me to have to talk about it, so hardened am I to the glamour of it all. I feel a stab of guilt at lying, at temporarily disowning my family, and I say to myself that I'm not ashamed of having been a housewife for more than two decades. It's just that I don't think the phrase 'housewife' will light Charles's fire. 'Designer', yes; 'divorcee', perhaps – it at least denotes a woman with some kind of past. But 'housewife', no.

'Say,' he says, shooting a glance at his watch: a Rolex, I notice. 'You know, there's a much nicer bar upstairs, if you fancied another drink?' I must look a little dubious, for he quickly follows it up with, 'Unless you're too tired, that is?'

'No, no,' I say quickly. 'Only I've literally just stepped off the plane. I'd like to pop back to my room to freshen up, if that's OK?'

'Sure.' He smiles. 'I'll meet you in there in, say, fifteen minutes?'

'Fine,' I say, and I head for the lift. As I wait for its arrival, I mentally rifle through the lingerie I've brought with me, panicking that I don't have anything suitable for such an occasion. The knickers I'm wearing, I realise now, are soaked through.

9

3

I'm just dozing off when I hear the card pass through the swipe and the door open. Mum tiptoes in, but I don't move. Although part of me is grateful for the good bed and the powerful air con after the long flight from London, I'm still mad at her for wimping out at the Hotel Aqua. If she thinks that's bad, she's going to have a shock when she sees some of the places I've highlighted in my copy of *Lonely Planet*. She's come along on the condition that this is my trip, but already it seems she's hijacking it, calling the shots. Perhaps she thinks it doesn't matter to me, when it's her money she's shelling out. But it does. I'm half Indian, after all, and I came here to see the real India, not the tourist version.

In the soundproofed quiet of the room, it sounds almost as if she's panting, and I wonder if she's been running, and if so, why? I continue to listen, holding my breath, and I hear her begin to mutter: 'Bloody hell ... damn ... sure it was ... shit ... this will have to do.'

Groaning as if in sleep, I roll over in the duvet and half open one eye. Mum is on her hands and knees on the floor, bent over her suitcase, holding up something for inspection in front of her. It's a bra, I realise as I open my other eye for a clearer view. And then I see her stand up, strip off her slacks and sweater followed by her undies, and put on a fresh bra and pants. I frown: why on earth is she changing into new clothes, rather than her nightdress? What is she playing at?

In the semi-darkness I see her step up to the full-length

mirror, look herself up and down in her underwear, place her hand on her belly and pull a little face. I feel a pinch of guilt, spying on her like this, and also a touch of sadness, seeing how her body seems to embarrass her. It's not a bad body at all, that's the thing. She's never made the most of herself; her clothes have tended to the frumpy, making her look older and more shapeless than she is. But for a 45-year-old woman, she's doing good. It's nothing a sharper haircut and more tailored clothes and a few sessions of Pilates wouldn't fix. But listen to me! Who am I to talk, with my oversize combat trousers and manly boots? I am hardly the height of femininity and chic!

She's holding up her hair now, and pouting at herself in the mirror, then trying out different smiles, and it makes me want to cry to see her. For whose benefit is all this? I wonder. I wish she'd just stop messing around and come to bed. This is driving me nuts.

I'm just about to sit up and tell her as much when she seems to come to a decision. Turning around she takes her one dress – a flowery affair she bought from M&S just before we left – and slips into it. Her sandals are next, and then she grabs the room swipe, opens the door and, before I can say anything, is gone.

I sit up and look after her. Where in God's name has she gone, this late and in a city in which she doesn't know a soul? I debate inwardly whether to go after her, but reason that she's a woman in her 40s and doesn't need her daughter to watch over her. But suddenly I'm wide awake, and I doubt I'll find sleep until I know she's back and tucked up in bed.

4

I pause in the doorway of the bar, sure he'll be able to see my hands trembling, see my pulse throbbing in my throat. The booze is wearing off, and I wish I'd helped myself to a little something from our minibar before leaving the bedroom to steady the nerves. But I didn't want to disturb Nadia, didn't want her to know what I was doing. Perhaps I should have left her a note – she'll worry if she wakes up and I'm not there. But if I go back now I'm worried the fear will overwhelm me and I won't come back again.

Charles turns on his bar stool, looks expectantly towards the door, and raises a hand in salute. I walk over to him, as slowly as I can, holding in my tummy. If I'd had my whole wardrobe at my disposal, I'd have come up with something more flattering than this sundress, but I didn't pack for evenings in glam bars. And this is one glam bar, with its stunning glass dome. I feel like I'm in a film.

Charles rises to meet me, a cigar wedged in the corner of his mouth.

'I'm sorry I took so long,' I say, and I wince as I think of myself standing in front of the mirror in my bra and knickers, jiggling my spare flesh in disgust. Not having deviated from the same partner in 25 years made me, I realised as I studied my reflection, largely oblivious to the way time was leaving its traces on my body. And Ravi was so fond of his creamy curries, the calories just piled on over the years.

But I force myself to stop thinking about all that as I return

Charles's frank gaze. This man is interested in me; either that, or he's using me to kill time, or to take the edge off his loneliness, at least for an hour or two. I doubt it, though: I may have been out of the loop for a quarter-century, but I remember the look in a man's eyes when he wants you. A lot of men wanted me, before Ravi. Some of them had me, but then Ravi stole my heart and my days of sexual conquest were over. Until now, perhaps.

I return Charles's gaze. Remembering the antics of my late teens has dissolved my nervousness, made me feel brazen, and suddenly I don't want a drink, don't want to dull my feelings with alcohol. The pants I've just put on are already sodden, and inside them my sex is throbbing a little, beating like a little heart. It's something I haven't felt in so long, I can barely contain myself.

'What'll it be?' says Charles, not taking his eyes from mine. On his lips there's a light but ironic smile, as if he knows full well what's going on in my knickers, what thoughts are playing themselves out in my mind. It's on the tip of my tongue to tell him to forget the drink, to remind him that we are adults and don't need to go through this charade, but he's already turning to the barman, ordering himself another whisky sour.

'And for my companion . . .'

'I'll have another martini,' I say and look round for a discreet corner in which we can tuck ourselves. But Charles is quickly at my shoulder.

'How about outside?' he says, pointing. I nod and let him lead the way, and he takes me out onto an open-air terrace with heart-stopping views over the ocean.

'Wow,' I say, and then I remember I'm supposed to be a worldly, well-travelled fashion designer. 'Is this table OK for you?' I ask, feigning an urbane disinterest.

He nods and sits down on one of the deep white sofas,

patting the space next to him to indicate where he wants me to sit. A waiter appears beside us with our drinks on a tray. We say nothing as he carries out the ritual of placing the coasters on the table, standing the drinks on top of them, laying out the nibbles and lastly putting down the bill in its sleek black-leather folder. All the while I am aware of Charles's eyes on me, and I look studiously out to sea, as if lost in my own thoughts, as if oblivious to the desire of this attractive American.

'Cheers,' he says at last, and I lean forwards, pick up my glass and raise it to him. We drink, holding each other's gaze, and then Charles sits back, looks at me appraisingly.

'So, you're in fashion, you say?'

I nod, wanting to change the subject. I hate lies, the way they spawn still more lies, once you've set the chain in motion. I wish I'd simply stuck to the truth – that I'm a tourist. But I was afraid of boring him, by not having a defined role in life, beyond that of mother, of course.

'And you?' I say to change the subject.

'Software,' he says. 'The Indians are leading the field, in many ways, so I decided to ride on their coat-tails, as it were. I started my own business a couple of years back, after leaving Microsoft.'

I nod again, but I couldn't be less interested. The martini is making me woozy, and I've suddenly remembered that I'll be prey to the effects of jetlag too. If I don't act quickly, I'll find myself passing out before we've made it back to his room. I lean forwards, affording Charles an ample view of my cleavage, take the olive from my glass and jab at it with my tongue, not taking my eyes from him.

That's all it takes. A moment later I feel his foot against my calf under the table, and I realise that he's slipped his shoe off. His foot advances in a sock so soft it must be made of cashmere, and I hold my breath as it travels over my bare flesh from my knee to my inner thigh. Then he presses it against my sex, and as he does so he gasps: he must have felt how wet and ready I am for him. I'm swooning back on the sofa now, my sex pulsing as he inches his foot over and, with bent toes, pulls back the fabric of my knickers. I look wildly around, checking that nobody is looking, but we are alone on the terrace now, cooled by the winds coming in off the Arabian Sea.

Charles has leant forwards now, and is delving under my skirt. Pulling back his leg, he replaces his foot with his hand, then parts my folds with his thumb and index finger, pinning them back like a butterfly's wings, and shoots his remaining three fingers inside me. He lets out a moan as I open up and swallow him like a mouth. It's been so long since I've wanted something this much, I feel like I might go out of my mind with it.

Looking up to check that we are still alone, Charles moans and saws his hand in and out of me. Already I can feel the intimations of my climax, like water rising. I tilt my head back, and he leans forwards and covers my exposed neck with kisses. I am grateful to him for that: overwhelmed by my appetite, I had forgotten the social niceties. To have carried out these acts on each other's bodies without any display of tenderness would have left us feeling cheap, and perhaps a little sordid, after-wards.

I clutch his shoulder with one hand, raise my head to kiss him on the mouth, and then he leans back a little and I watch as he unzips the trousers of his elegant suit and releases himself. Now he's tugging at his cock, eyes half closed, more moans escaping from his lips, the rhythm of his left hand obeying that of his right one still inside me. It's at this moment that we both lose it and, as my orgasm floods up and engulfs me, he increases the pace. Through the contractions inside me

I feel the warm jelly of him rain down on me, on my thighs and my pussy. Then he falls forwards on to me, where I lie on the sofa. He's laughing a little, and I laugh too. He looks down at my face and says, 'Shall we go somewhere a little more private?'

We're in his room – of course, we couldn't go back to mine, and in fact I decided to disclose to him in the lift that I'm travelling with my daughter. I've only booked us in for tonight, but if we end up staying longer, and if Charles is staying on too, my little factual omissions will definitely come back to haunt me.

He doesn't say much – merely remarks that I'm lucky to have a good relationship with my child. He confesses that he barely sees his own, but I sense with that comment he considers that particular conversation closed. In any case, the lift doors are opening, saving him from any prying that I might have been tempted to indulge in, and in a moment he's swiping his card and pushing open the door, standing back to gesture me in ahead of him.

'What a gent,' I say with a smile, and then I gaze around his corner suite, which makes our room look positively humdrum. It is not only up a few degrees in luxury, but has a curved wall and incredible views over the ocean. Not that Charles must spend much time appreciating the scenery – a laptop is open on the marble desktop, and in the ashtray beside it I see a half-smoked cigar. Happily, Charles doesn't seem to notice how impressed I am by it all, striding over to the sideboard to fill a glass for me. He turns back to hand me a large gin and tonic.

'Bath?' he says, and when I smile and nod, he invites me to sit down again while he calls his butler.

Ten minutes later, the bath drawn, the butler gone, my

g and t finished, Charles leads me into the bathroom, all black marble with cream striations, where a deep tub awaits me, the surface of the water strewn with rose petals. It's all I can do not to laugh – where, a couple of hours ago, my daughter was trying to check us into a dingy hostel, now I find myself in the bathroom of some swanky suite, in the company of a man so pointlessly rich it makes my head spin.

Charles has stepped up behind me, is nuzzling my nape with his mouth as he slips my sundress off my shoulders, taking playful little nips of my skin. As my dress falls away from me, I turn, wrap my arms around his neck and pull his face towards mine. At once his hands move down to my breasts, cup them, palpate them. At first he's gentle, but as I feel his need rising, the crush of his groin against me, he intensifies his grip, and with his thumbs he works at the buds in the centre of my nipples, alternately pressing and then flicking at them. I strain towards him in response, both pushing my pussy to meet the bulge of his cock through his trousers and taking a good handful of his buttock, pulling him towards me. It's so long since I've felt an urgency of this kind.

He drops to his knees and slides my knickers down over my hips at the same time, then brings his face to my pussy. I sit back on the rim of the bath for support, opening myself to him, willing him in. For a moment his tongue flicks at my clitoris, tantalising, then he clutches my hips with both hands and shoots his tongue inside me without hesitation. I let out an immense moan of pleasure, and my whole body goes rigid with shock. I look down and my knuckles are white where I'm clutching the edge of the bath so hard.

But Charles has other plans for me. Taking his mouth away from me, he turns me around and bends me over the bathtub, so that I'm down on my knees too, then prises my cheeks apart with his strong hands. For a moment I feel the bulb of his cock snuffling at me, around my back passage and then further forwards, around my pussy lips and my clitoris. I turn my head to one side, towards the wall at the foot of the bath, which is covered by a vast floor-to-ceiling mirror that's reflecting our antics back at us in all their Technicolor glory. My instinct is to wince, to grimace at my rampant double in embarrassment: what do you think you're doing, Valerie Kumar? is the first thought that flits through my mind. But then I notice the glitter in my eyes, the healthy pinkness and sheen to my skin, the 'O' of my mouth as I ready myself to take Charles inside me, and I think that I haven't looked so good, so young, so alive in years.

And then suddenly, as if he can't hold back any longer, he's driving himself inside, yelling out as he does so, as if he'll come again any minute. I close my eyes and feel my hands grasp at the water, helplessly, as if doing so will anchor me to some kind of reality, but all I catch are handfuls of petals, velvety to my touch, blood red. Then Charles reaches round me with one hand and jiggles my clitoris with a sure and sturdy finger, not letting up even as I beg him to stop, afraid that the orgasm I feel building up is going to tear me asunder. I'm surprised that I have the presence of mind, when it hits me, to reach back through my legs and give his balls a firm squeeze, bringing on a climax that both coincides with mine and equals it in its shattering force.

For a moment we both lay draped over the side of the bath, hands trailing in the water, his on mine. In my ear his breath is loud, ragged; on my neck I feel its heat. His chest hair feels oddly comforting against my back. For a moment I think guiltily of Ravi, wonder again what he's doing tonight. But then I force myself to cast him from my mind: I haven't enjoyed myself this much in years, decades even, and that was partly down to Ravi's failures. I'm not going to let him intrude on this incredible evening, and whatever else it has in store.

When Charles finally stirs and stands up, he scoops me up in his arms – a bit like a bride it occurs to me – and lowers me into the bath. He asks me if I'm OK for a drink, and I say I'd love another g and t. Then I lie back in the water and look down at my body, amazed at the pleasures it has afforded me after all this time.

5

I wake up, and it's a shock to see that Mum's bed hasn't been slept in. I sit up, panic rising in my chest, and then I remember her behaviour of last night, and I know it would be foolish to call down to reception and report her missing. She's somewhere in the hotel, I tell myself; I just hope she knows what she's doing. She's far from worldly wise.

I've slept quite late and, not wishing to miss Mum when she returns, I order a cooked room-service breakfast: she can bloody well foot the bill after all she's put me through, after leaving me alone without any kind of note as to where she might be and when she'll be back. If I hadn't spied on her little performance when she came back to the room, or the shenanigans with the underwear, I'd be more concerned than I am. As it is, I have more than an inkling of what she's up to.

While I wait for my food to arrive, I bathe and dress, wondering what the day ahead will bring. We're not scheduled to stay in Mumbai for long, just a night or two while plotting our next move, so Mum and I ought to get out and see the sights – if she's in any fit state when she does roll in. I've heard so much about this extraordinary place: the designer shopping malls and the chaotic bazaars; the stalls selling *bhelpuri* on Chowpatty Beach; the cages of the red-light district; and the red double-deckers that go nowhere fast, stuck in the infamous traffic jams.

Over my breakfast and several cups of strong coffee, I flip open my notebook-cum-diary that I bought especially for my trip. In it are lists and lists of things I want to see and do, divided by city and/or region. OK, I admit it – I'm fairly anal where things like this are concerned. But this trip has been the focus of all my energies for so long, I'm afraid of not making the best of it, of bypassing things and then regretting it later.

I take a pen from the bureau and put a little asterisk by the sights I consider a priority and the secondary attractions I think I might be able to fit in today. I don't even begin to consider what Mum might like to do; as far as I'm concerned, if she's not happy, she can go her own way. Already I'm astonished by her selfishness, by the way she seems to have claimed this trip as her own before it's begun.

Chewing the end of my pen, I ponder on this for a moment, wondering if I ought to be more lenient on her given the sacrifices she's made for us over the years. She's entitled to let her hair down now she's got the chance, isn't she? But even as I tell myself this I feel the niggles worming their way back into my thoughts. If I'd pulled the stunt she's pulled, she'd be furious with me. And there's no way I'd vanish like this without letting her know where I was, because I know how lost she'd feel in a city she doesn't know, a country she doesn't know, amidst strangers.

At last I get up, thrust my notebook into my little leather backpack – a present from Dad – and head out of the room. If Mum thinks I'm going to spend any more of this precious, longed-for trip waiting around for her, she's mistaken.

Within five minutes, I'm caught in the thick of Mumbai's notorious traffic, terrified but exhilarated. From the back of the rickshaw I caught on Marine Drive, I watch astounded as old London Routemaster buses crawl around corners, so overloaded that the back step almost scrapes along the ground, to the general unconcern of the passengers, who merely cling on and continue to read their newspapers. Cars and decorated trucks honk their horns to no avail, creating a merciless cacophony, and all the while scooters and bicycles dart between, often transporting not two but three or sometimes even four people – Mum, Dad and a couple of kids.

Before too long, I realise the pointlessness of sitting here motionless, and I pay my driver, adding a tip that I immediately know is way over the odds by the look on his face. Then I walk the short distance to the Gateway of India. I find the colonial landmark a seething mass of humanity: there to cater to all the camera-wielding tourists are snake charmers, balloon sellers and touts of all kinds, giving the place the atmosphere of a bazaar. I take a few photos with my new digital camera – another present from Dad – then I walk up to the Chhatrapati Shivaji Maharaj Museum, a gorgeous domed building with British-Gothic overtones. For a couple of hours I lose myself there, amidst the centuries-old statues of oriental gods, the exquisite miniature paintings, many of them showing erotic scenes, and the stunning decorative objects in jade, ivory and more, from daggers to jewel boxes. Afterwards, I walk up to Chhatrapati Shivaji Terminus, another Gothic building, more reminiscent of a cathedral or a palace than a station. I've no plans to catch a train here, but for an hour or so I just wander around, soaking up the atmosphere, looking at the carvings of monkeys, lions, peacocks and gargoyles.

My next plan is a spot of retail therapy – a budget version as befits a student, of course, at the Bombay Store emporium or the indoor Crawford Market. But I suddenly realise how tired I am, and thirsty, so I dig out my notebook and find an address within walking distance, back towards the hotel, where I can chill out for a while. The Mocha Bar sounds very European, but when I get there I find it all decked out in an Arabian style. I settle gratefully on one of the big floor cushions and order a panini and a Jamaican Blue Mountain coffee to revive me, then look round at the trendy clientele smoking hookah pipes and listening to the world music soundtrack. I could, I think, be anywhere in the world, but it doesn't matter. I know already that it will be hard to get up and leave.

It's not long afterwards, as I'm supping my coffee and flipping through my notebook for further inspiration, that I become aware of eyes on me. And sure enough, when I glance up, there's a good-looking guy watching me from across the room. As our eyes meet, he looks down at his magazine, but then he looks right back up and, as if having come to a decision, closes it, stands up and starts walking over to me.

I watch him as he moves: he's tall and athletic and, like me, doesn't look 'properly' Indian, such is the milky-coffee hue of his complexion. I imagine he's half and half, like me, and wonder if he too finds it disorientating sometimes – not so much due to how I feel about it myself, but to how other people often react. However, in his Diesel jeans and crisp white shirt, worn unbuttoned at the neck, he looks perfectly at ease with himself and at home in his skin.

'Manju,' he says as he comes to a halt by my table, holding out one hand. As I shake it he asks, 'Mind if I sit down?'

'Not at all,' I say.

'You're not waiting for anybody, then?' His accent is Indian but his English impeccable.

I shake my head.

He smiles, holds up a hand to gesture to the waiter. 'Another coffee?' he says to me as the latter arrives.

'Sure, thanks.'

'You here on holiday?'

'Yes, I arrived last night. I'm just getting my bearings.'

He laughs. 'It'll take you a while. Mumbai is one big mind-fuck.'

'I've heard. Probably not the best place to start, huh?'

'Well, there's certainly nowhere else like it. Futuristic five-star restaurants owned by millionaire cricketers, squalid slums ... it's a confusing place. You from London?'

'Sheffield.'

'Ah yes, I know it. Not first hand, but I have friends with relatives there.'

'It has contradictions, like anywhere.'

'Of course. But somehow, in Mumbai, they've become more extreme and mindblowing than anywhere else.' He steals a glance at his watch. 'Listen, what are you doing now? Fancy a spin?'

I look at my own watch. I really should be getting back to the hotel, to find out if Mum's resurfaced, but I know even as I think it that I won't. Why sabotage my chance at a person-alised tour of the city with this handsome, eloquent stranger after what she did last night? Mum can wait.

Outside, I'm surprised when Manju walks over to a powerful-looking motorbike and swings a leg over. From astride it he smiles back at me, patting the space behind him. 'Well, what are you waiting for?' he says.

'A helmet?' I suggest.

He laughs and shakes his head. 'Sorry.'

For a moment I consider declining the offer: the roads here are mad. But then I imagine myself walking back to my hotel, having a row with Mum, sulking for a bit and then making up in time to go out and find somewhere to eat, and I think to hell with it and place myself in the hands of the gods, whichever gods they may be.

We take off into the road, weaving our way through what would be lines of traffic in most other places but are a higgledy-piggledy mass of honking, fume-belching vehicles here. I'm grimacing as I cling to Manju's back, knowing that my life really is at stake here. Yet at the same time I feel a strange thrill inside, which I quickly realise is the thrill of being alive. Let him take me where he will. If I didn't come to India for adventure, then why am I here?

After a whirlwind, nerve-jangling tour of the city, dodging the ubiquitous 1950s-style black-and-yellow taxis, he takes me down to Colaba and then back up to Chowpatty Beach via the Eros Cinema near Churchgate, a beautiful art deco picture house with a rocket-shaped facade. Over nachos at the Cream Centre at Chowpatty, followed by a stroll on the sand, he tells me he is a film agent and asks me if I have seen many Bollywood films. I have to confess to him that I haven't, explaining that my father isn't really into movies so never took us to see Indian cinema or had any Indian videos in the house – he was always too busy working.

'You're missing out,' says Manju. He looks at me. 'Perhaps I should take you to see one or two. How long are you here for?'

I shrug. 'I'm not sure,' I say, 'but only a day or two, I think.'

'Shame. You can't be persuaded otherwise?'

I gaze at him. I've realised, by now, that he's not my type, in spite of his looks. There's definitely no frisson between us. But it's nice to have a friend already, and it would be wonderful to stay on for a while and get to know this fascinating city through a native's eyes.

Taking my silence for a 'no', he shrugs in turn, looks out over the water. 'Never mind,' he says. 'You have your plans. Let's just make the best of your short time here. Come.' He stands up and gestures back towards where his bike is parked. 'There are some people I'd like you to meet.'

* * *

We're in Seijo and the Soul Dish, a space-age bar in an office block in a place called Bandra West. After admiring the manga artwork on the walls, I'm talking – or rather shouting over the ambient house music – to Manju's friend Ajit, who has been introduced to me as a 'foreigners co-ordinator'. Without too much preamble, Ajit asks me if I've ever done any acting or modelling work, but when I say 'no,' he tells me it doesn't matter, that girls with looks like mine don't need any experience. I explain to him that I'm only staying in Mumbai another day or two, that I have plans, but he says that's unimportant too, that the extra money will come in handy for my travels. And of course, if I ever did return to Mumbai, having already done some work as an extra will stand me in good stead for more.

After my initial misgivings, my suspicions that he is spinning me a line, I warm to the idea. It might not be stardom – which is not something that has ever attracted me in any case – but perhaps a little of the Bollywood glamour will rub off on me for a while. And even if it doesn't, it'll be something interesting to tell my new friends about when I start uni next year, something a little out of the ordinary.

Just as we're discussing the finer details – there's a shoot tomorrow, not for a movie but for a soap opera, requiring extras for an airport scene – there's a sort of vibration in the air, as if something has materialised from another planet or sphere, and as Manju says, 'Nadia, meet my friend Asha,' I turn and am confronted by the loveliest of visions: a stunning Indian girl wearing the skinniest of skinny jeans and a fabulous halterneck top made of bejewelled sari material. The top leaves little to the imagination, and I realise what I haven't yet thought in any conscious way: that most women in Mumbai seem to be incredibly conservative in the way they dress, tending to choose blouses and trousers over skirts or dresses.

On the contrary, Asha's shoulders are bare and, in the neon light of the bar, so peachy in texture that they almost beg to be bitten into. In fact, Asha as a whole seems to glow from within, her skin is so luminous, of a softness that seems unreal, otherworldly. My breath catches in my throat as our eyes meet and she bestows a smile on me.

'Wonderful to meet you, Nadia,' she says, her voice husky and surprisingly deep. She touches my arm as she speaks, very lightly and briefly, and it's as if a rare butterfly has flown past and grazed my skin. Or as if I've been kissed by something from another dimension, something that I can't see. A shiver runs through me; one so violent that I think Asha must feel it. But if she does, she doesn't let on, turning instead to Manju and Ajit.

'Karishma and I,' she says, gesturing back to a darkened corner of the room, 'were just going to make a move to Juhu Beach. There's a private party at the J49 bar to celebrate the end of shooting of that new movie. How about it?'

Manju looks at me, and I nod. This is better than I could have hoped for on only my second night in India, and I'm buzzing with excitement, all thoughts of Mum cast from my mind.

'Great,' says Asha. 'I'll be back in a minute.' She flashes me another smile, one not entirely sincere, I suspect, and I notice that her teeth are unnaturally white. Still, real or fake, genuine girl or Bollywood confection, Asha is an amazing creature.

On the way to the loos, I wonder why it is always like this, why, even at home, at A-level college, I never really hit it off with boys. For a while I thought it was to do with race, thought that the kinds of boys who were attracted to the strange hybrid that I am, with my skin paler than a true Asian's but darker than an Anglo-Saxon's, with the blue eyes I got from my mother, were just not the right kind of boys for me. Not that I never had my pick of the good-looking ones. Far from it – it only ever seemed to be the good-looking ones who were attracted to me, to the point of boredom. After a while, I started to crave something more interesting, more edgy, than physical perfection. Yet the boys I really wanted, the long-haired rebels more into bands than studying or sports prowess, never seemed to even throw me a second glance, to the extent that I started to suspect they were afraid of me in some way, or at least intimidated or confused.

In the meantime, bored of my suave charmers, my football pitch heroes, always ditching them after a couple of weeks, I discovered a confusing taste for women, one that I'd never admitted to anyone. It hasn't led anywhere, is based on nothing more than fantasy, but it has thrown me into disarray. It all started in the hockey changing rooms one Friday just before lunch, when I glimpsed the head prefect, Carla, giving herself a firmer-than-average scrub-down in the shower. I stood, mesmerised, snatch growing ever wetter, as she rubbed at her muff, eyes closed, lips parted, oblivious to my presence – we'd both stood talking to the coach after the game, and were late off the pitch, hence there being no one else in the changing rooms. After a moment or two, she'd spread her lips with the thumb and index finger of one hand and, with the fingers of the other, began to massage her clit vigorously. I'd felt an intense burning sensation start up between my own legs – something way more powerful and instinctive than the slight itch I felt whenever my short-lived boyfriends tried to put their hands up my skirt.

And then she came, with a barely suppressed cry, and as she did so she opened her beautiful catlike green eyes and smiled at me as if she'd always known I was there. As if, even, she'd done it for my benefit almost as much as hers. Looking back, in the light of what happened afterwards, her behaviour towards me, I often found myself wondering whether there wasn't an invitation in those shining, post-orgasmic eyes, a beckoning. What would have happened if I'd cast off my own clothes and joined her in the shower? It's a question that will haunt me for the rest of my life, or perhaps until the day – if such a day ever comes – that I experience a woman sexually. But I didn't join her. Instead I fled, abandoned my own plans to take a shower and rushed from the changing rooms and back to the school bus without even changing out of my hockey kit, telling the sports mistress I felt faint. When Carla caught up and boarded the bus, I looked steadfastly out of the window, too embarrassed to meet her eye.

That night, alone in my room, I'd logged on to the internet in the privacy of my room and looked at girls. Girls of all shapes and sizes, girls of hues, girls in all kinds of positions. Some I liked, others I didn't. In that sense, my feelings didn't differ from those I had towards boys. Only with girls, I found I had curiously opposite tastes – whereas I liked my men a little rough, a little grungy, the girls who invoked an ache in my groin were all scrubbed and fresh, with shaven pussies and a clean look to them. I thought again of Carla, of the 'O' of her mouth as her orgasm had taken hold, of the way she penetrated me with her green gaze. If she hadn't been inviting me to actually partake of her, she'd enjoyed sharing her triumphant moment of climax with an onlooker, I was certain of that.

I lay back, pushed my pyjama bottoms down, noticing that the fabric was soaked right through, and fingered my snatch. Suddenly, after months of being able to resist all sexual advances on the part of boyfriends, I had to be satisfied. I had to know what it was like. And so, Carla's bewitching eyes in my mind, I slipped one hand deep inside myself and let the other hand mimic her actions with her clit. Within seconds the pleasure had mounted and I was writhing on the bed, palpating the swollen bead of my own clit, hearing moans escape from me and praying that the TV in my parents' room was turned up loud enough for them not to hear as I initiated myself in sexual pleasure.

My head thrown back against the pillow, my mouth frozen in some kind of fixed grin, I felt my sex widening as if opening itself up to something. And then suddenly there was a giving way inside myself, as the walls of my sex began to contract and relax and then contract again around my hand, and my clit...it's hard to describe. Afterwards I was so shaken and overcome that I could barely register how it had been, but if I had to put it into words, I'd say that my clit had exploded and behind my closed eyelids sparked a thousand different colours.

Remembering all this on the way to the loos in Seijo and the Soul Dish, I have to stop for a moment, steady myself against a wall with my hand. It's a few minutes before I've recovered myself sufficiently to carry on.

6

I wake mid-afternoon and jump up in alarm: Nadia will be worried about me. In fact, the poor girl will be frantic by now. Mouth dry, a sharp pain beating at my temple, cursing the first hangover I've had in years, I gather my clothes from all around the floor of the suite, dress hurriedly and leave the room. Charles isn't there, but I don't have time to wonder where he might be.

As I run through the hotel corridor to the lift, I'm aware that I look like a scarecrow, but I don't really care. All I can think about, at this moment, is how anxious and confused Nadia will be. I imagine she's probably even called down to reception to report me missing by now, and there'll be all kinds of explanations to go through when I do show my face, perhaps even bureaucratic procedures. Heavens! What if my disappearance has been reported to the police and I'm officially a missing person? How mortifying that will be. I'll have to fabricate some story about jetlag and one drink too many and falling asleep over a nightcap in a friend's room. No one will buy it, let alone Nadia, who knows I don't have any friends here, but there's no way I can tell the truth.

The truth ... hmmm, I hardly know where to start. In fact, it all grows a little hazy after the bath, the warm bath that enfolded me, continued caressing my skin after Charles's onslaught. I'd stayed there for about half an hour, letting it soothe me, calm me back down, and then when I'd finished my drink I'd climbed out and swaddled myself in a thick fluffy bathrobe. At that point I'd assumed I'd be dressing and returning to mine and Nadia's room and that the night was effectively over. I had no idea what time it was, but I guessed it to be the very early hours of the morning.

Charles, though, had other ideas. And all credit to him. He has incredible stamina for a man his age. As I'd walked back into the living room, he'd risen from the desk, having apparently been working on his laptop, and came towards me.

'Feeling nice and relaxed?' he'd said with a smile. As I smiled and nodded and thanked him for the bath and the drink, he slipped my bathrobe from my shoulders and pushed me gently down onto the armchair. Parting my legs with his hands, he brought his face to my pussy again, and treated me to half an hour of mind-blowing cunnilingus, exploring every tiny crease and fold with his mouth and tongue, kissing me, licking me, alternately softly and wildly, before putting his tongue inside me again, swirling it round and round until I was bucking on the chair, on the point of orgasm, then teasing me, pulling it out and encircling my hole over and over.

It got to the point where I wanted him inside me so much, I could have cried with frustration. And he knew it, bringing me to the brink time and time again, relishing my cries as he backed off just as I felt myself on the cusp of orgasm. When I just couldn't handle it any more, I took control, forcing him up from me and then turning him around and pushing him down onto the chair. Slowing the pace down a little, despite my frenzy, I climbed onto the chair above him, one knee on each arm of it, and untied the belt of his towelling robe. As I peeled back each side of it, his cock sprang up, almost comically eager for me. For a moment he stared down at it; we were both, I think, surprised and awed by the juices that were splashing down on his belly and groin from my pussy suspended above him. With two fingers he gathered some of the sweet liquid and brought it to his mouth, and as he tasted it he let out a moan of satisfaction. In response I grasped his cock, felt its warmth and smoothness against my palm, its steely readiness. It was time. I couldn't hold off any longer.

Sensing what I wanted, he rose on his taut buttocks as I brought myself down towards him, and he entered me, as sure and confident as a missile seeking its target. I leant forwards slightly, kissed him and, while our tongues and teeth clashed, I felt my clitoris mash against his belly. For a while I enjoyed the soft, slightly yielding pressure of him against me, but as his pace inside me quickened, I sat up and then inclined backwards slightly. My clitoris, my whole pussy, felt gloriously exposed to Charles's scrutiny, and indeed, after letting me rub at myself for a minute, Charles removed my fingers and replaced them with his own, not taking his eyes from my wide open parts.

His scrutiny both unnerved and thrilled me. Ravi and I, when we did do it, which was once in a blue moon over the past ten years or so, always made love under the covers, in the dark. If there'd ever been some kind of ID line-up of pussies, I doubt he'd have been able to pick mine out. Ditto with his cock. Any sense of discovery there'd ever been had dissipated over the years, as the demands of domesticity, child-rearing and Ravi's career had superseded all thoughts of a half-decent sex life. But as I said, even in the early days, we were hardly great goers.

And so I felt flattered by the way Charles was studying my pussy, relishing the way it was spread wide for him, the way it was responding to his movements. I also, for a time at least, felt a tiny bit self-conscious. The booze was probably wearing off a little by now, and I wasn't used to being studied in this way, at such close quarters. I have never lavished a lot of attention on my body, since no one else has paid it much notice. I've heard of Brazilians, Hollywoods and the like, but I'd be hard-pressed to tell you what they are exactly, and I wondered if Charles was surprised at how unkempt I was 'down there'. He seems like a man who knew his stuff when it came to bushes. Not that it bothered me, that he was undoubtedly a ladies' man with a new conquest in every port of call. Like I say, I was surprised and flattered that he had chosen me, and that he was taking such obvious enjoyment in my body.

We were in beautiful sync now. As he thrust into me, I pushed forwards to meet him and a delicious rhythm built up between us, punctuated by our moans. After a while, he took his hands from my pussy and gripped each of my bum cheeks with one hand, easing them apart, pulling me even more forcefully in towards him each time he thrust, then letting me swing back. As he did so, his fingers crept inwards towards my sphincter, and I felt a ripple of joy run through me as he started playing at my pink frill with his fingertips. Nobody had ever even been near there before and it was intoxicating. I couldn't even feel embarrassment, the sensation was so incredible. One hand on Charles's hip, I brought my fingers back to my pussy, jiggled my clit again, and suddenly the moment was near: it became clear that neither of us was going to be able to hold off for much longer.

I leant back a little further, intensified the pressure of my fingers, and Charles started twitching, losing the rhythm we'd been maintaining as he began to lose control. As I started wailing, feeling myself on the verge of opening up, he pushed one finger into the rosebud of my anus, and I came like I had never come before, with a full-throated scream of joy.

As the waves of pleasure receded with ever-diminishing contractions, I rode out his own climax, relishing the dig of his nails in the flesh of my buttocks, the grimace of ecstasy on his tanned, handsome face. And then I collapsed down on him on the chair, feeling as if I could sleep for a hundred years.

The lift doors open and I step inside, astonished and exhilarated by the events of the night.

7

The bar's toilets are hard to find, squirrelled away in little pods like something out of *2001: A Space Odyssey*. Mumbai, with its futuristic bars, its coffee shops selling exotic blends, its hip young things, has so far confounded all my expectations. Of course I knew in advance, from what I'd read, that this is a city of seemingly impossible contradictions, but no travel guide could have prepared me for what I have found. Yet I also know that, so far at least, I've seen the place from a privileged perspective. Despite knowing that this is not an 'authentic' India but one heavily tinged by Western attitudes and values, I find it seductive, compelling, addictive even. I want this evening to go on and on. I want to find out more about the mysterious Asha and her life, and meet more of the people who populate this chic milieu.

As I enter one of the pods, unzip my jeans and sit down to pee, I hear noises from the neighbouring cubicle. There's nothing so odd in that, except that it sounds to me like there are two people in there, two women. Hushed voices speak in a language I don't understand but assume to be Hindi. At first I think I'm overhearing a spot of recreational drug use, but the words are soon interspersed by little giggles and moans and gasps, and I quickly realise that it's something far more interesting.

Standing up but not flushing, I continue listening in for a moment, oddly excited. But then I start to feel self-conscious and hurry out to wash my hands and splash my reddened face with cold water.

As I'm turning to leave, I hear the pod door open behind me and, although I try hard just to carry on walking and not look back, I can't help but glance over my shoulder. I'm stunned to see Asha and another raving beauty stepping out, faces aglow.

'Oh hi,' breathes Asha when she catches sight of me. There's no trace of embarrassment either in her face or her voice, although they must know I heard something.

I manage a smile, pull open the door and walk back to the reassuring presence of Manju and Ajit at the bar.

At the party at Juhu Beach, it quickly becomes clear that Asha and her friend are not so out of the ordinary. They're spectacular, of course, but in this environment of young Bollywood stars and hangers-on, they blend in like peacocks in a whole flock of the shimmering creatures, and it's 'normal' people like me who stand out. Yet, although I feel out of place, Manju and Ajit make sure to introduce me to everyone who comes within earshot, and a few others besides, and I drink my fair share of luscious, fruity cocktails and begin to relax and think that this is all rather fun.

But my eyes keep going back to Asha and Karishma, who flit round the room from group to group, bedazzling all those with whom they come into contact. Even from several metres away, even over the din of the other conversations and over the music, I remain receptive to the brittle tinkle of their laughter. It must rapidly become obvious that I'm obsessed with them, because before too long they start repaying my glances, fluttering their eyelashes at me.

I try to focus my attention on the crowd I've just been introduced to. One of them, Manju has already told me with an unmistakeable note of pride in his voice, is the rising star of Bollywood, Vashu Chopra – a sure-fire heart-throb and leading man for the twenty-first century. We talk as a group, Vashu holding sway, and it's clear that he shares the others' high opinion of himself, which is usually an instant turn-off for me. But with his tousled hair, his two-day beard and the cigarette hanging out of the corner of his mouth, he's also undeniably sexy. He has attitude, and attitude turns me on. He looks like the kind of guy who will lead his career in the direction he wants it to go, rather than be led by it – a kind of Indian Johnny Depp. Perhaps self-assurance is not a bad thing, after all; perhaps it's just the natural consequence of knowing who you are. I wouldn't know.

It's weird, but after I've spent a few moments in his presence, and despite my being in this room oozing with gorgeous, nubile young movie stars and models, Vashu seems to be focusing his attentions on me and, sure enough, before long he's talking exclusively to me. The rest of the crowd drifts away gradually, into smaller satellite groups, and we're more or less alone. I quickly get Vashu's measure: after asking me the regulatory handful of questions about myself and my life in Britain, he uses my comments as a launch pad for a monologue about himself and his experiences during a recent promotional visit to London, where he was photographed by a bunch of prominent men's magazines. Among other things, he did a big fashion shoot for *GQ*. Of course, it's all very impressive and I can't help but be in thrall to the glamour of his life, as well as flattered that it's me he's picked out to hear all this. As much as I find his self-absorption and his swagger off-putting, his bad-boy looks and demeanour keep me by his side, listening in spite of myself. I find myself wondering if tonight is the night, and if I am destined to lose my virginity to a rising Bollywood star.

Yet as soon as the thought has crossed my mind, I'm thrown into even greater confusion when I glance across the room to find Asha staring at me, blatantly. She's holding her glass up to her mouth, but over the top of it her eyes twinkle with some kind of mischievous intent. Perhaps she's just teasing me, reminding me that she knows that I overheard at least some of what was going on between her and Karishma in the loos, and letting me know that she doesn't care that I heard, that she may even be happy that I did. Or maybe – and perhaps this is no more than wishful thinking on my part – there's something more to the frankness of her gaze. I remember Carla and her invitation. The problem is, I never know if I'm being invited to participate or just given permission to be an onlooker.

Sensing my distraction, Vashu has turned away, become embroiled in a conversation with an older, rather distinguished-looking man. I wonder if he's a director – he has an authoritative air to him. I take the opportunity to turn away from them, to slip unnoticed through the crowd and out into the night. Some fresh air may help me sort out my thoughts.

Sitting on the beach, I look out at the waves and wonder why it is that I have such trouble working out what it is I want. If only I knew, then I could reach out and get it, take life by the throat. Is it because I'm caught between two cultures, neither wholly one nor the other, not fully at home in either world? Or is it because I'm bisexual, because I don't know whether to go for boys or girls? Or is it for both of these reasons?

I lie back on the sand, staring up at the constellations, trying to play a game with myself. Who, in an ideal world, would be my sexual partner of choice? Would it be a hot blonde girl like Carla, or a dark beauty like Asha? Or would it be a boy, and if so would it be a white, lank-haired rocker, someone like Taylor Hawkins out of the Foo Fighters, or a Hindi heart-throb, one with a little bite – a Hrithik Roshan or a John Abraham, or even a less self-centred version of Vashu Chopra? Of course, I'm aware that I don't actually have to choose, that I could enjoy all of these. But at times I feel frozen, unable to act or to make the simplest of decisions, and I feel that my sexual disorientation is at the heart of this and needs to be tackled. It's not as if I want to settle down and get married and have kids, although I haven't ruled that out for the future. I'd just like to stop feeling so dispersed, to cease this habit of starting off down one avenue and then halting, becoming paralysed by the thought that I ought to have taken another.

After a while, my ruminations are interrupted by the sound of voices and, sitting up, I look over my shoulder and see Asha walking in my direction. She doesn't seem to have seen me, and she's not alone. She's not with Karishma this time either, but with another girl I can't see too well in the pale moonlight. Asha's leading the way, holding the other girl's hand as she leads her out towards the water.

I watch, entranced, scarcely daring to breathe in case their awareness of my presence breaks the spell. Asha leads her friend to the shoreline, and for a few minutes they stand looking out over the Arabian Sea, hand in hand, talking in low voices. Then Asha turns to the other girl, brushes her hair back from her face with both hands, and moves in for a kiss. The other girl responds voraciously, and my stomach somersaults as I watch them eat at each other's face like starving things. It's hard to believe that Asha has already had a girl-ration not an hour ago. With their hands they are pulling at each other's clothes, and I moan as I see items fall to the sand around them. Though the moon is on the wane, I can see the sheen of their nutmeg-brown flesh as it is revealed piece by piece.

The girl, whose hair is cropped relatively short around the skull but has a long fringe, is naked first; Asha's still got her skinny jeans on, though she's shucked off her wedge-heeled sandals. Her breasts are pert and lovely, seeming to rise up to meet the girl's. With one hand she's reaching between the other girl's legs, palpating her mound. And then she moves backwards, dragging the girl further up the beach towards where I'm sitting. Letting herself fall back onto the sand, she pulls the girl down on top of herself, then slithers out of her jeans. The girl falls upon Asha hungrily, sucking noisily at her tits as she delves between her legs.

I'm clutching my own snatch, pressing my fingers against my clit as I watch them thrash about on the sand, emitting low guttural sounds of pleasure, like the growls of playful bear cubs, issuing instructions to each other that I don't understand. Then Asha flips the girl over onto her back and takes her turn on top, and I watch as they grind their mounds together, grasping at each other's tits. I'd do anything to see the look on Asha's face as she comes, but her hair hangs down forwards over her face.

Suddenly they're climaxing together, and I'm rubbing furiously at my own clit, all the while trying to ward off an orgasm in order not to give my presence away. Asha is bucking on top of her friend and, as she achieves ecstasy, she rears up. As I'd hoped, she flicks her hair back and I see the contortions of her incredible face.

She falls away from the other girl, lies panting on her back. The girl is either embarrassed or in a hurry for some reason, perhaps anxious not to be caught out by a boyfriend waiting indoors, because she gets up quickly and hurries down to the shoreline to retrieve her clothes.

Asha is clearly in no rush. She stays where she is, and after a while I'm convinced she's asleep and dare to stand up and walk down to where she lies. In the milky moonlight I look down at her firm faultless body, and I tingle when I see, below the little tuft of her Brazilian, what looks to be a real diamond sparkling amidst her still-swollen labia – she's pierced. In spite of what I know to be right, I fall to my knees beside her, reach my hand towards her snatch. I haven't brought myself to orgasm yet, but I feel that I wouldn't need to if I touched her, that my cunt would catch fire. But she stirs, lets out a little sigh, her eyes still closed, and I bottle out, take my hand away and stand up.

I'm just turning away when I feel her hand on my ankle. 'Stay,' she murmurs, her voice even huskier than before. But I'm too afraid. The moment has passed, as the moment always passes, and I've lost my nerve.

I head inside, ask Manju to call me a cab. He gives me his telephone number, tells me to call whenever I'm next in town. I thank him for everything and promise that I will.

As I'm about to walk out of the door, Vashu catches me up, expresses surprise that I'm leaving. 'The night is still so young,' he says, and for a moment I'm tempted, really tempted. Not only am I furious with myself for turning down Asha, I'm also afraid that I'll be kicking myself later on, when I realise what I could have had with Vashu. Something about him, perhaps his self-confidence, tells me he's unbelievable in bed.

Then I shake my head. 'I'm sorry,' I say, and he shrugs and turns back into the room, probably on the scent of a fresh conquest. I'm not under any illusions that I would have been anything more than that to him. And probably to Asha too – she's clearly a woman of immense appetites, and I'd have been merely one more notch on her metaphorical bedpost. But that doesn't stop me, as I ride back into central Mumbai, from clutching at my snatch and wondering what might have been.

8

Nadia's not in our room, but when I venture down to reception and ask a few discreet questions, I find out that she's not reported me missing after all. The girl at the desk tells me she went out late morning, caught a rickshaw outside after requesting one of the free maps that they hand out here. She's obviously decided to do a spot of sightseeing, and who can blame her, though it is strange that she wasn't more concerned about where I might be.

I shrug, head upstairs, deciding to wait in the room rather than venture out myself. Truth be told, I'm more than a little sore – I haven't seen this kind of action in a very long time, not since before Ravi, and I don't feel I could do much walking around.

Upstairs, I settle on my bed to read one of the glossy magazines left on our coffee table. At once I find myself studying the male models with the eye of a would-be connoisseur, running my finger over bodies on paper, assessing how they might be in bed, what they might do to me, what it would be like to be with a man like that. Not that Charles is in any way wanting – he may be in his latter fifties, but his body is firm and honed, well looked after. And he has the benefit of decades of experience. Which is probably why everything he did to me hit the spot so exactly.

I thrust one hand down my knickers, thinking of Charles and what he did to me, but still flicking through the pages with the other, looking at the array of male flesh, imagining it against my own skin. I rub gently, aware I've already over-done it, yet addicted, it seems, to the pleasures to which Charles has reawakened me, to the potential that has lain dormant for so long, unable to be sated for more than an hour or two. The tide rises inside me, inexorable, and I lie back and cast aside the magazine, legs spread.

The telephone rings. Still rubbing at my lips with my fingers, I reach out my free hand and answer.

'Val, it's Charles,' comes the now familiar drawl. It's as if he's tuning into my thoughts, to my need.

'Hi, Charles.' I keep up the pressure.

There's a short silence on the other end of the line, then, 'Are you OK? What are you doing?'

I don't know what it is about this man but he brings out a wantonness in me I hadn't even known existed. 'I'm playing with myself,' I say, without hesitation.

For once I sense him caught off guard, stuck for words. Then he says, 'And what are you thinking about?'

'You,' I breathe. 'You fucking me, harder and harder, with your beautiful big dick.'

I close my eyes. In my mind I see him parting my buttocks again, his fingers sinking into my flesh. I moan. 'Oh fuck,' I say, 'I'm going to come. Oh, Charles, I'm ... oh, oh.'

A moan at the end of the line echoes my own, and I know he has brought himself to a climax too. The very thought of him sitting at his marble desk with his cock in his hand, jerking himself off as he listens to me, makes me come again, almost before the first climax has died away. I fall back onto the bed, receiver still pressed against my ear, listening to him pant, waiting for him to say something, anything, to break the spell, to bring us back to something approaching normality.

I'm relieved when he clears his throat, speaks again. 'Dinner?' he says.

I smile and say, 'I'd love to.'

* * *

I'd like to be able to say that I get to know Charles a little better over our risottos and Sicilian red wine in one of the hotel's restaurants, but he retains his air of mystery, avoiding my most personal questions and opening up only when the conversation turns to more general matters – India and its future development, first-class air travel, Iraq and American politics as a whole. I gather from titbits he drops here and there that he is divorced, has two kids in their late teens who have gone off the rails slightly, but personal revelations are scant.

Not that I want to make too many of my own. I speak of Nadia a little, of how this was really her trip before going to university to read media studies. I tell him I've spent most of my life married to a man named Ravi, but I don't give him the reasons for my divorce just as he doesn't tell me about his. In truth, I am still not clear in my own mind exactly what happened with Ravi. I suppose we just grew apart, imperceptibly, over the years, and when the kids became independent, I just lost all sense of myself and what my role in the world was. Which is why, I guess, I leapt at this chance of coming along with Nadia. Heaven knows what I'd be doing now if the opportunity hadn't arisen. Joining book clubs, going to yoga and aerobics, watching the same old soap operas. Thinking about how humdrum my life was back there seems surreal after what's happened in the last 24 hours.

After dinner, Charles insists we take a nightcap up to the rooftop pool. Who am I to resist? Once up there, we recline on loungers, kick our shoes off and make a toast to Mumbai and to the adventures it offers.

'Here's to many more,' says Charles, and he turns to look at me in the moonlight. 'Listen, Val, I know you're here with your gal, but your plans seem pretty fluid to me. So why don't you think about coming with me to Rajasthan tomorrow? I'm going for a couple of days, and I'd love to show you the sights. It's an incredible place.'

I look at him, touched that he has even thought of asking me along. Then I sigh, look out over the sparkling Arabian Sea. 'I'd love to,' I say, 'I really would. But what about Nadia?'

'Bring her along,' he says breezily. 'She'll love it too. And hell – I'll pay for a room for her if that's what's bothering you.'

My throat constricts. So he's banking on he and I sharing a room? Again, I'm touched, honoured that already, after only one night and a day, he sees us as an item. I roll over on my lounger, place one hand on his hip, then move it slowly to the zip of his trousers and take out his cock. For a while we lie there staring into each other's eyes as I slowly bring him off, but before I can make him come he's pushing my dress off my shoulders and, rising to his feet, pulling me up too. I stand before him in my underwear, looking around to double-check that no one can see us. But the pool is deserted; this isn't a busy time of year. As he reaches his hands around me to unclasp my bra, I swoon back. Then he bends down to pull off my knickers, giving my pussy a little kiss on the way back up and, sweeping me up into his arms, hurls me into the water.

I give out a little scream as I come up gasping, laughing, waving a fist at Charles in mock anger. He's stripped now too, and is standing on the pool edge with his cock raised in a kind of salute. He brings his hands together and executes an elegant dive, his muscles tautening even more with the effort of springing up and then arcing through the air. And then I shriek again as, before he's even come up for air, I feel his mouth on my pussy under the water, his teeth taking playful little nips at my clitoris. When his breath gives out, he surfaces, pulling me to him, and, with seemingly no effort on either of our parts, his cock slips inside me.

For a moment we just stand there, lost to the moment, looking at each other in the pale light. Then he pulls me over to one side of the pool and, as I lie back against the edge, arms outstretched to steady myself, breasts pale and jiggling, he humps me hard, feverishly, his mouth fastened on my shoulder so firmly I know his teeth will leave marks. At length, tiring a little, we climb out of the water and lie on the side like beached sea creatures. Then he turns me over and enters me again, and we both come with cries that sound like pain.

We're on one of the loungers, me sitting between Charles's legs with my head back against his bare chest, when Nadia appears. Modesty has prevailed, and we're partially dressed, me in my dress and Charles in his trousers. At first I panic, thinking that someone must have known where we were, and hence what we were doing, to have directed her to us. But it soon becomes apparent from the look of surprise on her face that she had no idea she would find me here. Then I notice that she's carrying a towel rolled up under her arm and I realise she's come for a late-night dip. Thank God, I say to myself, she wasn't here half an hour earlier.

On the other hand, as this is the first she even knows of Charles's existence, it must come as a shock to find me all snuggled up with him like this, so I jump up and walk towards her. I go to embrace her, but she seems to be sulking, so I don't force the issue.

'Have you had a nice day?' I say.

She nods and says peevishly, 'And so have you, by the looks of things.'

'Nadia, I'm sorry . . .' I begin, and then the words stop coming and I just stare at her, thinking about how all this must look.

She waves one hand airily, sits down on a nearby recliner and starts to take off her clothes.

I gesture back at Charles, where he's sitting finishing up his drink. He raises a hand at Nadia.

'Nadia, this is Charles Hoffmann,' I say. 'He's staying in the hotel on business.'

She nods and stands up in her bikini. 'Pleased to meet you,' she mutters, or something like it, and then she holds her nose and leaps forwards into the water without testing the temperature first.

Charles and I exchange looks, our Rajasthan trip in jeopardy unless I can do something to thaw the ice. I've taken enough liberties already; there's no way I can swan off up north with Charles for a couple of days of wild sex and leave Nadia in the lurch. For a while, as Nadia notches up the lengths, he remains where he is, seemingly contemplative, and then he gets up, walks slowly alongside the pool to where I'm standing watching my daughter.

'I was going to try to talk to her,' he says. 'But she looks like a tough cookie. I think I'll fade away into the background, let you guys sort things out.' He takes my hand, discreetly. 'I want you to come with me,' he says. 'I want you. Let's talk in the morning. My flight leaves just after midday so we can play it by ear.' He squeezes my hand. 'Sleep tight,' he says, and already I'm thinking of the night without him, of how I'll get by without his big beautiful cock within reach, seeking me out or waiting to be sought.

When Nadia's worked off some of her fury in the pool, we head down to our room and I order us some hot chocolate on room service as she showers. I don't want to rush her, but I can't miss this opportunity with Charles. I've never felt this kind of excitement about a man, at least not since my teens, and if I blow it I'll regret it for the rest of my life. The thought of living without the kind of sensations and emotions he has called up in me over the past night and day makes me feel sick. What would be the point of going on?

Nadia comes out of the bathroom, swathed in a bathrobe, pink and glowing from the shower, and I'm startled by her beauty. Of course, having seen her almost every day for the last eighteen years, this shouldn't come as a surprise to me. But when she's free of make-up like this, her wet hair pulled back from her face, free of all artifice, even I can still be amazed. I wonder at the fact that she never has boyfriends, or anyone who lasts more than a week or two. They're always incredibly good-looking, clean cut, polite – a mother's dream. But she never seems to form an attachment to them, to judge by her coolness when the relationships come to an end. I've never once seen her cry or even look downhearted about a boy.

At her age, I was wild, at my most sexually prolific. Just thinking about that time makes me wonder all the more at what happened after that, at the waning of my appetites when I married Ravi. I loved him, I suppose that was the thing, and so I accepted that sex wasn't a big deal for him. Or perhaps I hoped that I could teach him that it was a big deal. But the kids came along not so long after we got married, and in quick succession, and the exhaustion made me forget how wonderful sex can be. I lost myself along the way.

Now I'm forced to admit it: I'm a sexual being who has needs, vast needs. And Charles is a man who can answer them. I can't let him go, not now. I have to build a bridge back to Nadia – for selfish reasons of course, but also because she's my daughter and I love her and want her to have fun too. Who knows, perhaps she can discover herself during this trip, sexually as well as in all the other ways that are possible? Or is sexuality an integral part of discovering oneself?

'Mum?'

I'm still staring at Nadia but thinking about Ravi when I

realise she's trying to talk to me. I sit up in my chair. 'Yes, darling?'

'I said, who is that guy you were with?'

'I told you, he's a businessman staying in the hotel.'

'And you're – you spent the night with him?'

'Honey, I'm so sorry. I should have told you, should have left you a note. It's inexcusable. But to tell you the truth, I was a silly girl and had a bit too much to drink. I didn't mean not to come back. And when I did you'd gone out.'

'I wasn't going to wait around for you.'

'No, I realise that. I didn't expect you to. But I'm sorry I worried you.'

'And what about this guy, this ... Charles?'

'Oh, darling, what do you want me to say?'

'Well, nothing, I suppose. There's not much I can say. It's your life. You're old enough to know what you're doing.'

'I don't know about that,' I say with a chuckle, trying to inject some humour into proceedings. But when Nadia doesn't pick up the bait, I continue. 'He's a good man, I really like him. Perhaps I have rushed in a little, but – well, I'm on holiday, we're on holiday. We're not here for long, so there wasn't the luxury of time like there is in real life. It's not like we had time for two weeks of dating before making up our minds whether we were going to take things further.'

Her face relaxes a notch or two. 'Sure,' she says. 'I guess I can see that.' She looks down at her nails, and I wonder what she's thinking about.

'What about you?' I say. 'What have you been doing all day – and this evening?'

'Oh, nothing much. Wandering about, museums, seeing the sights.' She hasn't looked up from her hands, and I sense there's something on her mind, something she's not telling me about where she's been and what she's been doing, but I decide not to pry. I know her well enough to understand that it won't reap any rewards. She'll only talk if she wants to, and not necessarily to me.

I feel a jab of guilt. Perhaps this is all my fault. It's hardly as if I caused Katie to be ill and to drop out of the trip, but Nadia wanted to do this with someone her own age, a soulmate. Instead she's lumbered with me, and I'm not sure we've ever been close enough for her to consider me a candidate for the role of confidante. The last thing I want is for her to feel lonely.

I lean forwards in my chair, blow on my hot chocolate. 'Nadia,' I say. 'The thing is ... the thing is, like I said, I really like Charles. I feel this is something that could go somewhere. And ... well, he's making a two-day trip to Rajasthan tomorrow afternoon, and he's invited me along with him, and ...'

Nadia sits down, looks at me squarely. 'Rajasthan wasn't part of the plan,' she says. 'Or at least not yet. We'd agreed we'd head up to Delhi and Agra, then Varanasi.'

'We'd talked about that, yes, but nothing was set in stone.'

'It wasn't set in stone, but ...' She shakes her head. 'You're ... you're hijacking my holiday.' She looks around her. 'I certainly never intended to stay in a place like this, for instance. It's hardly "the real India", is it?'

'You don't even know what the real India is.'

'I know better than you. At least I've been outside the four walls of the hotel since we arrived. I've not been holed in a bedroom shagg –'

I raise a hand in admonition. 'Nadia, please.'

'OK, I'm sorry.' She does look contrite, and for a moment I watch her as she gazes across the room, lost in thought. 'Fine,' she says at last. 'It's no big deal. We were going to go to Rajasthan at some point anyway, and it would be mean-spirited of me to refuse on principle, so if this fling means so much to you, we'll go.'

I start at the word 'fling'. Is this all it will be? But I decide not to challenge her, knowing that is how it must appear to the outside world. 'You're an angel,' I say instead. 'We'll have a good time, I promise you. Charles will be in meetings some of the time so he won't monopolise me. I promise not to disappear again. And he...he's such a sweetheart, Nadia. He's even said he'll pay for your hotel room.'

Nadia's face clouds. 'I don't want that, Mum. I didn't come to India to stay in five-star hotels. And I don't want your...your lover's charity. Or bribery, perhaps I should say. I'll come along because we're travelling together, and because I don't want to spoil your fun. But I'll find myself a hostel, thanks very much all the same.'

'Fine. I'll tell Charles.'

'So what's the deal with him? I mean, presumably if he's here on business, he's not hanging around forever? You two don't have plans to go on together somewhere after Rajasthan?'

'Oh no, Nadia. Don't you think I'd tell you if that were the case? We haven't actually discussed it – the future, I mean. But I gather from what he's said that he's due in New York next week so I know he won't be around too much longer.'

'Well, in that case, don't get your hopes up, OK? I don't want you to be let down.'

I smile wryly, amused at the idea of my daughter giving me romantic advice. 'It'll be fine,' I say. 'I have a very good feeling about Charles.'

9

Sitting on the plane, having grudgingly accepted Charles's offer of a plane ticket – the only real alternative was a long overnight bus ride, which would leave me shattered and with little time in Udaipur itself – I look up from my glossy in-flight mag full of ads for stuff no one needs and study Charles as he taps away on his laptop. Mum, beside him, is reading a thriller, one hand on his leg, high up and close to his groin, as if she can barely keep her hands off him. Although Charles is way too old for me, and not at all my type, I can't help but feel a little twinge of envy that Mum has so obviously found someone who does it for her. There were never any displays of affection at home and, after all she's done for us, she deserves her moment. Only I hope for her sake this turns out to be more than a moment. She seems hooked on Charles, but I'm wary of his intentions towards her. He's a smooth operator, and she must know that – perhaps it's even part of his appeal. But is he more slippery than he appears?

I think back to last night, and it seems like a dream. In fact, when I did finally fall asleep, after sorting things out with Mum, it was to restless visions of Asha and Vashu. Of Asha on the beach, sitting astride the other girl and throwing back her head in a paroxysm of joy. Asha dozing, post-coitally numb, a diamond winking from between her glistening lips. Her hand on my ankle – another invitation I didn't dare take up. And then I dreamt of Vashu, lying naked behind me, his prick in his hand, straining for me, a little bead of pre-cum shining at its tip. But as I'm reaching for it, hand trembling, Asha appears in the doorway, smiles, walks towards the bed and impales herself on Vashu with a yelp, and I've missed my chance again.

I woke up with ripples of pleasure going through me, and I realised I'd just come in my sleep. Lazily, I put my fingers to my drenched snatch and worked at it again, slowly but firmly, until I was climaxing again, drawing out the moment this time, making it last, savouring every contraction, every throb of my clit, relieved that Mum seemed to be sleeping the sleep of the dead.

The plane lands and within minutes we're in a taxi heading for my hostel, which I booked on the internet before leaving Mumbai. There they drop me off; I wave goodbye, having arranged to meet them for dinner, and head inside. The Panorama, as described on the travellers' websites I looked up, is clean and comfy, and full of backpackers. I instantly feel more relaxed than I did at that stupid place in Mumbai. After inspecting my room – basic, but with a funky hanging hammock chair – I head up to the roof to appreciate the stunning view over the city and Pichola Lake, the largest here. In the middle of it I can make out the hotel to which Charles and Mum were heading, the Lake Palace, which truly is a palace, one that was constructed entirely of marble and seems to float on the lake like a mirage.

I must be mad to turn down an offer of a night or two in such a fairy-tale place, I think, but then I look back around me at the other travellers on the terrace and I remind myself of why I'm here. Mum and I have different agendas right now, and while she enjoys her five-star luxury and pampering, as well as Charles, I will set out to discover the city.

One of the other travellers, a guy in his late teens or early twenties with shoulder-length blond dreadlocks, is smiling over at me. 'Just arrived?' he says in a sunny Australian accent.

I return his smile. 'Is it that obvious?'

He comes towards me, one hand outstretched. 'Christian,' he says.

We sit down. He asks me where I've come from and what my plans are, before filling me in on his six months of travel around India. I drink it all in, and at length take out my notebook to jot down a few specific tips and recommendations. Without my going into too much boring detail about my mum's sexual reawakening, we establish that I'm as good as alone here, and Christian suggests that, since he's been here a week and knows the place pretty well, he shows me around for the afternoon.

As he's been talking, I've been shooting him crafty looks, and I like much of what I see. He's certainly more than a little rough round the edges, with his knotted dirty-blond locks and his ripped jeans. His face tends towards the pretty rather than the manly: full lips and big blue wondering eyes, full of enthusiasm for the things he talks about. Only time will tell if I like him enough to consider sleeping with him, but he will certainly make an attractive guide for the afternoon.

'We should start,' he says, 'with the Indo-Aryan Jagdish Temple with its amazing carvings, and then perhaps see the Crystal Gallery with its mind-blowing collection of crystal chairs, sofas, tables and even beds.' He adds afterwards, 'We could take a stroll around the beautiful Fateh Sagar Lake, and even take a boat out in it to Nehru Park with its boat-shaped café.'

I tell him it all sounds wonderful and thank my lucky stars again that I didn't take Charles up on his offer.

10

This is beyond what I have ever dreamt of, and so far beyond the limits of what I have experienced in my admittedly very limited life that I can scarcely allow myself to believe it is happening to me, that I am really here, in this fabulous marble palace in the middle of a lake, with this incredible man. He's sitting naked in front of me on the private terrace of our royal suite, talking on his mobile. I'm naked too. After arriving by boat and having a drink in the Lily Pond courtyard, we came here and made strenuous love on our vast four-poster bed. The opulent furnishings and fabrics made it seem all the more carnal. I felt like a wild animal as I clawed at Charles's back, at his buttocks, pulling him even further inside me, turning over so that he plunged into me doggy style as I fingered my clitoris with one hand and squeezed his balls with the other.

He probably thinks I'm exhausted, that I'm glad of the respite, but in fact as I lie here watching him, admiring his strong lower back, the curve of it into his buttocks, I'm already plotting my next move. In fact, I won't even wait for him to get off his call. Inching forwards on my lounger, I reach round him and wrap one hand firmly round his cock. His whole body stiffens and then his shoulders start to shake. I can feel the effort it's costing him not to cry out. I start to pump his cock, cradling his balls with my other hand, and I feel my pussy start to flood the recliner beneath me.

Charles cuts short his call with an excuse about the line

being too bad for him to hear properly all of a sudden. He turns to me, but instead of lust on his face there's fury.

'What the fuck do you think you're doing?' he snarls, yanking my hand away from his groin. 'That was an important call, to a big potential client. You could have cost me millions.'

I recoil, afraid for a moment that his anger is such that he's going to slap me, but instead he stands up, looking down at me. 'You have absolutely no idea what's at stake here,' he says, and he turns on his heel and stalks inside, swearing under his breath.

I sit flabbergasted, blinded to the incredible views over the shimmering lake by his outburst. I tell myself that I haven't known him for long, that I misread him, underestimated his seriousness, at least in certain respects. But he has made me feel like a child, and it's an unpleasant sensation, to be scolded like that at my age. I was only having a laugh, encouraged by his nakedness. If it was such an important call, why didn't he dress and go inside to his desk, instead of flaunting his beautiful body in front of me?

Of course I need to say all this to him, but already I know that I won't, that a mumsy housewife like me won't come out tops from a 'discussion' with a business brain of his calibre. No, I've learnt my lesson, and I've also learnt a little about Charles Hoffmann and what makes him tick. What I can and can't get away with.

Nadia takes the hotel boat over to us. We planned to meet on shore, but Charles insisted on staying at the Lake Palace in the end, and I didn't feel able to argue with him after the incident between us. Nadia didn't seem to mind too much, although she did ask if she could bring a friend with her, and also told me they won't stay too long since there is a screening of *Octopussy* this evening on the rooftop of her hotel. Some of the Bond film was shot in the city, she explained, and so there are regular showings in certain cafés and budget hotels.

Dinner, which we opt to take in the less formal of the hotel's restaurants, is quite a sober, even stilted affair, in spite of the presence of Nadia's new 'friend', a chirpy Australian she met at her hostel. He is a very nice boy, or should I say young man, in fact, and probably the only thing that saves the meal from disaster. Nadia still hasn't warmed to Charles and the lingering atmosphere between the two of us probably only serves to make her more wary of him. Charles, meanwhile, is clearly starting to tire of her frostiness; his annoyance with me probably makes it even harder for him to tolerate being given the cold shoulder.

I am glad when it is all over, although I dread being alone again with Charles. As Nadia and Christian head back for the boat, I look after them both enviously and hopefully. Perhaps he will be the one who finally melts my daughter's heart, or at least makes her happy for a time. Sometimes I feel she is more than a little lost, without being able to pinpoint a reason why. She is beautiful, bright, has attracted more than her fair share of handsome boys. So why is there this sadness to her?

On our way back to the suite, however, Charles puts his arm around me, pulls me towards him. 'Listen, Val, I'm sorry for bawling you out,' he says. 'It was out of order.' He stops in the corridor, turns to face me and takes me in his arms. 'I appreciate the gesture, I really do,' he goes on. 'You're one incredibly sexy lady and I love the fact that you keep coming back for more. It's horny as hell. But please, just think next time – there are few things that I would turn you down in favour of, but this is a huge deal for me and I need to be focused.'

I nod, smile at him. 'I'm sorry,' I say. 'I wasn't thinking. It won't happen again.'

'Oh that's a shame,' says Charles. 'I was rather wondering ...'

He reaches round and grasps my buttocks, pulling me up towards him, so that I can feel the rock-hardness of him against my lower belly. I reach up, bring his face to mine, but we don't kiss for long, impelled by our desires towards our suite and the four-poster that awaits us there.

11

'Your mum seems nice,' says Christian on the way back across the lake. 'But that guy she's with is a creep.'

'You think so?'

'Don't you?'

I wrinkle up my face. 'I don't like him,' I say, 'but I don't know why. And he makes Mum happy, so –'

'She didn't seem so happy over dinner.'

'No, you're right. She wasn't her normal self. I think they must have had a row or something. The atmosphere between them had definitely changed.'

'Well, I'm sure they'll sort themselves out. You say she just met this guy?'

'Like, two days ago, in the hotel bar of all places. He picked her up.'

'Or she picked him up.'

I look at him sharply. 'My mum's not like that,' I say, and he apologises, pats my hand and says he didn't mean anything by it.

He's a sweet guy, and when he does that I take his hand and we sit in silence for a while, contemplating the twinkling shore as we approach it. After a minute or two, I turn my head and glance back at Mum's hotel, which looks even more other-worldly when lit up and reflected in the inky waters as it is now. I wonder what she's doing at this very moment, and hope that she's happy, that she and Charles have sorted themselves out, even though I agree with Christian that he's basically a creep and wish she'd never met him. I hope more than anything that she can relax and enjoy herself in that amazing hotel; it may not be to my taste, but she deserves a spot of unashamed luxury after the life she's had.

The boat reaches the shore and we climb out, our hands unclasping. I start back in the direction of the hotel, but Christian catches hold of my wrist, eases me back and, twirling me round by the shoulders, pulls me into his arms. For a moment he just stands looking down at me, eyes sparkling. 'You're amazing, Nadia,' he says at last, and he leans in for a kiss.

I step back, my wrist still in his hand, trying to assess my feelings at this point. There's part of me that just wants to let him lead me back to the hostel, pull my clothes off and take the prize of my virginity, rid me of the cursed thing. I know that he will be gentle and respectful. But as always, I hesitate: am I straight or gay, do I like white or brown flesh? Yes, I could easily sleep with him, and then we will both go our separate ways, no matter how good it was, and we will remember each other with fondness. But is he the one who really does it for me, the one I've been waiting for? If the question poses itself, then the answer must be no.

He's not the kind of guy to take offence or lose his temper with me, and we walk back to the hostel in a companionable rather than an embarrassed silence. At the foot of the stairs up to my room, I turn to him, feeling that he deserves an explanation.

'I don't really understand it myself,' I say. 'You're an attractive guy, and ... it's not that I haven't thought about it today. I've thought about it a lot. But ...'

'It's all right,' he says, one hand on my shoulder, unthreatening, reassuring. 'Neither of us is sticking around, and if there's not any future in it ...'

'It's not even that,' I say ruefully. 'I have no objection to one-night stands. I'm just so confused about myself.' I couldn't bear to take him to the brink and then back out – he's too nice a guy for that.

He frowns, perplexed, and then leans forwards and kisses me lightly on the cheek, musses my hair. 'You're a great girl,' he says. 'I hope you find someone who makes you happy.'

'Ditto you,' I say, smiling regretfully. 'Thanks for everything. Maybe I'll see you in the morning?'

He shrugs. 'I don't think I'll hang around much longer,' he says. 'I'm through here.'

'Where next?' I ask.

'I'll decide when I get to the station,' he says with a grin and another shrug.

I look at him in admiration. How wonderful it would be to be so spontaneous, to put oneself in the hands of fate, I think, as I walk upstairs. How wonderful not to think of the consequences, not to have to play things out in advance.

On my bed, despite my weariness, I think of all the people I've met over the past few days, of all the chances I've had and squandered, and of my life back home. It's always the same story. I came here to escape myself, and also to find myself. It sounds like a paradox, but I really feel that if I shed my skin, the protective layer I wear back in Britain, then the true me will be revealed, my needs and desires acknowledged. But instead I find that I'm just the same old me – fearful, fucked up, incapable of decision or action. What will it take to shake me free?

I lie down. We missed the film, but it's no big deal. Perhaps Christian has gone up there now, has started the process of forgetting me already. Not that I flatter myself that he is in love with me, but he was clearly very taken with me. I pull my top off, then my bra, release my breasts and clasp them in my hands, run my thumbs over the creamy-brown nipples and watch as they spring to life. Then I pull my skirt up above my thighs, till it's all bunched up around me. I let go of my breasts, pull the gusset of my knickers to one side and palpate my clit and lips, thinking of Carla, of Asha. So different yet so beautiful, with their wet little beavers, all clean and shaven, with the look in their eyes, provoking me, asking for a reaction, willing me to do something.

For a while it's hard to make myself come, however much I think of them, however much I visualise their dripping wet snatches – wet, perhaps, for me. Wide open and waiting for me. It's only when I imagine them sitting there, at the end of my bed, arms around each other, hands on each other's thighs, watching me bring myself off, that my orgasm comes, and I scream out in the night, feeling lonelier than I've ever felt before.

12

I'm due to meet Nadia this morning, for breakfast and some sightseeing on land, but when Charles's alarm call goes off at seven-thirty, I decide I need at least another few hours in bed. Last night shattered me – and not only physically. Charles took me to places I'd never even known existed, never dreamt could exist, and in doing so revealed to me how much of my life has been only half lived. It's as if I've been inhabiting a dream for the past twenty years, or perhaps all my life, and now I'm wide, wide awake.

There was pain involved, of course, along with the pleasure. Or should I say: it was as if the pleasure was bound up with the pain, as if they were the two faces of the same experience. Certainly, from the way Charles acted, reacted, it was as if reaching the summit of his own personal pleasure involved a large dose of hurt. 'Exquisite pain,' he'd called it, during one brief moment of respite, jaw clenched, head thrown back on the pillow, eyes tightly closed, beating the bed with his fists. 'Fucking exquisite pain.'

It wasn't long after we got back to Charles's suite that I realised things had changed between us, shifted to a new level. Perhaps, thinking about it now, Charles was still angry with me about the incident on the terrace and wanted to punish me. But even as I say this, I think, no, it would have happened anyway. These are things that are in Charles, awaiting a catalyst. Our little 'misunderstanding' of earlier that day might have been the trigger, but these desires are part of Charles, who he is. I see that clearly now.

'Strip!' he'd barked at me as we were barely over the threshold, and my pussy turned to liquid. But as I began to unbutton my shirt, looking over at him, I was surprised to see the back of him as he walked away from me, over to the minibar to get himself a drink. He didn't offer me one, but stood in the window gazing out at the view. I recognised that I couldn't hold a candle to the sight of the lake at night, of the shore opposite, lit up as if by fairy lights, but I was shocked by his apparent, some might say studied, indifference.

At length, without even turning around, he said, 'Are you ready?'

I was indeed naked by then, my clothes in heaps on the floor around me, shivering slightly with a mixture of desire and fear, mouth parched. What was he going to do with me? There was something different in the air, a kind of threat, but one that excited me. I clutched my pussy with one hand, afraid that my juices might start to rain down from me.

He turned at last, but the room was still unlit, and all I could see was his silhouette in the window, the outline of him; his face was shadowed and undecipherable. 'To the bed,' he said simply. Then he added, 'On all fours.'

I didn't answer, afraid that my voice would sound high pitched and girly and break the spell, but crossed the room and positioned myself as he had bidden. For a few moments there was silence: nothing beyond the plash-plash of the lake water against the wall of the terrace outside. Then footsteps came towards the bed; Charles still had his clothes and shoes on.

He parted my buttocks with his firm hands, as if inspecting a fruit for ripeness, then brought his face to me. I let out a cry as I felt his fingertips around it, digging in, prising me apart to allow his tongue an entry point. Unable to stop myself, I brought one hand to my clit and started vibrating it frenetically, listening to myself whimper. I didn't know if I wanted it to stop or go on forever.

When Charles surfaced, I knew there was nothing I wouldn't do, no way in which I wouldn't humiliate myself, to ensure that he carried on, that he concluded what he had put in motion. But of course he had no intention of stopping there. As I looked over my shoulder, I saw that he was loosening his belt buckle and then the button and fly of his expensive slacks. The cock that he unleashed was proud, majestic – I suddenly felt unworthy of it. My pussy seemed so everyday, so unexceptional: not ugly, for certain, but I'd hardly taken care of it. Charles could see a hundred better ones anywhere he cared to look. Especially in a place like this, full of idle wives free of domestic cares, with nothing better to occupy themselves than afternoon-long plucking, waxing and bleaching sessions at the beauty parlour.

But reminding myself that I *was* here, that it was *me* that Charles had picked out and chosen to invite on this little jaunt, I spread my knees a little wider on the bed to facilitate his explorations, to let him know that I was ready and willing, that I consented to whatever he had in mind. Within a few seconds I felt the tip of his cock pushing against my backside. Beside it, Charles's thumbs pressed into my flesh, stretched it, inched it apart a little more at a time. It hurt, God knows it hurt, but it was a sweet-tasting kind of pain, a sublime one.

I heard Charles spit and knew he was coating his cock with his saliva. My heart thudded: I dreaded what was about to happen, feared not being able to bear it, and yet I wanted more than anything else in the world to know what it felt like. Ravi and I had seldom diverged from the most staid and conventional positions and the idea of anal sex had never even presented itself. It seems amazing now, looking back, that we lived that way for so long, but I suppose that once the rules are laid down in a relationship, the boundaries drawn, people rarely question them, and forget that other things lie beyond. I certainly had.

His cock was at me again, pushing harder now, and I felt myself begin to give, felt my muscles loosen their hold and allow Charles purchase on me. Instinctively, I pushed back and up a little, very gently, reaching back with my own hands to peel my buttocks further apart as Charles's fingers continued to work at my opening. And then, all at once, he forged through and slid right in, and I shrieked in both pain and rapture. There was an incredible tightness to the way I fitted around his cock that felt both dangerous and full of erotic potential. There was no way, as there is with vaginal sex, when you're not feeling into it, or when you've come and you're a bit numb for a while, that you could just ignore it, just go with the ride.

He started thrusting, gently at first, as if finding a way, assessing the terrain, seeing how much I could take. I wanted so much to touch myself at this point, to take up where I'd left off with my clitoris, but I knew that if I did, I'd come straight-away, and if I did that, then he'd probably come too. From the grunts he was emitting, his head on my shoulder, I knew that it was already hard for him to hold back and that when he did come, he would come hard.

I started pushing backwards and forwards on him, meeting his rhythm, accepting it, but letting him know that I was ready for him to increase it, that I could take it. He began thrusting harder, moving in a little deeper each time, as my resistance gave way. Between my spread legs, I could feel his balls bouncing against me, the soft fur of them. With my free hand I reached between my legs, caught hold of them and massaged them against my perineum and lips. Charles moaned, stopped pumping. 'No,' I heard him murmur, and I knew he wouldn't be able to stave off his orgasm for long once he started moving inside me again.

I parted my legs a little further, to their absolute limit, so that I could accommodate him fully. Taking the signal, or unable to stop himself from going on, he jerked himself into me full pelt, to the point where I knew he could advance no further. For a moment he stopped, breathing heavily by my ear, a low moan escaping from his throat. With one hand he sought my pussy opening, slid three fingers inside, and then he started moving again, plunging his amazing cock right in and pulling it far back, to the point where he was about to be released from me, over and over. I hardly needed to attend to my clitoris: the combined action of his fingers inside my pussy and his cock in my anus had me rising, rising, until I felt I was suspended over the bed, losing all contact with the earth, opening up for the greatest climax of my life.

And it was. I tore at the bedclothes with my hands, having at last let go of my clitoris, tears pouring down my cheeks, a strange animal wail issuing forth from my throat as I felt both my pussy and my anus open and contract around Charles. He, too, lost control, riding my bucking form like the most experienced of horsemen, gripping my hip with one hand as if letting go would send him hurtling through the air. It seemed, for a while, as if he would keep coming forever. When he was at last spent, he collapsed forwards onto me, and I in turn fell forwards onto the bed, still crying a little, awed.

I don't know how long we lay there, or if at length I fell asleep beneath Charles, even with his weight on me, but when I sat up he wasn't there. I couldn't see him in the room, but noticing a chink of light coming through the bathroom door reasoned that he must be having a bath.

I knelt up, crawled up the bed, wrapping the sheets gratefully around me. If only Ravi could see me now, I thought, and

I felt a sudden pang for him. I hoped he wasn't lonely. Would our marriage have survived had he done to me the things that Charles was doing to me now? Would he have done them to me if I'd asked him to, to please me? I didn't think so, and yet it had never occurred to me to ask him. If I'd known how good it was, then I think I would. He'd have resisted, certainly. He would probably even have been disgusted. But perhaps I could, over time, have persuaded him to see such things as part of the way we loved each other, rather than the sordid acts that some people thought they were. I would have loved, I thought as I lay there, to share not only my pussy but my anus, the most intimate area of all, with Ravi, to have him worship it with his mouth and cock the way Charles had that night. To celebrate it.

I didn't care that I was a bit sore, a bit bruised and crumpled. Charles had shown me a new source of pleasure, one more shattering than I had known existed. It hurt, yes, but in a curious, compulsive way that made me want to go on and on, hurt a little bit more. It was a testing of limits, but also proof that limits are only there to be tested, to be challenged and shifted back every time. Next time, and I prayed to God there would be a next time, I wanted Charles to push me further, to set me a new challenge, to show me that anything is possible.

I played lazily, sleepily, with my clitoris, astonished by my new appetite. Then, as if responding to my thoughts and my mood, Charles stepped out of the shadows on one side of the room and I realised he'd been standing there all along, in the darkness, and not bathing as I thought. I wondered what he'd been doing, if he'd been watching me. He stepped forwards, and I understood that he had indeed been waiting for me, waiting for me to wake up. I couldn't see his face again, but I saw that he had something in his hand. For a time I couldn't guess what it was, but then as he grew nearer

I made out something consisting of straps and a cock-shaped apparatus. A dildo, I muttered to myself. He's got a dildo.

I thought of my vibrator at home, hidden away in a shoebox at the bottom of my wardrobe. It was seldom used, but over the years it's probably saved me, time and again, when the frustration got too much. Certainly, there were days when, having driven home through the grey streets of Sheffield after taking the kids to school or doing the weekly round of the supermarket, or after switching off the Hoover and thinking What next?, I'd lain back on the sofa with my legs open, pulled my knickers to one side and given myself a quick orgasm to cheer myself up. Usually it was like that – a quick fix, a brief blast of ecstasy to blow away the cobwebs and recharge myself for the drudgery. Occasionally it turned into something more. Running a bath rich with scented oil, I'd rub a handful into my pussy, furtively at first, and then dragging it out, luxuriating in the feeling, until I'd have to go and hunt out my vibrator, climb into bed, and spend a good half-hour pleasuring myself, often nearly letting the bath overflow I'd get so carried away. It was a rabbit vibrator, so I'd generally spend at least half that time teasing my clitoris with it, submitting myself to its delicious frisson and then moving it away when I felt my climax building up, exploring my wet lips with it, and sometimes the flesh around my arse too. Finally, unable to deny myself any longer, I'd push it inside me, turning on the G-spot stimulator full of beads, the swivelling head and the clitoral attachment to give myself one mighty orgasm. After that, the domestic chores were so much more manageable.

So I was no stranger to sex toys. I just didn't know what Charles had in mind, as I watched him approach the bed. I could see his eyes now, in the moonlight streaming in through one window, and there was a dangerous glint to them. His face was deadly serious. This was not a man who took his sexual gratification lightly, as it had first seemed to me, when he so casually brought himself off on my pussy on the terrace of the Dome bar. This was a man who meant business in everything he did.

He handed me the dildo, and I understood at once. I knelt up, inspected it to make sure I was clear how it was to fit on me, and then wrapped it around me and buckled up. Charles, meanwhile, was looking around for something at the bottom of the bed. Having found it, he stayed where he was, gestured for me to join him there. I crawled down towards him, the harness secure around my waist, the dildo flopping beneath my belly, and he held his belt out to me. There was a commanding look on his face, as if he would brook no dissension, but beneath it I thought I saw something imploring in his eyes, a kind of need.

I snatched the belt from him, clasped him roughly by the shoulder and twisted him round, so that he was backed up against one pole of the four-poster. He leant his head against it, chin jutting into the air, and closed his eyes. His breath, I noticed, was coming in quick shallow gasps. Pulling his arms back around the pole until his wrists met, I wound the belt around and around them and then, with the slack, tied him to the bed. His cock was erect. For a moment I stood back and admired the sight of him in the moonlight: naked, eyes closed, lips parted slightly, as if he were letting out a long silent moan; he was resplendent.

I stepped forwards, brought the tip of the dildo to that of his cock, let it graze it, flirt with it for few seconds. He inhaled sharply, arched his back against the pole and, as I withdrew my fake dick, tried to follow it with his own, all too real. A bead of liquid shone at its tip. Reaching for it with my hand, I held it tightly for a moment, amazed that a cock could be so beautiful. It was all I could do not to reach down and finger myself at this point, but I recognised that this was not my moment, that this was not about me. I had had my pleasure, more pleasure than many women can hope to enjoy in a whole lifetime of sexual encounters if they're with the wrong men. This was about Charles, about some need in him for submission, for falling out of control. I went down on him, slurped and jabbed at his cock with my tongue, took his balls in my mouth in turn and then together while I shuttled one hand up and down his shaft.

Yet this was not what he wanted, what he really wanted, and we both knew it. Belly-down on the bed, I yanked Charles's legs wide apart and pulled his knees up. He opened his eyes then, looked down at me, a peculiar half smile flitting about his lips. I met his gaze, then looked away, slid my hands between his legs and, pulling aside one buttock with each hand, looked at his anus. Like the rest of him, it was clean and neat, a lovely thing. It seemed like the most natural thing in the world to want to get close to it and, in any case, I wanted to repay the compliment he had paid mine by so obviously taking pleasure in it. I licked the fingers of one hand, brought them close to him, let them flutter about his hole to get him used to the idea for a moment. Then I pushed them slowly in. He growled, as his body jerked off the bed towards me. I took his cock back into my mouth and syncopated its movements with the thrusting of my hand. Charles jerked like a puppet against the bed pole.

Before he could achieve release in my mouth, I reached around and loosened the belt from the pole and untied his hands. Sensing my next move, he turned obediently around, knelt forwards. I pulled each hand around the pole again, retied them. His head was down like a dog's, but the arc of his back, the upwards turn of his buttocks were proud.

I wet him with my mouth, plentifully, calling forth all my reserves of saliva. I wished we had some lube, would have expected him to provide some since the dildo was clearly a stalwart in his luggage. The fact he didn't suggested that this was such a common practice that he no longer needed it, that he would yield easily enough. I wondered if he did it mainly by himself or with other sexual partners. The thought gave me a little stab of jealousy. Who were these sexual partners: fellow travellers, like me, who he picked up in bars, or regular lovers? How many women had satisfied him with this very dildo before? And – the question came to me from out of the blue but seemed to be obvious as soon as it had posed itself – were any of his partners men?

I felt a kind of surge of anger – anger that I couldn't have Charles to myself, that he was the kind of man I would have to share if I were to have him at all. These past couple of days I'd been kidding myself, telling myself we were an item, that I was embarking on a new and lasting relationship that could somehow be worked around his globetrotting lifestyle. I hadn't thought it all through consciously; I suppose in the back of my brain there lurked the notion that, divorced and with no job, I'd tag along with him.

Now I saw clearly, as I knelt back up, wiped my mouth with the back of my hand and brought the dildo towards his moist hole, that Charles was not the type of man to be satisfied with one person, that his appetites were too great and too varied. Keeping hold of him would mean accepting I could only ever have a little piece of him, for short periods of time. I knew that I was not a woman for whom that would be possible.

I drove the dildo into him with a kind of fury. His torso jerked forwards, his head back. I grabbed a handful of his hair, pulled it even further back, sank my teeth into his shoulder, pushing deeper, ever deeper, and then retreating slowly. For a while I continued this slow motion, teeth still in his flesh. Then I increased my pace and, as my clitoris bashed against his lower back, sending shockwaves through me, I clasped my nipples between my fingertips and pinched them hard, then harder still, until Charles and I were crying out in unison. As the dildo worked its magic on his prostate from inside, he took his cock in his fist and began pumping in time to it, and it was only a few seconds before I saw the jet of white shoot out from him, spatter down onto the bed.

As he collapsed forwards against the bed pole, gasping for breath, I let myself fall back against the bed behind me and, twisting the dildo round so it hung down over one hip, masturbated frenetically. As I flooded the bedclothes beneath me with my come, I looked over at Charles, still clinging to the pole like a shipwreck, with a mixture of love and hate fizzing inside me.

I lie on the bed, chafed and a little heartbroken. Beside me is the note Charles left for me when he went out this morning: *Meetings all day. Back for dinner, I hope. Have booked you in at the spa at noon – enjoy.*

Nadia is furious with me, hung up on me. I can understand why – I let her down again, and again because of Charles. She called him 'that bastard', told me I was acting like a teenager letting my head be turned, that it was insulting to her to have come this far with me and then be brushed aside in favour of some stranger. How could I explain to her what the past couple of days has meant to me? To do so would mean telling her how flat things were between her father and me, how lacking our relationship was in crucial respects. Although we've put her through the pain of our divorce, I'd rather not go into such intimacies with her, and in doing so make her see that we probably only stayed together so long because of the kids.

I'd do anything for my daughter, and she knows it. But we have plenty of time before us to sightsee, and today – today, I can barely move. My body isn't used to all of this. The promise of spa treatments is the only thing that's keeping me going, although I'll have a hot bath first, see if that helps at all. Of course, again, I can't tell Nadia the reason I'm so wrecked is that I was awake through the night, being sodomised by Charles, then sodomising him in turn. She probably wouldn't believe me anyway. So I had to blame it on drink, and she will probably infer the rest anyway, or part of it. She'll remain miffed for a while, but she's an eighteen-year-old between A levels and university, and I think she'll come round by the end of the day. Even mums have the right to let their hair down every once in a while.

13

I feel so alone. Christian has gone; he checked out first thing this morning according to the receptionist. Although he'd told me he was going, his absence makes me sadder than I expected. I think of him at the dinner table last night, at Mum's hotel, and of how wonderful he was handling Mum and Charles, despite the sour mood that hung over the table like stale lake mist. He was a blast of air in my life, potential boyfriend material, but what do I do but give him the brush off, as per bloody usual, and then go to my room and wank myself silly over a couple of girls I'll never see again. It doesn't make sense. It makes me sick to think I could be in his room right now, in his bed, skin against his taut, tanned body, satisfied, for once, by something other than my own hand.

And then there's Mum. We'd had this loose arrangement to breakfast together, then have a look around Udaipur – Charles had mentioned at dinner that he'd be in meetings most of the day. Of course, if anything had come about with Christian and me, I'd have preferred to spend the day with him. But that shouldn't have been a problem: Mum seemed to really like him at dinner, so there's no reason he couldn't have tagged along too.

But no, it's too much to ask that she should spare a few hours of her precious company for the daughter she's travelled 6,000 miles with. When I got through to her room, she answered the phone in a scarred, groggy voice, told me she wasn't feeling up to it. I asked her why, and she said she'd overdone it on the booze.

Of course, I knew that was only half the story. Maybe she did have one or two too many, but I'm pretty sure there was more to her exhaustion than that. I'd rather not know, of course. I'd rather not think about her and the creep at it like rabbits till the early hours. It hurts that she's letting this affair with Charles take precedence over time with her own daughter.

Thinking about it now though, I wonder if I've been a bit harsh on her. After all, I didn't mention to her that Christian has left, so she's probably thinking it's no big deal my being let down by her, that I'll be happy spending some time with him. But how would I even begin to explain to her what happened last night? The way I receded as soon as he advanced, only to go and pleasure myself in my room and then nearly cry this morning when I found out I'd never see him again. It's idiotic. Who am I to judge her for giving herself over so entirely to this thing with Charles? At least she's taking her opportunities by the throat, living her life at last. The same can't be said of me.

But I don't regret what I said to her about Charles, harsh as it may seem. There's something cold and calculating about him, even for a businessman obsessed with wealth and status and power over other people. I'm worried that she's falling for him, and that he's going to let her down badly. As far as I'm concerned, the sooner it's over between the two of them the better. In fact, I think I'm going to have start calling the shots today. Udaipur is devastatingly beautiful, but it's dead to me now that Christian is gone, tainted by my memories of him. In fact, its very beauty nauseates me. Of course, there's poverty here as everywhere else in India, but the lovely bits are just too lovely, a parody of loveliness, and I find myself longing for grime and squalor, a bit of real life.

I pack my things, shoulder my rucksack. I'll go find some breakfast, and then I'll head for Mum's hotel and tell her we're leaving town today.

14

Sitting here in the shade of a mango tree, trailing one hand in the pool as I sip my champagne and feast on strawberries, I'm really rather glad I didn't go out sightseeing with Nadia, in spite of my lingering guilt. I have to keep reminding myself that I deserve all this, that I've had very few treats in my life and that I'm not unworthy of it all. And anyway, if Charles and I are over, as I suspect we are, then I may as well take advantage of his generosity until we part ways.

I haven't thought too much about when that will be. It largely depends on what happens with Nadia and that lovely boy Christian she brought to dinner. If she's hooked on him and wants to stay in Udaipur a while, then I can't begrudge her that after my own selfish behaviour. I'm sure there's plenty to see and do to keep me occupied while she gets her share of romance, or sex, or whatever it turns out to be between them. A mixture, I hope.

Charles is leaving soon anyway; he was vague when he mooted the idea of my accompanying him here, said 'a couple of days', but I suspect he's scheduled to move on tomorrow. I've no idea where to – he hasn't talked about the future at all. It wouldn't surprise me if he asks me to carry on travelling with him. Despite his little outburst of yesterday, he seemed satisfied with me last night, more than satisfied at the time. I think I've passed the test. And he's evidently fond enough of me to splash out on expensive little treats.

And some treat it was. In a gorgeous room surrounded by

erotic frescoes of bathing Rajasthani princesses, flickering with candlelight, I was given a speciality Mewar Khas signature treatment that Charles had picked out for me. The masseuse told me that it was derived from a pre-bathing ritual once practised by royals to prepare for their wedding day. Beginning with a sandalwood, turmeric and herb scrub to exfoliate my skin, followed by an aromatherapy massage, it was just what my tired, aching, rather bruised body needed, although the irony of Charles having chosen a bridal massage for a woman who is about to leave him didn't escape me.

But that, in a way, is the problem – I'm no longer the type to wait around all day for her busy, successful man to come home, divine though the massage was. I couldn't live like this every day, it's just not in my blood. A lifetime of domestic servitude clearly isn't desirable or something that I miss, but it has instilled in me the inability to be idle, at least in any sustained form. I feel, bizarrely, like a trophy wife, or a geisha, or a mistress – there to service my man, whenever he shows up, whenever he has time for me. The rest of the time I must entertain myself or be entertained in some costly way. It really just isn't me. Even lying here beneath the mango tree, sipping my champagne, I feel like a phoney, an interloper in a world to which I don't belong. Perhaps I'm mad, but I've realised I don't want the kind of life I would have with Charles.

I rise at last, head back to my suite to call Nadia, hoping that I can reach her on her mobile. If I can't, I'll pack and go to try and find her at her guesthouse. The Panoramic, did she say? Yes, that was it. I can't remember its location from the taxi ride – I had other things on my mind – but the boatman will be able to tell me where that is.

I'm just approaching my suite, composing in my mind the letter to Charles, thanking him for the massage and everything else, when I see a figure skulking at the end of the corridor.

It turns, and I realise it's Nadia. She steps towards me and beside her, leaning against the wall, I see her rucksack.

I smile. 'I'll just going to pack,' I say. 'I won't be more than fifteen minutes.'

She grins, opens her arms for a hug.

15

Mum blossoms as we travel through Rajasthan, taking in the blue city of Jodhpur, with its clusters of traditional houses painted a pale indigo, originally to denote that Brahmins lived in them, and the pink city of Jaipur, colour-washed in the nineteenth century, according to my guidebook, in order to emulate the light-red sandstone used in Mughal cities. She delights in the vibrant colours, not only of the buildings but of the women's saris, and of the scintillating fabrics on display at the many markets that we visit, alongside pungent blood-red chillies, whole and in powder form, heaped on the pavement or spilling forth from sacks. With her little digital camera she takes thousands of photos, and her wheel-along case is soon filled with swatches of material; over lunches and dinners she talks endlessly of her youthful ambitions to be a fashion designer, stifled – I presume, although she never says as much – by marriage and motherhood.

I don't mind that she goes on a bit – I'm just grateful that she is free from the clutches of Charles and that I didn't have to force the issue. She had made the decision herself, although she hasn't explained to me why, or not in much detail. She just told me she didn't think she was the kind of woman who could live the life of an idle wife or mistress. I sensed there was more to it than that – after all, no one would force her to live that way. Even if she had stayed with him, had travelled around with him, she could have forged a life for herself, could have even started up as a designer just as she's talking about now.

No, something happened between them to make her back off, but I'm not going to probe. It's her own business. And perhaps there are some things about one's own mother one is better off not knowing anyway.

For my own part, I'm starting to question the choices I've made, the life I've plotted out for myself. I'm due to begin a degree in media studies in London next year, but being in India has made me wonder about it all. Here in Rajasthan there are acute water shortages, and I've read that half of the children under three are malnourished and half of the women are anaemic. I don't know what can be done about the devastating droughts that plague the region, but thinking about it makes my life back in Britain, my petty troubles, my future plans, seem utterly meaningless. Although media studies is no longer the joke subject it was ten or so years ago, I wonder what relevance it will have to the world, beyond preparing me, perhaps, for a job in marketing or PR or journalism. And is that really what I want to do with my life?

I try to enjoy travelling, and Mum and I start to have a good time together, but all this is just another layer of confusion to add to my overall feelings of not knowing who the hell I am. It's tempting to talk to Mum about it all, but I'm embarrassed, especially about the sex side of things. How can I tell her I'm torn between boys and girls, that I don't know if I like snatches or dicks best, that I might well be bisexual? That not being able to decide is making me miserable and frustrated, and losing me people I start to care about? Mum's led a fairly cloistered life and I'm pretty sure she's never had a bisexual or gay friend, or not one that she's known to be such. And then there's the race thing, and I don't see how much help she can give me with my feeling of being stuck in the middle, neither one thing nor the other. Sure, as a white woman married to an Indian man when such things were much less common than they are now, I'm sure she's had more than her fair share of prejudice to contend with, her own battles to fight. But she remained white; she never tried to become Indian in habit, dress or whatever. So I don't think she could empathise with this split I feel in me, this sense of never quite fitting in, of standing out.

We agree on going on out to Jaisalmer, the 'golden city', this time, perched on a ridge of honey-coloured sandstone and crowned by a fort. From there, we've heard, you can take a camel safari out into the Thar Desert and sleep under the stars. I've also read, on a travellers' chat room, that the city is slowly collapsing, its historic buildings crumbling like biscuit after piped water and underground sewers were installed to service both the growing population and the increase in tourists. Together with monsoons and a huge earthquake a few years ago, seepage from these conduits into foundations has made the whole place unstable, and almost led to the loss of the city's oldest palace.

It's the perfect opportunity for me to fill Mum in on some of the evils of the five-star hotels she loves so much, and to insist that we forgo staying in one in favour of something more eco-friendly – a town-house hotel called the Killa Bhawan, recommended on the same green talkboard. When we arrive, Mum is not at all put out – the rooms are brightly painted, in shades of crimson, lime green and orange, and there are amazing views from the three terraces, especially at sunset when the declining sun seems to set the whole city alight. There are no baths, but Mum says she can cope with that, especially when the friendly staff talk to us about the restoration projects underway. She finally seems to understand that visiting a place can't just be about taking from it, that you have to treat it with respect, at the very least, and even picks up a leaflet on the Jaisalmer in Jeopardy campaign. The same staff also advise us on a reputable firm – a two-brother outfit – with whom to book a camel tour, since the choice is vast and the quality is said to vary wildly.

We go to bed happy to be here. Mum, it seems, has forgotten all about Charles – or at least, if not forgotten, then is secure in the knowledge that she did the right thing by leaving him. As for me – well, I do think of Christian with fondness, but we knew each other for such a short space of time, I can't really miss him. And I've come to the conclusion that if I'd really wanted to, I'd have gone for it. I shouldn't keep doing my head in about missing opportunities: I'll know when the right one comes along.

We've opted for a short tour, venturing only a short distance into the desert and spending a single night there. There are longer safaris, but we need to get moving soon. Mum has made arrangements to meet someone down in Goa, and we certainly won't be flying this time, so we'll need several days to make the trip.

Our camel driver, Rajesh, came to our hotel to fetch us after lunch; we'd spent the morning exploring the streets of the fort, one of the oldest inhabited ones in the world, with its intricately carved *haveli*s. It is he who is leading us out into the sand dunes now, on our plodding, farting camels, while his brother Abhay drives ahead in a Jeep, to the spot where we will set up camp tonight, the Sam dunes. He has not only bedding but cooking apparatus and the ingredients from which the pair will magic up our evening meal.

Rajesh doesn't have his own beast, instead either walking along beside us, chiding the camels along with a big stick, or taking it in turns to ride pillion behind me or Mum. Or that's the theory, but he spends more time with me, since my camel is the most unruly, constantly threatening to break into a gallop and separate from its mate. Seeing that I am struggling to control it and that I'm a little panicked, he climbs up behind me and puts his arms around me to hold the reins and exert a little authority on the camel. His English isn't great, but every time the camel lets out another fetid fart, we laugh together, and Mum, a few metres ahead, looks back and smiles at us.

Rajesh must be in his late-twenties, his brother a good five years older, although their faces are slightly weathered from the elements, like the buildings of Jaisalmer itself, so they may be a few years younger than they first appear. They're both lean and fit from their sorties into the Thar. I wonder at this strange life they lead, taking tourists out into the seemingly endless sand dunes, day after day, spending their nights beneath the vast open sky. Do they have families back in Jaisalmer? What occupies their thoughts as they walk or ride, for the thousandth, the five-thousandth time, towards an ever-receding horizon?

You'd think you'd relax, on such a journey, but largely deprived of noise and other stimuli, my mind is working over-time. Seeing the women, still wonderfully colourful in their albeit ragged saris, walking long distances to collect water in clay jugs that they balance on their heads, or carrying massive bundles of laundry, also on their heads, to the river, to spend their whole day scrubbing at it, is giving me a fresh perspective on my comfortable life in the West. In many ways I feel like a voyeur: after all, I have paid this man to bring me here, to show me this place. But not liking all of what I see is making me question my right to even be here, if I can't help improve the lot of these women, if my very presence is adding to their problems. How dare I come and take the water for which they have to walk miles every day?

Of course, it's not all angst: there's incredible beauty here too, especially in the form of a couple of deserted villages that we get off to explore. I take plenty of photos and consider emailing the student newspaper of the college I am to attend next year to see if they are interested in commissioning a feature on the Jaisalmer in Jeopardy campaign. I wrote for my school newspaper, and it's an obvious way for me to help put something back into this country.

We arrive at our destination just as the sun is beginning to go down and, as Rajesh and Abhay build a small fire on which to brew up some reviving *chai*, Mum and I go for a walk over the dunes, which are shaped into waves and crests by the desert winds. As the sun sinks towards the horizon, these dunes change colour almost perceptibly, and we hold our breath, awestruck, at the otherworldliness of the setting.

There's not much to do here, clearly, and, as soon as we've finished our *chai*, chatting as best we can with the brothers but hindered by their limited English and our non-existent Hindi and Marwari, they begin to prepare supper. Mum and I sit beside them on the sand, watching them chop vegetables, helping out where we can, talking between ourselves.

As the light diminishes and the stars wink into life above us, I study Rajesh while he stirs the potato and green bean curry he has prepared, then rolls out the *roti* and forms the *kadhi* dumplings with his hands. The latter, though gnarled from the camel driving, are quick, dextrous; his arm are sinewy. Like his face, his body is interesting, bears witness to a life spent largely in the open, amidst nature. I envy him in a way: everyone has their troubles, but this seems such an uncomplicated life, to a large extent free of the material possessions that we in the West claim are essential, claim as our right.

I find myself strangely attracted to this silent weather-beaten man hunched over his fire, lost in the task of preparing our dinner; there's a mystery to him, an impenetrability that arouses me. There'd be no need for small talk, with Rajesh, for any of the nonsense involved in becoming someone's lover – the chat-up lines, the playing hard to get, the mind games. I'd just put my hand on his strong wiry arm and he'd understand and lie back on the sand, unwrapping his skirtlike *dhoti* from around his hips and under his groin to reveal his lean brown thighs. Kneeling on the sand, I'd strip, slowly, savouring the feel of the desert breezes on my bare skin, the feeling of communing with my surroundings. His prick would be straining for me in the moonlight, and after wetting it with my mouth, sucking at it as I fondled his balls, I'd straddle him and ride him through the night, wordlessly, feeling every sensation intently, the lack of other stimuli heightening everything, until our fucking became like a prayer or a hymn to nature.

Startled back to reality by Mum's voice, I look across at her. She's accepting a bowl of curry from Abhay, thanking him in slow, over-enunciated English. I take mine in turn, and we sit in near silence, sharing our meal with the brothers, hearing the cries of animals we can't identify ring out in the encroaching darkness. Mum looks slightly apprehensive all of a sudden, but given that Rajesh and Abhay don't react to the sounds in any way, I decide that there can't be anything too threatening out there.

After dinner, Rajesh shows us over to our 'bed', which he has made on the top of a large dune with a flattish top. Mum and I laugh nervously: it seems almost absurd to be spending the night so exposed to the elements, now that we're here; a little foolish to be roofless like this.

The brothers retreat and, as we undress and change into our pyjamas in the darkness, we see them sitting in the Jeep, the ends of their cigarettes flaring and then dying back, over and over. The low chunter of their voices is reassuring. We climb into bed, pull the cover up and say goodnight to each other.

It takes a long time to get to sleep, what with the snuffling noises of the animals against an almost eerie quiet, and the sky above us is so breathtaking I can hardly bear to close my eyes. Beside me, Mum is restless too, but we don't talk. Now that our feelings of foolishness have dissipated, there's something almost religious to this experience and neither of us wants to break the spell.

But sleep must claim me at last, for I awake with a start and, reaching across for Mum to reassure me, find that she's not there. I nearly flip – perhaps the animals we heard aren't so harmless after all. Who are these people we've come out here with anyway? The guest house recommended them, but for all we know they could be inexperienced chancers with little knowledge of the desert and what lurks here.

I leap up, look around, waiting for my eyes to grow accustomed to the darkness. Noticing the embers of the fire still smouldering, I begin to walk towards it. The dark bulk of the Jeep reveals itself not far away. I turn around. I don't want to call out, in case I attract unwanted attention from some predatory creature, so I'll just have to creep around on the sand until I work out where Mum has gone. Perhaps she's just answering a call of nature, seeking out a spot in which to pee. Perhaps I'm overreacting.

After fifty metres or so I come to a halt. Mum *is* answering a call of nature, but not the one I'd imagined. On the ridge of a nearby dune, I see the silhouettes of two figures rolling around in a passionate embrace, and now that I'm close I can hear their moans. One of them is female. I turn away, start running back towards our bed, not wanting to see any more.

16

I haven't smoked in years, but when I hear Nadia start snoring and know that she's finally dropped off, I get up and walk over to the Jeep to crash a cigarette. The older camel driver is sitting in the driver's seat; as I climb in the passenger seat, he motions into the back and I see his little brother asleep there, curled up beneath a sheet.

'No sleep?' he says, and I shake my head and gesture around me.

'Too beautiful,' I say, and he seems to understand, smiling and nodding.

For a while, the time it takes to smoke my cigarette, we sit in silence. I think about Charles, wonder what he's doing now, what he thought when he read my note. Did he call me a traitorous bitch or did he, as I suspect is more likely, shrug off my departure, get on the phone to some little friend in his next port of call? Was he sleeping now, or wakeful in some plush hotel suite in another city, taking his dildo out of his case, handing it to his companion with that commanding yet needy gleam to his eyes? Has he even given me a second thought since I've gone?

I glance over at Abhay to find him looking at me. He smiles shyly. There's nothing commanding to his expression, and I realise that what first turned me on in Charles, the way he decided in a flash what he wanted and set out immediately to get it, brooking no dissension, is exactly what turned me against him in the end. He was calling all the shots and I was his puppet.

I place my hand on Abhay's thigh, lower down towards the knee. I don't want to scare him away, want him to know he can trust me, that I won't push any further if he doesn't want me to. He places his hand over mine, lightly, looking down at it and not at my face, and I feel his fingers trembling. Then he seems to come to a decision.

'Not here,' he says, glancing up at me, head jerking back towards his sleeping brother, and he lets go of my hand while we climb out of the Jeep. Then he walks round the front of it, takes my hand again and leads me over the dunes without a word. For a while we stand kissing, his hands moving lightly over me, flitting over my nipples, erect beneath my flimsy pyjama top, and then I feel an immense need for him inside me and, taking off my top and slipping out of my pyjama bottoms, lower myself to the sand.

'No,' he utters. 'Wait.' I watch as he unties his *dhoti* and then unfolds it so that it forms a sheet. His thighs are muscled and lean from all the walking and camel-riding; over them rises his cock, bobbing a little, eager for me. I lie down on the *dhoti*, rub my pussy lips, in a hurry now to feel him within me. It's only been a couple of days, but already I feel deprived, in need of satisfaction beyond the pleasure my own hand could bring me. Abhay slides into me easily. I raise my buttocks a little, bear downwards to meet his tentative thrusts and welcome him in. In response he slides his hands under my buttocks, lifts them a little higher, then a lot higher, looping them over his shoulders, so that now he's kneeling and I'm up on my shoulders. The position, which I've never tried, allows him to get in really deeply, and also exposes my clitoris to his gaze. He admires it for a moment, then brings one thumb to it, starts brushing it with the pad.

Suddenly he stops, looks to one side, as if he's heard something. For a moment he squints into the darkness, one finger over his lips, then he shakes his head as if he was imagining things, or as if whatever it was – I don't know what kind of animals might roam this desert at night and I'd rather not spook myself by letting my mind dwell on it too much – is of no import. I take advantage of the hiatus to gradually lower my hips to the ground again and turn over. Feeling more assertive than I ever have in my life, I guide Abhay down, so that he's sitting up, and then I climb aboard him and slot myself down over him. He clutches my buttocks hard as I slide myself up and down his pole, his mouth and tongue on my nipples, kissing, sucking. Then I lean back, my eyes filled with starlight, and, bringing my hand to my clitoris, bring myself to orgasm with him inside me – an act that, in turn, causes him to climax too. As my own carries me away, I sink my teeth into my hand to avoid screaming out into the night and waking the others, or drawing the attention of animals to us. Abhay, when he comes, does so open-throated but silently, head thrown back against the *dhoti* as his whole body convulses against mine.

Afterwards we say nothing. What is there to say? This will never happen again and there's no point in making it out to be anything more than it is. But I already know, as I head back to my makeshift bed on the dune, that I'll never forget my night in the desert and my taciturn but hot-blooded camel driver.

17

I wake up and Mum is beside me again. For a moment I wonder if it was all no more than a dream or me imagining things in the dark strangeness of the desert night. But then I see the telltale sign on her neck, like a little red weal, and I know that it is true – that Mum seduced one of our drivers. Of course, it could be that it was one of them who seduced her, but I can't imagine it. They both seem quite restrained, and there was certainly no flirting going on over *chai* or dinner.

She looks beautiful as she lies there, her hair streaming back over the thin roll-up mattress that Rajesh laid out on the sand for us, and although I still feel a little squeamish about having seen even as much as I did, there are other emotions at play – I'm happy that she's happy, or is at least having a good time after all those years of near-slavery. I'm envious and resentful too – not only because this was supposed to be my time of discovery, not hers, but at the fact that she seems able to act on her desires and I don't. In fact, here I seem even less able to act on my desires than I did at home, and part of me is wondering whether that might not be down to Mum's presence. If I were travelling alone, or with Katie, would I feel freer to follow through on my impulses? Am I held back by the thought that she might find out what I've done and disapprove?

I don't say anything when she wakes up, but as we pack up our little camp and load it into the Jeep while Rajesh feeds and waters the camels in readiness for the ride back to Jaisalmer,

I catch a look exchanged between Mum and Abhay that tells me all I need to know about what happened last night. At least, it wasn't Rajesh. I've that to be grateful for.

Our combined journeys down to Goa, via Delhi, take a couple of days despite our catching an 'express' train, and so I agree to go first class. Mum may be sprightly for her age – in fact, a bit of a goer, as it turns out – but the second-class accommodation seems a little basic to me. In any case, I hardly feel that I'm selling out by giving Indian Railways a little more of our cash. It's hardly Hilton that's profiting from me.

I wasn't at all keen on coming to Goa because of its association with hippies and rave parties but also because it's now full of package holidayers too, but as soon as Mum got involved with this trip she was keen to meet a colleague of her yoga teacher, Christopher Mulholland, who runs a beachside retreat in the state. But now that I'm here, I'm really rather glad I agreed. I've never done yoga before, to my shame, but sitting with Christopher – Chris as he insists we call him – in the kitchen of his old Portuguese house-cum-studio in southern Calangute, my hopes are awakened that practising it will help me to achieve a degree of mental peace and clarity that will put an end to my inner turmoil and confusion. As well as resulting in better physical health through the alleviation of postural/structural problems, Chris explains as he pours from a pot of wild fennel tea, the Iyengar yoga that he teaches can help to release emotional tensions, which facilitates deeper self-knowledge and hence greater self-confidence.

It helps, too, that Chris is drop-dead gorgeous. He must be in his early thirties, roughly midway between Mum's and my ages, and simply oozes charisma in an indefinable way. I suppose that's what charisma is, really: a mysterious extra something that you can't quite put your finger on. He's tall and quite willowy, without being overly skinny, and you can tell even from his everyday movements – the way he stretches up to a high shelf for the tin of tea, the way he bends to tie an errant shoelace – that he is incredibly limber. His hair, which he keeps tied back in a short ponytail, is prematurely greying, but that only seems to make him even more attractive, lend him an authority and dignity beyond his age. His face is serious and pensive, as befits his beliefs and morals, yet there's a twinkle to his eyes, a kind of mischief flitting behind them, as if just waiting for the opportunity to show its face.

I feel, too, that he's a soulmate. He talks to us passionately about the huge environmental problems that exist here too, which, again, include water shortages through overdevelopment, combined with over-fishing and iron-ore mining. He doesn't take offence when I ask him if he doesn't feel implicated in all of this by attracting tourists to the region to take part in his workshops, but merely sighs, leans back in his chair, frowning slightly.

'I'll confess,' he says, 'that I have had my qualms, my sleepless nights, about the whole issue. But I came here as a hippy, a long long time ago, before much of what you see today existed. Yes, I took my fair share of psychedelic drugs, danced under the full moon, acted like your stereotypical arsehole under the guise of being a free spirit. But that got boring more quickly than you'd think. I wanted to stay. Who wouldn't? But I realised that I needed to be part of the community and to give something to it. So I went up to Pune to train in Iyengar yoga, and then I came back and set up here. I haven't showed you round yet,' he goes on, 'but I'm serious about the environment. All the water used here is recycled, the lights and showers are solar-powered and there are eco-loos. The guest rooms are furnished with a mixture of colonial antiques and items made locally from sustainable bamboo, the carpets are made of natural coir and there's no air-con – you open your window if you want some air. Oh, and the food is all organic and veggie.'

I listen to him talk, nodding approvingly, and feel like I might be falling in love. What I know for certain is that were Chris to make a pass at me, all hesitancy would fall away from me, that I would do whatever he asked of me and more, that I would give myself to him without holding anything back. The knowledge that I've met such a person at last thrills me enormously; I'm afraid, of course, but it's a kind of delicious terror at what's in store, an overwhelming sense of anticipation and pure bodily longing.

Chris is looking at Mum. 'Val, I know you said you'd stay only a day or two, but if you don't have immediate plans to be elsewhere, there are a couple of places left on this week's course. I had two ladies cancel at late notice. I won't charge you, of course – it's on me.' He smiles, and I feel light-headed. 'Although you will have to pitch in, as everybody does, with the cooking and other chores.'

Mum looks at me. 'What do you think?' she asks, and I can tell by the excited look on her face that she really wants to do this. She's been doing yoga for a couple of years back in Sheffield, and has told me how great it makes her feel, both physically and mentally. It strikes me now, looking at her so relaxed, that it might not be a coincidence that she started practising yoga not so long before things fell apart between her and Dad. Did the yoga bring *her* mental clarity, awakening her to the possibilities to which domestic routine had deadened her for 25 years?

'I'm game,' I say with a smile, 'if you are.'

Chris claps his hands and stands up. 'Great,' he says. 'Now if you don't mind, I have to check my internet bookings and deal with other mundane matters. But I'll see you ladies later for dinner with the other guests.'

We start early the next day, with meditation on the beach to greet the rising sun, followed by a yoga session in the cool studio with its cow-dung floor. Conversation at dinner last night was dominated by a couple of American women, who monopolised Christopher's attention, and I'm eager to see him again, to be able to just admire his magnificent physique as he talks us through the moves in his slow, measured, calming voice. From time to time he does the rounds of the space, checking our alignments, whispering encouragement, sometimes nudging people into a slightly better position with a light touch of his hand. I find myself purposefully positioning my leg or arm a little askew in the hope that I will be the recipient of one of his touches, but I never am. It crosses my mind that the other students – all women – may be employing the same strategy in order to win his attention.

Afterwards we breakfast in the courtyard, cross-legged on low-level cushions, blue kingfishers perching on the branches of the trees overhead. We feast on the freshest, sweetest payaya and watermelon, tiny bananas, home-made muesli with curd made from local buffalo milk and organic coffee and *masala chai*. I try to catch Christopher's eye several times as I eat, to let him know, more than anything, my profound admiration for his values and the way he has chosen to live his life. But as in the yoga studio, he remains somewhat aloof, without losing any of his friendliness. I tell myself that he's just being professional, that it would be out of order for him to show any favouritism towards his guests just because he has a personal connection to a couple of them, and a tenuous one at that.

But this reserve only serves to enflame me further, and I'm glad when Mum tells me that she's going for a stroll up the beach, giving me an opportunity to sneak back to our room for a wank. Rolling around on the bed, my hand between my legs, three fingers inside myself, I close my eyes and imagine it's Christopher who's pleasuring me, Christopher with his thoughtful green eyes, his guiding hands easing me into the correct position for orgasm. When I picture in my mind's eye his lithe, supple body between my thighs, imagine the feel of his mouth on my breasts, I swoon back and start coming, beginning slowly but building up until I wonder if I'll be able to stand it.

Afterwards, showering, I whistle with a cheerfulness I haven't felt in a long time. Christopher, I tell myself, is the man to unlock me from my inhibitions and sexual confusion. And tonight, after we've all eaten and retired to our rooms, when Mum has fallen asleep, I intend to creep to his room and persuade him of that fact.

It's 11 p.m. and the house is silent. I've been almost frantic with anticipation, but dinner – a South Indian buffet of *channa masala* with mint, vegetable *bhaji*, lemon rice and hot home-made breads – went on forever, and then Mum took hours to go to sleep. She, too, is a fan of Christopher's teaching and has borrowed a book from him that she was insistent on reading in bed.

Now, as I slip down the hallway towards Christopher's room, the only sound is that of my heart thudding in my chest, and I have to ask myself what the hell I think I'm doing. What am I going to say to him when he opens the door? What pretext am I going to drum up to account for my disturbing him late at night? Should I come out with it – tell him I'm there because I want him, feel that I can't live another moment without him? Or shall I pretend I need to talk to him about some aspect of yoga and then, once ensconced in his room, try to seduce him?

You'd have thought I'd have worked all this out in my head while I was waiting for Mum to turn in, but the truth is that I was too terrified to think about it, that I dithered and faffed and avoided the issue of how exactly I was going to go about achieving my aim.

I'd have been wasting my time anyway, as it turns out. As I arrive at his door and raise my hand to knock, still not knowing what I'm going to say, deciding to play it by ear, I hear the tinkle of female laughter from inside, accompanying that of Christopher. Scared that I'm going to be caught standing here, looking like a fool, I flee, running on tiptoe back down the corridor. Entering my own room like a thief, I undress in the darkness and climb into my single bed beside Mum's. My disappointment is as bitter as the darkest chocolate.

It's infernal, the next day, waking up and knowing I can't have him. Infernal seeing his beautiful body, his noble face, in the yoga studio – watching him demonstrate the positions, his cock bulging magnificently in his tight Lycra shorts – and knowing that someone else has a claim to him. And of course the irony is that this morning he does touch me, does come up behind me to tweak me, adjust me, correct my alignment, and I melt inside while willing him so hard to stop taunting me. When he walks away, it's as if my body still bears the traces of his touch, like bruises, or like fluorescent handprints. I feel marked, and deeply unsatisfied. I have no appetite for breakfast; I want only to go back to my room and masturbate while I still feel the ghost of his hands on me. But I don't, because I know it will make me feel worse – empty inside, and even more cheated of the thing I most want in the world.

At breakfast, nibbling at a piece of fruit, I look around at the other women in my group, trying to catch a glance, a gesture, that might indicate to me who it was that I surprised in Christopher's room. None of them are supermodels, but none of them are yoga novices like me, and they all have firm, fit, well-looked-after bodies. They treat themselves well, eat well, and it shows in their fine, glowing complexions. None are what you'd call unattractive, and I realise with a shock that what I thought to be my major asset – my youth – counts for nothing in such company. There's no reason that Christopher would choose me over any of them. To him, I'm probably just a silly schoolgirl.

I keep a lookout for a sign, but it doesn't take long to twig on to the fact that *all* of the students – and there are a good dozen – are flirting with him to a greater or lesser degree, and that includes my own mother. Some are better at it, more subtle, than others. The two Americans, who I had actually assumed to be lesbians, are puffing out their ample chests, being overly jokey and girly, pathetically desperate for Christopher's attention. He's not playing ball, sharing himself around everyone judiciously, generously, fairly, giving a little of his time to everyone, responding to questions but taking care not to get so embroiled in a conversation with any one person that he's at risk of ignoring the others. But everyone, I'm certain of it, is responding to his charisma in some way, letting him know they're up for it if he is. I'm left with the impression that it could have been any one of them in his room last night. Or more than one, it occurs to me, and I shoot a spiteful glare at the Americans. They look just the sort who would try to get him involved in a threesome.

I try not to be cross that Mum's flirting too. She's not making a fool of herself as the Americans are, just twirling her hair absently around one finger and looking at Christopher a bit glassy-eyed, as if she's been hypnotised. Maybe I'm wrong, maybe she's not even flirting but just spaced out by our second morning of meditation and yoga. But I don't think so; there's definitely a funny look to her face, and why not? Why should she, out of all of us, remain immune to Christopher's charms? On the other hand, having seen how she's behaved recently, having witnessed the flowering of her appetites, I wonder if I shouldn't warn her not to try her luck with him, since he's already having an affair?

The opportunity presents itself that afternoon, when we take a taxi up to the famous weekly fleamarket at Anjuna. There, while we're browsing the stalls of T-shirts, sarongs, jewellery, carvings, chillums and spices and admiring the tribal women in all their finery, our talk turns to Christopher and his classes, and I ask Mum what she thinks of him.

'Oh,' she says airily, fingering a fine amber necklace, 'I think he's a very gifted teacher. Inspirational.'

'But what about *him*?'

'What about him?'

'Do you like him?'

'Of course. He's a very pleasant man. Kind, thoughtful.'

Either she's hiding her true feelings or she's oblivious to his charms, which I can scarcely believe. But I'm clearly not going to get any more out of her, and certainly not without revealing my own feelings for him, so I change the subject.

We end up staying out for dinner, feeling that we should experience something of Goan cuisine beyond what's on offer at Christopher's guest house. At a hotel near the market known as Grandpa's Inn, we find a wonderful restaurant with a veranda and a garden, bursting with old-fashioned charm. For a while I'm able to stop thinking about Christopher and just enjoy Mum's company and the feeling of being in the real India.

When we're back at the guest house, however, and once more within Christopher's domain, thoughts of him take over my mind again. I'm so sure that he's the one for me. Not necessarily for my whole life – I'm sussed enough to know that at eighteen few people meet a partner who will suit them all their lives, through all the changes and upheavals to come. But sure that he can teach me to relax and let go, to give of myself. Not just because I fancy the pants off him, but because of the yoga techniques in which he's trained. If anyone can unlock me, it's him.

I drift off with Christopher's face in my mind, and wake suddenly, who knows how long later, desperate either to see him or to find out which of the students he chooses to spend his nights with – which of this week's students, at any rate. This leads me to the realisation that it may not have been any of them I overheard last night: Christopher may have a girl-friend from outside, who came by after we'd all gone to bed. She may be a long-term thing.

I've no idea what time it is, but I get up, slip out of our room and tiptoe down the corridor beset by a sense of déjà vu. I'm amazed at my daring, at my obstinacy, but tell myself that these must be proof of my feelings for him, of their serious-ness.

I arrive at his door, pause this time, and sure enough my heart sinks to hear a woman's voice inside. This time I don't run away, though; this time a kind of horribly jealous curiosity takes hold. I bring one ear to the door, hold my breath and listen closely for a few moments. Against a background of creaking furniture and liquid being poured into a vessel, I can make out certain sentences or fragments of sentences.

'... find you incredibly attractive ...'

'... too old for you ...'

'... experience that younger women just can't provide ...'

'... Chris ... oh, that's ... oh, don't stop now ...'

My heads reels back, jerks away from the door in shock. I pray I'm mistaken, but even as I do I know that I'm not, that it's my mother's voice I heard in there. She's gone and done it again, only this time she's gone too far. This time she's taken my man, the only one who could cure me, the one I know could have made me happy if only we'd been given the chance. But no, she's barged in there, just as she went storming in with Charles, and then with Abhay, seducing men left, right and centre, acting like some sex-starved maniac. Which is what she is, really. A lonely old woman who hasn't had any in years and now can't see a man without throwing herself at him like some floozy.

Mum doesn't come back all night; I know because I don't sleep at all. Rage boils inside me. I toss and turn and throw off the sheets, throw open the window to the night air and the mosquitos, gnaw my nails to the quick and even think about going out to find a late bar where I can drink myself into a stupor. When it becomes clear she'll be out all night, becomes clear that she is not only having sex with him but spending the night in his arms, I have a little weep and then I try to think more rationally. Mum wasn't the woman in Christopher's room the first time I went to call: she was asleep in our room when I left. Of course, the first woman might not have been sleeping with Chris, may have been in his room on some kind of legitimate business, but the whole thing seems more than a little dubious. Beneath that caring, mild-mannered exterior is it possible that there lurks a wolf, a cad who sleeps his way through his students on a weekly basis? Even now that he's in bed with my mum and I'm nauseous with envy and disappointment, I don't want to believe such a thing of him.

18

I don't know what possessed me. Sure, I did find Chris attractive, right from the start, but I just assumed he was too young for me and that I wasn't in with a chance. I've never had a younger man before Abhay, and he doesn't count – stuck out in the desert like that, with a woman's hand on his thigh in the dark, he had nothing to lose. Chris, on the other hand – Chris is continually surrounded by nubile young things contorting their lovely bodies in front of him. Why choose me over any one of them? I still don't know. All I know is that when he touched me in yesterday morning's yoga class, pushed my thigh back into alignment with my torso, it was as if some kind of electric shock ran through me. I let out a little gasp, and our eyes met and I realised that he might be interested in an older woman after all.

It was torture, being away from the guest house for the rest of the day, although I loved the market and enjoyed spending time with my daughter, of course. When she suggested staying out for dinner, I was a little miffed, but reasoned with myself that if anything was going to happen between Chris and me, it wouldn't be at dinner in front of all the other students. The trick would be to get him alone, and I didn't see how that might be possible given that the others were always around. And then I remembered what he'd said about borrowing books, and I realised I had the perfect excuse for calling round later that evening, after Nadia had gone to sleep.

As Nadia slowly dozed off in her bed, I lay quietly in my

own, softly fingering myself under the sheets. I was so over Charles, so happy to have broken away from him when I did, but the memory of his beautiful cock and the way it felt as it parted my lips and pushed inside me was still there, ripe, almost tangible. Charles, though, was older, and although he'd kept himself fit and lean, his body couldn't begin to compete with Chris's. I had high expectations of what would happen if Chris did invite me into his room, if he did acknowledge the electricity that had passed between us.

Afraid I would make myself come if I carried on thinking rather than acting, I climbed out of bed and changed back out of my pyjamas and into a tight yoga top and leggings. I was so much more confident about my body since arriving in India – I had Charles to thank for that too. He had made me feel desirable for the first time in more than two decades, and feeling like an erotic being again seemed to bring on non-stop horniness. I hadn't realised I was so frustrated, so repressed.

I opened the door quietly, crept along the hallway in the direction of Chris's room. I had it all worked out in my head, had even looked up, at the guest house's internet station, the title of the specific book I was going to ask to borrow. I suppose I was nervous, but there was nothing really to lose. If Chris didn't want me, then I would be sorely disappointed, but at least I would have tried. It's the not knowing that's the hardest thing to bear, in my experience; the regrets at what could have been.

I stood outside his door, hoping that he wasn't asleep. It was getting late. Then I heard a sort of shuffling noise, as if he were walking about inside, and before I could change my mind I lifted my hand and tapped at the door. It opened.

'You're here,' said Chris. 'I thought you'd come.' He stood back to let me in.

'You did?'

'This morning,' he said. 'It wasn't just me, was it? You felt it too?'

I smiled. 'Like an electric shock,' I said shyly.

'That's exactly it.' He stepped forwards, took my hands. 'I really find you incredibly attractive,' he said.

I felt myself start to melt. His gaze was direct, probing, as if he were seeing into every part of me. I felt naked even before I'd started to undress. This was a man, I thought, who could really know a woman. With Charles, it had all been on the surface, physical fireworks that had burnt themselves out quicker than I had thought possible. Chris was something else entirely, and I had the feeling that sex with him was going to take me to another level altogether.

'I'm...I'm flattered, and surprised,' I replied at last.

'You are? Why?'

'Well, because...I don't know. I thought I'd be too old for you. You're surrounded by beautiful young woman all the time and...'

He waved one hand dismissively. 'Beauty can get boring,' he said. 'I look for something else, the sign of a life lived, of experience. An experience that younger women just can't provide.'

He'd moved his hands up my arms now, to my shoulder and neck. For a few moments he massaged them, applying pressure at certain points.

'Oh Chris,' I muttered. 'That's so good.'

Then he turned me around, planted kisses around my hairline while continuing to massage my shoulders from behind.

'Chris...oh, that's...oh, don't stop now...'

I pulled up my yoga top and brought my hands to my breasts. The nipples were hard little nuts of arousal. Leaning back into Chris, who continued to kiss and palpate my shoulders expertly, I plucked at my nipples with my fingertips, feeling as if I were in danger of falling backwards in space and that the delicious pain I was inflicting on myself was the only thing tethering me to the Earth. Then, gently but assertively, Chris took me by the shoulders, turned me around and guided me over to a chaise-longue positioned beneath his window. He lay me down against it and stood over me for a moment, pensive, then he helped me out of my top and my leggings.

'You have astonishing skin for your age,' he said. 'You're radiant.'

I wanted to tell him that I was flushing with desire for him, that until I came to India I felt grey and old, as crumpled as a used paper bag. But instead I decided to keep my mouth shut and revel in his compliments, in the fact that a forty-something like me could arouse a fit younger man like him, one who could take his pick of younger, sexier women.

'How do you want me?' I said.

He smiled and said, 'What's the hurry?' Turning back to his bureau, he chose from amid a number of little brown bottles with white labels attached, then knelt beside me and unscrewed the lid.

'What's that?' I asked him.

'Ayurvedic oil,' he said, pouring some of the unctuous golden liquid into the cupped palm of one hand, then putting the bottle on the floor and rubbing his hands together until both were coated with it.

'What's in it?'

'Oh, heaps of stuff. Sesame oil, asparagus, Indian nightshade, sandalwood, cardamom, musk root ... the list goes on.'

'What will it do to me?'

'It'll tone your skin and muscles, and it'll also alleviate symptoms of *vayu*: nervousness, insomnia, depression and anxiety.'

'I don't have any of those.'

'I'm not saying you do, Val. But everyone can benefit from

a boost to their overall strength, skin health, intelligence and digestion. From overall rejuvenation.'

'I guess so.'

I was lying on my back, legs slightly apart, and he remained fully clothed. He placed his oily hands on my belly, rested them there for a moment, eyes half closed, as if assessing something, feeling for something inside me. Then he began massaging my belly with long, slow, sweeping movements, using only his fingertips in the lightest, featheriest of touches. I felt the same electrical charge as when he touched me in the yoga studio. Part of me just wanted to open my legs wider and invite him into me, but what he was doing to me with his hands was so gorgeous, so new to me, that I knew it would be folly to speed things up. I had to find it in myself to delay the sex, no matter how earth shattering it promised to be.

After a while he rolled me over on the chaise-longue, asked me if I was comfortable, and began to locate my pressure points – *marmas*, he told me they were called – and to focus on those, occasionally also using techniques he described as thumbing and cupping. The latter involved him cupping one hand over the other so as to achieve strong pressure; he concentrated on my lower back while using this technique, saying it would improve my circulation. Thumbing, meanwhile, which focused on my shoulder blades, was good for my lungs and for releasing overall pressure.

It was interesting listening to him explain the philosophies and aims of Ayurveda as he moved his hands around my body; his voice was like an extra hand in some ways, caressing me, ironing out my kinks and areas of tension I hadn't even known existed. After a while I even forgot about the sex and just submitted to the pressure of his fingers on my back, then my arms, my legs, my feet and finally my head.

Then he stopped. I remained still, belly down, face to one

side with eyes closed, wondering what was going to happen next. Here I was naked before him, slick with fragrant oils, still wet for him. Surely that wasn't it? Surely he didn't expect me to just stand up, thank him, get dressed again and leave?

His hand made its presence felt between my legs: two fingers slipped inside me, and I realised he was checking if I was ready for him. I knelt up, impaling myself firmly on his fingers, and rested my arms on the end of the chaise-longue. He took his hand away, put his arms around my waist and lifted me into a standing position from behind, so that my bum was up in the air and my arms hung down, my hands touching the floor. His own waist was sandwiched by my lower thighs, by the muscles just above my knees.

'The wheelbarrow position,' said Chris, and I felt the tip of his cock hover around my pussy, teasing it. I wondered how he could hold himself back. I was half crazy with the need to have him within me. I pushed on my hands, trying to strain back and up onto him, but he had a will of iron, resisting my movement. I closed my eyes, swooning with desire. And then all at once he pushed himself inside me, reaching round and pressing my clitoris at the same time, and it was as if I was flooded with a kind of blinding holy light. I didn't come, or at least not genitally, but it was as if my brain itself was orgasming, and I cried out.

Chris stood me up, one hand on the side of my head, the other arm looped under one of my arms, binding me to him, with that second hand clasped over my breast. I felt the smooth skin of his chest on my back.

'The bodyguard,' he whispered, close to my ear, his breath hot on my skin. For all his control, his composure, his breathing was coming in saccades now, as if it were an effort not to come. His cock was still deep inside me. The position didn't allow for much thrusting but it was intense – similar to doggy-style but more intimate, since I was partially turned side on to him and our faces were close.

As if sensing that I liked the latter aspect, Chris now pulled out of me, to turn me around to face him. With one hand he eased up one of my legs, which I bent at the knee, and kept hold of it, re-inserting his cock. This allowed for greater movement in and out, and I discovered that by holding onto his shoulder with one hand, I could stimulate my clitoris with the other. I was finding it hard not to rise to orgasm when Chris pulled out again.

'Let's see just how flexible all this yoga has made you,' he said, and he lifted my leg up further. To my surprise, it kept on going all the way up to his shoulder, where he rested it. He pushed back inside me, and the sensation was greater still. This time I didn't need to masturbate my clitoris, as it was pressed up against Chris's lower belly and stimulated by his thrusts as well as contact with his skin.

'The dancer,' he breathed. 'I thought you could do it. Well done. I told you all that yoga would come in handy.'

As it became obvious that neither of us could hold off for too much longer, Chris lifted my leg and brought it back down to his waist. Placing one hand under each of my buttocks, he then lifted me up so that both of my legs folded around his waist. I wrapped my arms around his neck, and for a moment we kissed, deeply, exploring each other's mouth with our tongues, voraciously. When we pulled apart for breath, with his hands still cupping my buttocks and his cock still deep within me, he began walking across the room. I squeezed as hard as I could with the walls of my pussy. Then, unable to go any further, he lowered me slowly to the floor, onto a flokati rug, and started banging away at me so hard, I saw stars. It was as if all of his self-control had evaporated in one second and some primeval need had overcome him, making him almost animalistic. His excitement excited me, and I yelped and thrashed my way to orgasm beneath him, clinging on as if by letting go I would sink and never resurface. He came a few seconds later, head pulled up and away from me, teeth gritted as if in pain.

Rolling off me onto his back, he lay panting on the floor.

'That was incredible,' I said, turning onto my side, placing my hand on his chest, sweeping it down to his belly and back. He groaned a little in agreement but didn't open his eyes. I stood up, crossed the room to his bathroom and took a shower, douching myself vigorously. My clitoris still quivered a little with the aftershock, as if the sex had not numbed it but only made it even more sensitive. I teased at it with my fingers, pressed my fingers into my hole. I could do it again, I thought; already, I wanted him again.

Walking back into his bedroom-cum-study, I saw that he was still on the floor. His breathing was deep and regular, but I didn't think that he was asleep – he had crossed his hands over his belly. Now, keeping his eyes closed, he sat up and assumed the lotus position. He was meditating.

I climbed into his bed and rested my head against the pillow. I didn't want to leave yet, and I didn't want to break into his meditation either. Unsure how long he intended to go on for, I thought I might as well get some sleep. Horny I may still have been, but I was tired too. All this rampant sex was starting to catch up with me. I closed my eyes and let myself drift away.

I awoke to see Chris dressing on the other side of the room. I sat up.

'What time is it?' I said.

'Time we were at the beach,' he said. He wasn't unfriendly, but I wasn't sure he was that thrilled I had stayed the night without asking. He was so laconic, so slow to express any kind of emotion, that it was difficult to tell if he was annoyed or not.

'I didn't want to disturb you,' I said, 'by saying goodbye. And it felt rude just to go off like that ...'

'I should have explained,' he said. 'I always meditate, afterwards, to dispel the sadness.'

'The sadness? But it was amazing!'

'But "after sex, every animal is sad", as the old Latin proverb goes. Or better still: After the ecstasy, the reckoning.'

I swung my legs over the side of the bed, looked around the floor for my clothes, loath to continue the discussion if Chris was going to get all heavy on me. Not that I didn't agree: I knew exactly what sadness he was talking about, and I admired him for doing something positive about it. But I didn't want the memory of our night together to be infected with melancholy; Chris could meditate all he wanted, it wouldn't take away the joy of it all, or make me want him again any the less urgently.

19

When Mum appears at Christopher's side for the beach meditation the next morning, she invokes quite a few double-takes and spiteful side-glances from our fellow students. I open my eyes several times during the session to catch one or two of the others in a state far removed from karmic bliss – giving Mum the evil eye, one might almost say. At breakfast the atmosphere is leaden – quite the opposite of what it was yesterday morning. But Mum seems heedless to it all, she's so obviously loved-up; already, I can tell, she considers him and her to be an item.

I decide there and then to leave, with or without Mum. I can't stay here, not with my feelings for Christopher as they are. It would have been hard enough to see him hooked up with any of the women here, but I know in advance that I couldn't physically stand to see him and Mum together for the next five days. And beyond that, what? What is going to happen next? I don't want to be around to find out. Either they'll get together properly, if Mum has her way, or he'll turn out to be a Lothario and she'll get her heart trampled all over.

Back in our room, she tells me she spent the night with him.

I choke back sour laughter. 'No shit,' I reply. 'You're gone all night, and then you show up clinging to him like a leech. I'd kind of worked things out for myself.'

'I'm sorry,' she says. 'I suppose I should have warned you, but it was all so sudden. We just –'

'I don't want to know,' I interrupt. 'Please, just stop talking about it. Only...'

'Only what?'

'Only... I don't know. Just be careful, that's all.'

'Be careful of what?'

'Of Christopher.'

'What about him?'

'Well, haven't you noticed how all the other women in the group flirt with him, to one degree or another?'

She opens and closes her mouth like a fish. 'Well... yes, I suppose they do like him. But he's a charming man and a great teacher. They admire him.'

'They more than admire him, Mum.'

'What are you saying?'

'Well, I... I couldn't sleep the night before last, and I went for a walk and happened to go past Christopher's room. There was... I heard another woman in there with him.'

She pales, stares at me, then pulls her chin up, looks assertive, combative. 'That doesn't mean a thing,' she says. 'There could be any number of reas –' She stops herself. 'What did you hear anyway?'

I shrug. 'Laughter. Giggling.'

She looks relieved. 'Well, it could have been anything,' she says. 'Someone going to borrow a book perhaps. Remember, he did offer at the class that day. In fact, weren't those his exact words: "If anyone wants to borrow any of B. K. S. Iyengar's works, you know where I am."'

'But at eleven o'clock at night?'

'Well, yes, perhaps that is a little late, but this is hardly an orthodox set-up is it? It's all very free and easy.'

I frown. Perhaps it's a bit too free and easy, I think, and I look hard at Mum.

'Listen,' I say more gently. 'I really don't want to stay here any more. There's something . . . I don't know, something bothering me about the whole place. I think you should come with me.'

'What?' Incredulity breaks out on her face. 'Leave, after what's happened with me and Chris? You've got to be joking.'

'I'm just trying to protect you.'

She's struck silent for a moment, then her eyes become slits and she steps a little closer to me. 'That's bullshit,' she almost spits. 'You're jealous, that's what it is. You said it yourself – all the women here want Chris. You gave yourself away.'

I'm cringing inside at being found out, and even more at Mum having guessed that I have feelings for the man she's sleeping with.

'That's rubbish. He's bad news, that's all, and I don't want you to get hurt.'

'You're the one who's talking rubbish, and there's no way you're forcing me to leave. I . . . I'm falling in love with Chris and you're not going to spoil that for me. I'm sorry if I got there first, but you never had a chance anyway – he likes older women.'

'Well, he would say that, wouldn't he? He would tell you what you wanted to hear, if it helped to get you into his bed. I wonder what he told the woman he spent the previous night with, and all the women before that?'

'Oh shut up, just bloody well shut up.' Mum raises her hand and for a moment I even think she's going to strike me. I've never seen her like this, have hardly ever even heard her swear. Then she sits back on her bed, starts to cry.

I turn to my wardrobe, pull out my rucksack and then begin to make piles of my clothes on my bed, in a hurry now just to be gone. I have no idea where to, but the further away from Christopher and Mum the better.

20

I feel a sort of pride, which I know to be pathetic, on arriving at the beach session with Chris rather than with Nadia, on making it obvious what's happened between us, particularly given that I'm the oldest woman in the group by a few years. I feel a bit bad for Nadia too, that I didn't think to go back to our room first and forewarn her. Not that it's particularly her business who I do or don't sleep with, but I suppose it would have been polite to tell her first. And she may have been worried upon waking up to find me gone – although my recent performances have probably made her a little more sanguine in such circumstances.

She looks uncomfortable and, yes, cross, when I show up with Chris, and some of the other women give me the most fearsome stares, really quite hateful, which is when I realise what a catch he must be. But I tell myself that the prize is worth any amount of flak and animosity they may have lined up for me. I close my eyes and don't open them again until the end of the session, although I know that not every-body is doing the same. I can feel eyes on me as I try to reach a higher plane of consciousness where nobody can get at me.

After being given the silent treatment at breakfast, I go back to my own room with Nadia and tell her that Chris and I are an item, although even as I say the words it crosses my mind that I haven't actually discussed this with him, that I've taken it for granted that we will carry on, perhaps because we didn't just have sex but spent the night together, albeit without him exactly agreeing to my staying there.

The outburst that follows shocks me, and it rapidly becomes clear to me that Nadia, although she claims to be trying to protect me, is actually jealous, that she – like everyone here – wants to be Chris's lover. I try to explain to her that he prefers older women, but she counters that by telling me I've fallen for a line, that Chris will tell anyone what they want to hear. I can't believe that of him; can't believe that a man so passionate about the environment and social awareness would be such a cad when it comes to personal matters. Nor can I allow myself to countenance what she tells me about having overheard another woman in his room the night before last. I simply will not believe that he's the kind of man who would line women up like that, who would have his students coming through his room like so much human traffic. She's wrong, and part of me seethes at what her jealousy makes her say to try to stop me from seeing Chris. She even seems to think, at one point, that she might persuade me to leave.

And so it becomes a choice between Chris and my daughter, and Chris wins out. He has to, on principle as much as anything else. But for the rest of the day I feel empty inside. Perhaps he was right, about 'the reckoning'. Only falling out with one's own child is a little more serious than a twinge of post-coital melancholy. And there's another niggle in my brain: was Nadia telling the truth about there being another woman in his room two nights ago, and if so, who was it?

21

It's a long schlep back northwards to Kanha National Park, but I'm in no rush. The travel, always slow in India, is rather therapeutic, and I'm thinking that some time in a natural setting and away from too many people will give me the space to sort my head out. It would be wonderful to see some tigers too, more or less in the wild, but I've been told that that's rare even here – in the very place that inspired *The Jungle Book* and where some of the world's most significant tiger research was carried out.

Not having Mum around any more means I can check in to a shared log hut and not feel that I'm selling out. Not that they're at all bad – each has six bunks but plenty of space, and an adjoining shower and loo. They're clean and well maintained, with a wooden terrace where one can sit and appreciate the peacefulness of the reserve. I imagine myself sitting out there with a cool drink, writing in my journal. Despite all my copious note-taking, I've never kept a diary before – my life has never seemed interesting enough to record. But with my fall-out with Mum over Chris, and my recent experiences in Mumbai – Asha's face in particular surges into my mind, her lovely lips forming the barely audible word 'Stay,' as her hand falls on my ankle – I wonder for the first time not only if my experiences are worth the trouble of writing down, but whether some of this buzzing confusion in my mind might be eased by my putting my thoughts down on paper. If it might help me work out what it is that I want.

I'm just about to head for the small provisions shop near the huts for some chocolate when a couple walk in laden with heavy backpacks and look around them. Noticing me, the girl, blonde and green-eyed like Carla, smiles, says: 'Are any of these beds free?'

'I've only just arrived myself,' I say, 'but none of them seem to be taken.'

'We'll chance it then,' she says. 'OK, Dean?'

The guy with her nods. 'Fine by me,' he replies, slipping the rucksack from his shoulders. 'I'm just glad to get this thing off.'

I watch him as he moves, admiring his strong brown limbs. Like the girl, he's fair-haired, deeply tanned, and his body shimmers with little blond hairs. He's wearing shorts and a vest top; on his feet are heavy walking boots. His hair flops down over his face, bleached blonder at the front by the sun, but I can make out a sturdy, square jawline and eyes the blue-green of the Arabian Sea. He's gorgeous, and I feel a spike of envy at the girl for having netted herself such a prize.

But my envy dissipates immediately when the girl steps forwards, having divested herself of her own backpack, and, shaking my hand, says, 'I'm Sue, by the way. And this is my brother, Dean.'

I look at him again, feeling my cheeks flush. Suddenly knowing that he's available, or at least not travelling with someone who has a claim to him, makes me feel timid, tongue-tied. He's smiling at me, and I love the fact that beneath the unkempt hair, beneath the stubble and the grime of travel, he has bright white teeth and an overall feeling of cleanness. Like I said, I like my men grungy, but only on the surface. Underneath it all they have to have a pride in their bodies, a good standard of hygiene.

'You travelling alone?' asks Dean, and my belly somersaults.

I feel, when he looks directly at me, pinning me with his aqueous gaze, when he addresses me in his slightly dry, husky voice, as if I've lost my moorings and am adrift in time and space. It's both a wonderful feeling, a delicious giddiness like when you've drunk champagne, and a frightening one. But on balance I feel good, relieved that someone has come along to take my mind off Christopher. This, I feel, is a sane enthusiasm – Dean is closer in age to me, and also isn't surrounded by hoards of acolytes desperately vying for his attention.

I nod, not wishing to talk about Mum, at least not for the moment.

'Heading south or north?' he says.

'South, basically. That is, I was in Goa, so I've made a diversion back up north. But I plan to end up in Kerala, at some point.'

'You don't sound like you're too rigid,' says his sister, her voice approving. 'We've met so many people with these huge itineraries, these six-month plans, lists full of things to tick off.' She looks at Dean. 'We're much happier just kind of going with the flow, aren't we?'

'So you don't have any plans at all?' I say.

She shrugs, lifting one hand to her head to smooth down her hair, and I notice for the first time that she has really quite magnificent boobs. Like her brother, she's wearing a vest top, and I see as she raises her arm that she has no bra beneath it. Her breasts are large but very firm. Her vest rides up with her movement, revealing a taut, flat, brown belly. She's on the tall side, too. I think again of Carla, standing in the shower, bringing herself off as I watch, and I have to close my eyes for a moment and block Sue out, afraid that my eyes will give me away, will reveal my thoughts and fantasies.

'I guess we're just vaguely drifting down south too,' she says. 'Meandering. There's no rush, no real plan behind it all, but I wouldn't mind some time on the beach in Kerala. I heard it's a lot less hectic than Goa.'

Dean has turned away from us, to rummage in the rucksack he's laid on his bed. Straightening back up, he turns to us, waving a little tin in his hand. 'Just going out for a smoke before dinner,' he says.

Sue smiles affectionately at him, and we both watch him as he strolls out, his body as supple and confident as a big cat's. When I turn back to Sue, she's looking at me in what seems a slightly odd, appraising way, her lovely feline eyes a little narrowed. But I quickly decide I'm probably imagining things, or that that's the way she looks at everyone she's just met. As she unpacks her stuff, I sit on my bunk and we chat idly about the places we've been to so far, and about our lives back home. Sue tells me that she has just finished a degree in digital photography and hopes to make enough money from snaps she takes during this trip to set up her own studio when she gets back to the UK. Her younger brother, who often models for her, she tells me, is taking a year out from a sports management degree.

There's plenty to talk about, and after she's finished packing we head for the canteen-like restaurant together, to carry on getting to know each other over *dhal* and rice and vegetable curry. Dean, I discover, is much quieter than his older sister, without being unfriendly: she tends to dominate the conversation and, although I love her vivacious chatter, I find myself hoping that I get the opportunity to talk to Dean alone. Only then will I know if I stand a chance.

Above all, I'm keen to find out more about their plans, even if they contend that they don't really have any. If they are heading in the same general direction as me, with the same ultimate destination in mind, they might be open to taking a fellow traveller on board. I'm feeling a little apprehensive at the prospect of making my way around by myself, and if I can hook up with like-minded souls, then all the better. Especially if there's the prospect of a romantic entanglement with one of them.

But the last thing I want to do is scare them away by coming on too strong or by seeming too desperate. If it's going to happen, it has to be at their suggestion or invitation. Having said that, there's nothing stopping me from planting the seed in their minds.

We all turn in early, shattered by our respective bus journeys to Kanha, mellow from the beers and the company, and most of all mindful that we have to be up at dawn if we want the chance of going out on an elephant and seeing a tiger. At five the next morning, we are standing beside one of the beasts, watching our driver check the attachments on the huge six-person seat on its back. The reserve is not busy, and Sue, Dean and I are lucky enough to have one of the animals and drivers to ourselves. Though sleepy eyed and tousle haired from bed and lack of coffee, we are all excited at the prospect of going out. Seeing a tiger is far from guaranteed, but as the dawn mist clears, we may – according to our guide – be treated to sightings of panthers, hyenas, sloth bears, Indian bisons, barking deers, porcupines, mongooses, parakeets and more.

I position myself so that when we are helped up onto the pachyderm's back, I'm on the same side of the seat as Dean, hoping that I might get a chance to chat to him, to get to know him a little better, especially as Sue will probably be busy taking photographs. She's already fiddling with her Nikon, oblivious to my subtle machinations, so it's looking hopeful.

We mount, and I settle into my place beside Dean, as planned. In the half-light he smiles at me in anticipation of our adventure, and I smell his morning breath in the space between us – honeyed and not at all sour, like a child's. My own breath catches in my throat at our proximity: though still more stubbled, he's godlike, with a bone structure to die for. It strikes me that though they are both indisputably lovely, he and Sue don't really look that alike, beyond the superficial similarities of their colouring. Though her frame is athletic like his, her face is softer, plumper, less delineated. And those large breasts tell me that her svelteness is probably less genetic than striven for, paid for in hours at the gym or spent pounding the pavements in jogging kit.

Dean is wearing a fresh pair of shorts, and his leg beside mine tantalises me, begs to be reached out and touched. I feel like a malnourished person put within reach of a particularly juicy-looking, nutritious fruit, taunted by it. How is it, I ask myself, that I have held out this long without giving myself up to someone? I've had the chances, many chances, and none of the potential partners has been what you'd call shabby. And the wanking – it's been good, but it's only part of the story, of my story. What is stopping me from getting it underway?

Dawn slides away from us like a curtain being parted, revealing a world of wonder. Behind us, Sue is lost to her art, photographing away, gasping as she sees a new animal and tries to capture it from a different angle before it gets away. It's all she can do to stay on the elephant and not leap down and pursue her prey through the undergrowth. Dean and I are more restrained, though enchanted, and, as hoped, I have the chance to chat to him a little, in an unforced way, about what we see. After a couple of hours, I notice our legs have moved closer together on the elephant's side. All I need to do is ease mine over a fraction and I'll be touching him. I do so, and my whole body tingles. He doesn't react, but nor does he move his leg away.

We return for a late breakfast, without having seen a tiger

but satisfied with our outing, and then Sue and Dean declare that they want to take a midday nap after our early start. For a while I stand and watch our driver hose down the elephant, freeing him of mud and dust, then I return to our hut. Dean and Sue's bunk is on the opposite side of the room from mine; my bed, like Dean's, is on the lower level. Quietly I lower myself onto mine and lie there looking across at him as he sleeps. A ray of sunlight coming in through the window illuminates his angel's face like a strobe. I reach down and massage my snatch through my denim shorts. At the same time I feel an incredible weariness seeping through me, an ages-old ache in my bones. I don't want to do this any more. I want the real thing. I want Dean.

A movement above Dean makes me whip my hand away in any case, and I glance up to see Sue looking down at me, a funny expression on her face – knowing, ironic. I blush, wondering how much she's seen. Not that she can do anything about me fancying her brother, or about him fancying me, if it comes to it. But I don't want to make a fool of myself when I don't know if my feelings are reciprocated. And like I said, I don't want to scare them away if there's a chance they may ask me to travel south with them.

'Hey,' says Sue after a moment. Sliding her legs over the side of the bunk, she lets herself dangle for a moment and then drops the last couple of feet to the floor, eschewing the ladder. She's wearing only a pair of knickers, black with little pink polka dots, and her figure is revealed in all its ripeness. As my eyes take her in, I notice that her breasts are dark golden like the rest of her – evidence of topless sunbathing. I can't help but wonder what's beneath her knickers, whether she is tanned there too.

I don't have to wait long to find out: without any warning she bends forwards, slides her knickers down her long brown legs, and stands back up. The beauty of her cunt makes my mouth fall open: pruned, neat and compact, strawberry blond, with a little streak of hair above a clit peaking cheekily, invitingly, out. I look from Sue to Dean. He is still asleep. I look back at Sue, wondering. What does she want of me? Is she merely undressing in front of me, changing out of her knickers, or is she flaunting herself, trying to tempt me? I think back to our conversations of yesterday evening. There was no mention of a boyfriend, either now or in the past, but then again I didn't talk about myself in that way either. It doesn't mean she's a lesbian, just because she didn't go on about blokes. There are, after all, plenty of other things to think about. And just because she's standing here stark naked in front of me doesn't mean she's on offer. Just because there's a wet patch in my own knickers doesn't mean she's mine for the taking.

And if she was going to do that, would she really do it in the same room as her sleeping brother, who might wake up at any moment? No – no matter how laidback a family they come from, no matter what their attitude was in terms of walking round the house naked, I can't believe that she'd make a move on me under such circumstances. Rolling onto my back, I close my eyes.

'I think I am tired after all,' I say, faking a yawn, and after she doesn't reply for a minute, I open one eye slightly and look over at her. She's bending over, her back to me, slipping on a new pair of pants. She was only getting changed after all. I keep my eye open, admiring her sweet pink sphincter.

I do sleep, but it's a restless sleep, full of visions of brown flesh, tempting me, of golden hair, of eyes on me, waiting for my reaction, for my decision. Though I feel, already, that I'm madly in love with Dean, his sister's body has intervened to tempt me, to remind me of my indecisiveness, of my duality.

Am I destined to forever swing between poles, never to properly live because I'm unable to choose between the lives that beckon me?

I'm almost glad, when I awake, to find that they've gone to dinner without me. I cross them in the doorway of the canteen and, telling them I'll catch up with them later, dine alone, glad of some time to try to gather my thoughts. Should I travel on with them, if they do offer, or will that just be making life complicated for myself? How can I spend time with them, together, if I want both of them? And if something does happen with one of them, how will that leave me with the other? Will my ambivalent feelings just disappear in a puff of smoke if I make a decision one way or the other, or will I always be wondering 'What if . . .?' Always be craning my head and trying to peer down the route not taken to make sure I haven't made a mistake.

When I get back to the hut, Sue is sitting on the terrace with a book and a drink, legs unfurled in front of her. She has a bikini top and shorts on, and the sweep of her belly glints with the lightest of blonde down in the light of the setting sun. She moves a sarong from the chair beside her, pats it.

'Siddown,' she mock-drawls. 'Sorry we missed you for dinner. I wondered if we should wake you but you looked so sweet, lying there. Like a little girl.'

She's looking into my eyes and I think I see tenderness there. But is it the tenderness of friendship or is it something more? I hold her gaze, trying to fathom her out, daring myself to confront all my desires and demons, and suddenly she raises one arm at the elbow, then extends it. I hold my breath. Is she going to reach over and touch me? If she does, what am I going to do?

I look around us. There's nobody here, but somebody could walk by at any moment, catch us at it. And what about Dean?

Where is he? If something is to happen between Sue and me, I don't want it to spoil my chances with him.

But she doesn't touch me, instead she just lets her forearm and hand hang over the armrest of her chair. Perhaps she sensed my hesitation, my inner conflict, and decided not to push me. In a way, I wish she would – or wish that somebody would. I need a push. Need somebody to force the issue.

After a few moments, she asks me if I want some of her beer, and I say, 'Thanks but no,' and make my excuses. Despite the long nap, I feel unendingly weary.

'Are you sure?' she says. 'Dean will be back in a minute. He's playing pool with a guy he got talking to from another hut. We thought maybe we'd play cards, share a joint?'

I shake my head. 'I'm feeling a bit dodgy, actually,' I say weakly. 'I'd better give it a miss.'

'Fine,' she says, turning back to her book, and I walk inside and climb into my bunk with a heavy heart.

I've no idea what time it is when I wake up or am woken up, but it's pitch black inside the hut. I wonder what it was that roused me, and then I know – there's someone sitting on the edge of my bottom bunk, hand rested lightly on my leg beneath my thin sheet. It's a warm hand, slightly clammy. It's a hot night.

I half sit up, throat dry, panicky and yet excited. Of course it could be anybody – the huts are hardly secure. But in all probability it's Dean or Sue, come to force the issue. It's time.

I peel back the sheet. Beneath it I'm wearing a long T-shirt with nothing underneath. I pull it up, giving my snatch a quick rub as I do. Already I'm wet. In fact, I've never felt more ready for anything in my life. The hand comes back down, alights on the front of my thigh. Already I'm arching my back, throwing back my head; the anticipation is almost unbearable. I open my legs a little wider, imagine my snatch on display, wide open and juicy. Of course, whoever it is can't see it, but it doesn't stop me from feeling daring, provocative. They'll have sensed the movement, known that I was opening myself up for them.

The hand moves up my leg, infinitesimally slowly, and I reach down and pull myself wider apart, as if I can't be open enough. Fingertips graze my exposed clit and I spasm, face contorted in the blackness, trying to suppress the moans that are bubbling in the back of my throat. After a moment, as two fingers are slipped inside my hole, I bring my hand to my mouth and bite down on it to stop myself from crying out. But a hand takes it away, and I feel a mouth on mine and submit to a full-on kiss, to the questing of a tongue that prises open my lips. Teeth clash with mine, and I'm lost, lost, falling through space, unable to reach up and feel for my seducer's hair, which would let me know who they are.

The head pulls away and a line of kisses is planted all the way down my neck and then my torso, in a straight line down to my snatch. While the same mouth that kissed me busies itself with my clit, sucking and licking and flicking, hands fondle my breasts, fingertips squeeze my nipples. My T-shirt is bunched up around my neck. I press myself more fully into the hands; with my clit, equally, I seek the mouth as much as it seeks me. Finally, unable to deny myself the knowledge any longer, I lower my arms from where they've been stretched up above my head and clasp the sides of the head at my groin. Long hair.

I come, violently, from the workings of her mouth on me, but as I buck with the contractions of my orgasm she places a hand back inside me, and I hear her whimper with pleasure. It must be more than she can bear for, after a moment, while I'm still in the throes of my climax – it feels like it will never end – she rolls over on to her back beside me. Crushed up against me on the narrow bunk, she brings herself off with her free hand, mouth opening and closing on my shoulder to silence herself as she loses it.

Afterwards, she gets up, lights a cigarette and, lying back next to me, smokes it in the darkness. For a long time we're silent, and then she rolls over and puts her hand between my legs again, inserts one finger inside me.

'That was wonderful,' she whispers, leaning into me for a nicotine-infused kiss.

I return the kiss. I can't deny that it was wonderful, and I feel like dancing with joy that I've done it at last, that I've been fucked, and royally so, by this incredible girl. But there's an undeniable sour edge to it too – a part of me, and a large one at that, wishes it could have been Dean who came to me in the night, who took from me what I so much needed to give away.

Yet as our faces meld, as Sue takes my hands and brings them to those beautiful big breasts of hers, presses her neat blonde bush against mine, I reach down for her with jubilation, and feel, as her legs part, life itself opening up for me.

I find her, the next morning, sitting on the terrace in her bikini top and sarong, looking through the photographs she's taken on the digital camera. She smiles up at me but doesn't say a word, instead handing me the expensive-looking piece of kit. On the screen on the back there's a clear shot of some erotic sculptures on the outside of a temple.

'Khajuraho,' she says at last, as I examine it, then leans over and shows me how to scroll through the following images. As she does so, her arm, blonde and downy, brushes mine. My flesh rises in goosebumps despite the heat of the day, already intense.

'We stopped there on the way down from Delhi – this was one thing I absolutely insisted on seeing. It's a World Heritage site, very famous. It was covered up by jungle for a long time, and only about twenty of ninety temples have survived. Interestingly, the erotic sculptures are only on the outside of the temples, not inside.'

'How come?'

'One theory is that it was a reminder to people to leave their worldly desires outside, before stepping inside to worship. On the other hand, the temples were built by the Chandella monarchs, who were followers of Tantrism. You've heard of that, yes?'

'Only that Sting and his wife were supposed to practise it.'

'Well, basically, Tantrism holds that the gratification of earthly desires is a step in the achieving of nirvana.'

I feel the weight of her gaze on me as the subject of sex comes up, or is brought up, but I can't return it. I carrying on staring down at the camera screen, pushing the button with my thumb to advance to the next picture. It's more of the same, or more or less: this time a blissed-out-looking male stands between two bare-breasted women, one arm round each of them. The following one shows a man taking a woman, bent over at the waist, from behind. I look up at Sue, unable to avoid her eyes any longer, and she's smiling at me with a combination of tenderness and lasciviousness. For a moment I think she's going to make direct reference to the events of last night, and I cringe inwardly, shooting a glance back into the room where Dean sleeps on. But then she reaches her hand back out for her camera and, while she's switching it off, says: 'We were thinking of moving on today. There's only so much wildlife you can take, and my arse hasn't recovered from that elephant ride yet. There's no way I'm going up on one of those again in a hurry.'

'But I thought you enjoyed it.'

'Oh, I enjoy anything when I'm taking pictures of it.' She fingers her camera affectionately. 'Sometimes I think I only take pictures to make the world more interesting.' She glances at me, as if she's about to say something, and I wonder if she's seeing me through the lens of her mind, if she's thinking of me as a potential subject. The thought makes me a little horny, and I realise that I wouldn't be averse to taking my clothes off for her not only in a personal capacity but as a model. Something about revealing myself in this way, under the cloak of clinical detachment, is a turn-on.

'Anyway,' she says, 'we were talking about moving on, and we wondered if you wanted to travel down to Bangalore with us? It's supposed to be amazing.'

'In what way?'

'It's the Indian Silicon Valley, one of its richest cities, full of cool bars and lounges. A real head-fuck, apparently. Full of beautiful young things. I'm counting on getting some great photos. The India no one expects, beyond all the commonplaces.'

Asha flashes up in my mind again, and now I've tasted Sapphic delights with Sue, I regret all the more my squandered opportunity on Juhu Beach. A beautiful Bollywood actress invites me to lie with her on the sand and I run away. I must have been out of my tiny mind! I'm resolved never to miss out again. When something takes my eye, I will reach out and grab it, grab it by the throat. Life – it's a cliché but one that rings true in my mind right now – is not a dress rehearsal.

'Well?' Sue's looking a bit impatient now, aware that my mind is straying.

I smile at her. This is not the kind of woman, I'm sure, who would have passed up on a chance with Asha. Sue has unlocked me to myself, after all this time. Sue acts. Perhaps if I stick around with her, some of her decisiveness will rub off on me. And, of course, there's Dean to take into account. I may have slept with Sue, but nothing has changed the way I feel about her brother. This thing between her and me might only be a passing thing. When the novelty wears off, there's no telling what might be possible with him. I'm assuming that Sue's not going to tell him what happened between us last night, that she wouldn't do so without asking me first. And if and when she does, I'll explain to her that until I'm less ambivalent about my sexuality, I'd rather we kept things to ourselves.

'I'll come,' I say.

She grins. 'That's great,' she says. 'I'll tell Dean.'

22

The night Nadia left, Chris welcomed me back into his bed, but I wonder now if that was as much out of sympathy as anything else. I was distraught, even though the choice had, at least on the surface, been mine. In truth, I felt I'd been forced into it, had driven Nadia away, and I needed consolation. I'd told him as much at dinnertime, out of earshot of the other women, of course, and he'd said I could come round at ten.

The night was unforgettable, and for a while I did manage to erase thoughts of Nadia from my mind, worries about where she might be and whether she was safe. The mother in me, the one who wondered if it was right for an eighteen-year-old to be travelling on her own in India, was subsumed by the woman, the woman whose appetites had been pent up inside for 25 years, until just a few nights before. I'd rushed to Chris's room, at the appointed hour, and he'd barely brewed me a herbal tea when I'd dragged him over to the bed and gone down on him with a relish I'd never known before. Halfway through, he'd eased my head away, but it was only for a moment, while he reached into a bedside drawer and pulled out a metal cock ring, which he slotted over himself, explaining that he was in danger of coming too soon and that it would help him hold back.

Afterwards, however, when I brought my head away of my own account, moist for him, he'd stood up and gone to his table, poured me a cup of the fennel tea. Passing it to me, he'd left the bedroom, and from the adjoining room I heard running water. When he came back in, he gestured towards the bathroom.

'Our bath awaits,' he said.

I gazed at him, puzzled. Surely the bath was supposed to come afterwards, once we were sated, sweaty, covered by each other's fluids? But he was serious. Already he was turning and heading back into the bathroom and I had little choice but to follow him if I wanted to retain his attention.

He was climbing into the bath and, as I approached, he turned and looked at me seriously for a moment, then held out a hand to help me in beside him. His tub was large, with the taps set in the middle rather than at one end. I smelt some essential oils – sandalwood and perhaps also ylang ylang – that he must have added to the water. I sat down, let the water caress me, looked at him expectantly.

His head was back against one end of the bath, his eyes closed, as if all thoughts of sex had evaporated from his mind like the steam rising from the surface of the water. As if to remind him, I slipped one foot between his legs, brushed his cock and balls with the ends of my toes. He reached down, pushed them away, gently but firmly.

'Not yet,' he intoned.

I wanted to sit up, yell at him for leading me on. Here I was, a woman in need of consolation; a woman, moreover, who needed consolation precisely because of all that she had given up for him. And all he could do was run us an oily bath and look as if he was going to fall asleep.

He opened his eyes, fixed them on me, a little sternly I thought.

'You're in too much of a rush,' he said. 'The great Western disease. It seems to have got even worse since I left the West. It's a veritable epidemic now. It affects not only people's work lives but also their most intimate activities, and that's a danger to health.'

I stared at him. I was frustrated, horny as never before, but what he was saying made a strange kind of sense. What was this urgency I felt inside me? Sure, I was making up for lost time, for the barren years with Ravi, but there was something else to it too, at least this time – the panic need for a sort of oblivion.

'Sex,' said Chris as if tuning into my thoughts, 'is not a kind of forgetfulness, another way of numbing ourselves, like drugs or alcohol. On the contrary, it should awaken us, not only to ourselves and each other, but to life as a whole, to the universe in all its mystery and complexity.'

'So we're doing it wrong?' I said. 'Not us – you and me – specifically, but humanity as a whole?'

'The vast majority, yes. All those who see it as a ten- or twenty-minute race to orgasm, yes. All those who think that orgasm is the natural or inevitable endpoint. Whereas initiates know that the true purpose of intercourse is intimacy.'

I frowned. 'But don't you need intimacy to start with?' I said.

'Yes, ideally,' he said. 'But it is an intimacy that is to be deepened through sex. That is its true purpose. In the service, of course, of enlightenment.'

It was time for me to lean my head back now, zone out. I'm all for a spot of yoga or meditation to flush out the mind and tone the body, but if he was going to get all serious with talk of enlightenment and nirvana and karmic this and karmic that, then he'd soon realise he was going above my head. Not that I actually objected to anything he had to say. Yes, I do love coming, I do strive to climax and feel cheated if I don't when having sex, but I appreciated what he was saying about hurrying to the end, experiencing sex as little beyond genital stimulation. Perhaps that had been part of the problem with Ravi and me – with him exhausted from long days or nights at the hospital and me from motherhood, we regarded sex, when we did have it, as a quick in-and-out, the scratching of an itch.

Chris's hand was on my shin now, but in a non-predatory way; he was washing me, in fact, slowly and gently, as if I were a piece of delicate porcelain he feared dropping. With his fingertips he barely skimmed the surface of my skin, and his touch left me shivery with pleasure, a pleasure that had something of the sexual to it, but something much deeper too. I'll never be able to put it into words; perhaps that's where its very power lay, in its resistance to language, to being communicated. It made me feel extraordinarily sensual and yet, for once, there was no burning sensation between my legs, the urgency to be filled and satisfied. It was a kind of bliss that didn't need an orgasm, that wasn't rising towards some goal, towards satiation.

He washed my whole body, every last crease and crevice of me, and it took an age. But he was right: what was the hurry? We had all night. When at last we climbed from the bath, he massaged me a little, as he had the previous night, with Ayurvedic oils. Then he wrapped me in a silk kimono, laid me on the bed and read some poetry to me, from something he told me was called the *Amarushataka* or 'One Hundred Poems of Amaru', compiled in the eighth century.

'Hear his name and every hair on my body's aroused.
See his moonlike face
I get moist like a moonstone everywhere.'

Eyes closed, I felt myself smiling, caught up in a sensation of luxuriance and lazy sensuality, and glad now that Chris had foisted me off him after the blow job, even if it had seemed a bit of an insult at the time that he could resist me and my wet pussy. I felt relaxed and indolent, yet at the same time, as Chris had suggested, more alert – both to my own body and to his body, and to the world at large. It was as if what he had done to me – the washing, the massaging, the poetry – had revitalised me, re-energised me. I was infused with passion for him yet, curiously, in no need of actually fucking him. And that, for the moment at least, seemed healthy. Especially after all that had happened with Charles. It was as if Chris had put a brake on me, reined my appetites back in just as they were becoming excessive. And in any case, would it have been good for me, having sex with him to make myself feel better about, or at least forget, for a time, Nadia? Any relief it afforded me would have worn off as quickly as the effects of my orgasm.

No, Chris, in his serious, thoughtful way, had seen through my desperation and known what it was that I really needed that night. For that, for the respect he had shown me in not taking advantage but instead in making me feel cherished, comforted, he earned my thanks.

That, however, was the first night after Nadia left. And since it was our second night in bed together, albeit one in which sex didn't occur, I didn't feel that it was out of place to suggest we spend some time together that day, after the meditation and yoga sessions. Truth be told, I didn't know how Chris passed his time when he wasn't leading these sessions. I guessed he had to tend to his vegetable patch, shop for provisions in which he wasn't self-sufficient, deal with the boring admin of running his own business. But I didn't imagine he was busy all day and I thought that as a couple we might do something together.

His refusal was curt, hurtful, a plain refusal without any real explanation beyond the statement that his day was 'all accounted for'. The look on his face suggested that it was an imposition on my part even to have made the suggestion and made me realise how much I'd been taking for granted as a result of being allowed into his bed. Were we a couple after all? Did he even fancy me? I'd been touched by the way he'd refused to take advantage of my distress the night before, but now I wondered if the simple truth was that he didn't really want me, had only submitted to me that first night because I'd thrown myself at him.

I suppose I should have had some self-respect and taken myself out for the day. God knows I'd spent enough of my life cooped up in our family home in Sheffield – you'd think I wouldn't miss the opportunity to do a little unfettered exploring in this most colourful of countries, especially on such a gloriously sunny day. But I just couldn't pull myself together – as if Nadia hadn't been enough, now Chris was giving me the brush off, and I felt old and worn out.

Of course, I was being oversensitive. But as it turned out, I had reason to be suspicious: mid-afternoon, I heard voices in the courtyard and looked out of my window to see Chris sitting out under the trees chatting and laughing with a pretty young woman. I didn't recognise her from the yoga sessions. For a while they sat sipping at *lassi*s and talking, and then they rose and headed inside. I ran to my door, opened it quietly and tiptoed out and along the corridor in the direction of Chris's quarters. Sure enough, he and the girl were walking towards them.

I grimaced. Why had I placed my trust in this man after what Nadia had told me? Suddenly the compliments he had paid me during our first night together appeared to me in their true light as just so many smarmy lines. Nadia had been right. He told people what they wanted to hear and naive little me had lapped it up. Bloody old fool – a couple of compliments and I was anybody's. Pathetic, really.

But I had to be sure. I continued along the hallway, then halted outside his door and pressed my ear to it. I was aware, of course, of the risk of being found out, but at that moment I was smarting so much I didn't care. If he discovered me there, then all the better – I could confront him.

At first I could make out nothing beyond a low murmur of voices, with nothing distinct. Then I made out the woman's voice.

'Could you just explain that a bit more fully?' she said.

'Well,' I heard Chris say. 'The only time we ever really think about breathing, in any kind of conscious way, is when we are having trouble doing it. Yet conscious breathing can be a powerful aid in sexual growth.'

It was enough: there he was again, spinning lines, and I was damned if I was going to stick around and listen to him beguile another poor victim. I ran off down the corridor, not caring now if my footsteps could be heard, tears in my eyes.

In our room, now my room, alone, I wept. Then I swore at myself, told myself to stop feeling sorry for myself and decided to confront Chris about his visitor. I had no hard evidence that he was seducing her, after all, and before jumping to conclusions I had to be clear about who she was and what their relationship was. So I splashed my face with water, applied a mask of make-up and made my way to dinner.

Chris was there, of course, surrounded by his fawning pupils. As always, it was difficult to get his attention, but this time it appeared to me as if all the other students were ganging up on me, working together to shoulder me out and get me away from Chris. If we can't have him, they seemed to be saying, then neither can you.

At last I found an opportunity to speak to him without being overheard, as he was making his way out of the door to replenish one of the dishes in the kitchen. Unlike earlier, when he had seemed so offended by my suggestion we spend some time together, he was gentle and kindly, and I wondered if I'd misinterpreted his behaviour, or perhaps just caught him at a bad moment, when his mind was on more pressing matters. He was, in spite of everything, a businessman, I reminded myself, and there were bound to be pressures that even the meditation couldn't fend off.

Perhaps sensing that I was upset, he touched my hand briefly. 'Come to my room,' he said. 'But not before eleven. There are things I need to sort out. See you later.'

It was hard, filling the hours between dinner and the hour at which Chris would admit me to his inner sanctum, and I ended up going for a walk on the beach to de-stress me. As I strolled, I thought about the previous evening: about the bath, the massage; about Chris's insistence on taking one's time, on not hurrying. I'd thought he'd been talking strictly about sex, but now it seemed to me there might have been a message to me in there too, a message about our relationship as a whole. Let's take our time, he seemed to have been saying, and this morning I'd gone and nearly blown it by coming on too strong. Perhaps he was also thinking about his professional reputation. He might have felt safe entertaining me in his quarters late at night, but would it be right to be seen spending time with me during the day? He couldn't have failed to notice that by appearing with me at the meditation session after our first night together he'd incited animosity among some of his students, which probably wouldn't do his credentials a great deal of good. Yes, now that I thought about it, that was undoubtedly why he'd taken such a step back, had seemed almost frightened at my innocent-enough proposal.

He answered the door, at eleven, swathed in the same silk kimono in which he'd wrapped me the previous night. He looked relaxed, friendly.

'Come in,' he said, standing back and gesturing me inside.

Inside, I relaxed too, relieved to feel welcome, my heart lifting at the prospect of whatever was to happen that night. I had no idea what he might have in mind, but it was guaranteed to be something out of the ordinary. First, however, I needed to set my mind at rest about his visitor of earlier in the day.

I sat down in an armchair; the chaise-longue was too obvious, too full of implications. I looked at him. He was so damned handsome, albeit in a slightly womanly way, that my resolve wobbled. What did it matter who he had entertained here that afternoon? What did it matter that I only seemed important to him at certain times of day, and an encumbrance again afterwards? So long as I could experience some of that sweet and tantalising loving again, that feeling of our bodies slowly becoming one – not in some carnal sense, but on a spiritual level – then I didn't care. I wanted him.

Chris was regarding me thoughtfully, but when I held his stare it seemed to me as if he were almost looking through me. Perhaps that was just the effect of his fathomless blue eyes, which seemed to contain as many secrets as the oceans of which they reminded me.

'You seem . . . agitated,' he said.

I grimaced. 'Bad day,' I said.

'Anything I can help you with? You know I'm always here to listen. Being a yoga teacher is not only about guiding you through the right poses. In a way I guide people through their lives.'

This seemed more than a little arrogant to me, a tad presumptuous, but I knew from past experience of yoga classes that people did feel more open with each other after doing yoga together – with their classmates but especially with their instructor. It was as if the opening up of parts of one's body involved in certain of the postures – Utthita Triko-nasana, for instance – encouraged one to open up one's soul too, or whatever you wanted to call it. My own yoga teacher back in the UK had in fact become a kind of confidante during my divorce, and she had taught me various ways of controlling – but not repressing – my emotions through yoga.

Now, however, I *was* repressing my true feelings, was holding back on the questions I needed to ask, for fear of losing Chris. Which was ridiculous. My hold on him was tenuous, perhaps even imaginary. Looking back now, I see I had nothing to lose by confronting him, not really. But once again, as I had been, briefly, with Charles, I was caught in the trap of sex. My body was winning out over my mind.

'It's nothing a hug won't sort out,' I said at last. For a moment he continued to just look at me, which was more than a little unnerving. Then his chest rose and fell, as if in a sigh, and he stepped forwards and, taking my hands, helped me to my feet.

'I need a little loving,' I said. 'I need to feel like a woman.'

He pressed his face into my neck. 'That can be arranged,' I heard him breathe, emitting a warm exhalation onto the skin beneath my ear.

I reached down for his cock, fondled it through his loose canvas trousers. The breath became a moan. I moaned too, my pussy aching for him, and reached for the elastic top of his joggers.

'Whooa,' said Chris.

I stopped, pulled my head back. 'What's wrong?' I said. 'Did I do something wrong?'

He shook his head. 'Not as such. But you are my pupil and I've been trying to teach you about the value of patience, of slowness, of holding off. Have you taken in anything I've said?'

I shook my head, more than a little stung at being called his 'pupil'. Was that all I was to him? Were we not lovers, gone far beyond that relationship?

'The breath,' I heard him continuing, 'is the key. Yet the only time we ever really think about breathing, in any kind of conscious way, is when we are having trouble doing it. Yet conscious breathing can be a powerful aid in sexual growth.'

Sensing something hypnotic to his voice, as if he was trying to put me under his spell, I stepped back, shrugged his hands from me.

'You could at least come up with something original to use on me,' I said. 'A different line. At least do that for me.'

He was frowning at me. 'What do you mean?'

'I mean... well, I was walking by your room earlier and I heard you say those self-same words to someone else, another woman. I can understand... I wouldn't flatter myself that I'm the only one in your life. But I think I'm deserving at least of being seen and treated as an individual, not the latest item to be plucked off a conveyor belt and then discarded.'

He was waving his hands at me, fanning them up and down. 'Calm, calm,' he was saying softly. 'You're getting this all out of proportion, seeing it out of perspective. There's no question of anybody discarding anybody.'

'Then what?' I said. 'What perspective should I be taking?'

He guided me over to the chaise-longue, applied slight pressure to my shoulders to indicate that I should sit down and then lowered himself so he was sitting beside me. His hands were still on my shoulders. He cleared his throat, spoke slowly.

'Yes, there was a woman in my room earlier,' he said. 'Her name is Jasmine. What you have to understand, Valerie, is that this is my business as well as my home and as such I have meetings and classes and tutorials of one kind or another all through the day, day in, day out.'

'So who was she, this... this Jasmine?'

'She's an acolyte.'

'What's an acolyte?'

'A student.'

'She's learning yoga?'

'No, I am her guru in spiritual matters.'

'What does that mean?'

'It means that she focuses on me during her meditation, as a sort of earthly deity.'

'A god? Don't make me laugh.'

'I'm deadly serious.'

'But you ... you were talking about sex.'

'Look, Valerie, all of this is extremely complicated and more than I have the time and energy to explain to you, especially at this late hour. Now –' he turned to his bookshelf, then back to me '– if you really are interested in all this and are not merely annoyed because I had the cheek to consort with another woman, for very valid reasons, then I suggest you take this away with you tonight and spend a profitable couple of hours reading it.'

I took it, humbled by his words. I had let jealousy get the better of me. I'd not only made a fool of myself but I'd blown my chances of spending the night with him. At that moment I could see myself through his eyes and it wasn't a pretty picture: a middle-aged woman, attractive but by no means beautiful, throwing herself at a younger man, using her pain over her daughter as an excuse. The pain, of course, was real, but sex would only make me forget it for a short time. I knew that. But I was desperate for Chris anyway. I was wrong about the hypnosis: he'd put a spell on me already.

I stood up to go, hand at my throat. 'I'm sorry,' I said.

He took my hand, pulled me gently back down. 'I'm sorry too,' he said. 'I spoke too harshly and you don't deserve it. I just want you to understand that I have a business to run, a reputation to maintain, and discretion is key to that.'

'I understand. I'm sorry. I'll go now.'

'Stay.'

I looked at him in surprise and felt like I was falling into those blue eyes, falling into a beautiful blue sea from a great height, exhilarated even as I knew that I may fall so deep I might never come up again.

'Shall we do a calming exercise?' he said, his voice small and echoey as if it was coming from far away, from another realm. 'I think we could both benefit from it.'

'Sure,' I said, as if from a dream.

He crossed his legs on the chaise-longue and indicated for me to do the same, and, like him, to rest my hands on my knees with my palms facing up.

'Now, hold my gaze,' he said, 'however uncomfortable it might feel, however uneasy it might make you. Never look away. Take soft but deep breaths and try to go beyond my eyes, into my soul. When you've achieved that state and feel you can hold it, listen to my breathing and try to breathe at the same pace, in through your nose and out through your mouth. Don't look away. Let's see if we can keep that up for ten minutes.'

I did as he bade, but we can't have lasted more than three minutes, five at the most, before desire took hold and he leant in towards me, wrapped one hand round the back of my head and pulled me towards him for a kiss. It was a wild, almost vicious kiss: our teeth clashed, our tongues seemed almost to wrestle with each other. There was nothing calm about it. As we kissed, Chris pushed me, quite roughly, back against one end of the chaise-longue and, reaching below my skirt, pulled my knickers to one side and slipped one whole hand inside me. He began to pump it in and out, quite rapidly, and I was jerking and gasping beneath him, astonished by this sudden onset of naked, uncontainable desire. What had happened to all his talk of calm, of harmonised breathing and sacred intimacy? He was fucking the living daylights out of me and I couldn't imagine there was a spiritual thought in his head.

I reached around him, pulled down his trackpants and clawed at his slender arse as I felt my orgasm grow near. His spare hand, until now clutching my breast, moved down; with it he spread my pussy lips and glided his cock in. Then he pushed my legs and feet as high as they could go, which was quite high due to several years of weekly yoga and the last few days' intensive practice – I was pleased to discover all the hard work had paid off. Then he rode me fast and furiously, plunging in and out of me, yelping with pleasure, and I thrust back against him, matching his movements.

I wanted so much to come, knowing that when I did it would be hard – one of those almost painful orgasms that makes you clench your teeth, wondering if you are up to it, if you can withstand it. But I wanted to play him at his own game too, the game of deferral he was so keen on. Let's see, I thought, how he likes it when the tables are turned on him and it's his turn to wait.

Pulling myself from underneath him, despite his protests, and turning my head, I scanned his bookshelf with my eyes, looking for inspiration. I saw a silk scarf, intense purple in colour, and reached back for it, then bound it around Chris's head to cover his eyes. He moaned again and I knew that, much as he enjoyed control, he also, like Charles, got off on relinquishing it. Power, I thought, must be a double-edged sword, authority tainted by responsibility.

Looking back at the shelf I saw his Ayurvedic oil, also just within my reach. Unscrewing the lid, I poured myself a good palmful, then slathered his cock and balls with it, slowly, making sure to coat each millimetre, to saturate each pore. For the first time I noticed that he pruned his pubic hair: he wasn't wholly shaven, but it was kept neat and trimmed with scissors and maybe also clippers. This must account, at least partly, I realised, for the intensity of the sex we'd had two nights before, when he'd instructed me in various positions that were dear to him: the wheelbarrow, the bodyguard and so on. There'd been a definite feeling of unusual intimacy that I now saw was in some ways the result of how closely his denuded cock and balls fitted my spread lips, how our bodies felt almost moulded together.

I moved my hand up and down his straining shaft with long slow movements, deliberately drawn out. From time to time I touched my pussy, anointed it too with a little of the amber oil. But I was anxious not to rush; perhaps I wasn't such a bad pupil after all. Could I, I wondered, become one of Chris's acolytes? A lot of what he said struck me as so much mumbo-jumbo, but I couldn't deny that sex Chris-style was the most erotic I had ever experienced. Although we hadn't known each other more than a couple of days, I felt a powerful intimacy with him, and not only when we had sex – this was only, after all, the second time – but even when I was just looking into his eyes, those magical, complex, faraway eyes. Did I want to take this further and achieve, like him, a new plane of consciousness, and would he agree to take me there? Did embarking on such a journey with someone make them fall in love with you, and was there a chance that Chris and I could make a go of it together? I felt a shiver run through me: perhaps I wouldn't be going back to the UK at all, but making a new life here, in Goa, with this wonderful, enigmatic, desirable man who enflamed, it seemed, just about any woman he came into contact with.

I lowered my head, took first one ball then the other in my mouth as I continued my hand movements, flicking at them with my tongue, sucking at each in turn. Chris writhed beneath me like a snake, his lovely slim pelvis almost gyrating, his eyes still blinded by the scarf. All at once the sex I had with him appeared to me as a kind of dance. In fact, hadn't we tried out a pose called the dancer last time? There was an added dimension of rhythmic vehemence, which had been lacking in my lovemaking with Charles, in all of my love-making. This was a new level, another dimension.

But there was only so far I could hold back myself and so I swung one leg over him and eased him back inside me. It felt like belonging, and I wondered for a moment if I was going to cry. I squeezed my eyes closed to hold back the tears at the same time as I squeezed my inner muscles. Chris tightened his hands on my hips in appreciation and encouragement, a gurgle escaping from the back of his throat.

'Again,' he urged, and I pumped my muscles around his cock and felt both of our climaxes swell like a mighty storm gathering. Only rather than the usual short sharp shock of it all, the sweet brevity of orgasm, these climaxes went on and on, like ripples or waves, not deliciously painful but sweet and blissful and comforting, telling me that all was well in the universe. That anything was possible.

23

Bangalore, as Sue said it would, fucks with your mind. As in Mumbai, terrible poverty remains, juxtaposed with displays of almost obscene wealth and decadence, with a consumerism that rivals that of the West. It doesn't seem to bother Sue, though, as she flits around the city in the back of a rickshaw, shouting at the driver to pull over when she sees something or somebody photogenic or controversial enough to grace her viewfinder. I find myself wondering if it's possible to have moral scruples, as a photographer, or if one needs to be utterly detached in order to document these kinds of things at all.

We're staying in the Chandra Vihar, a cheapie close to the city's hectic wholesale fruit and vegetable market. After two days of bus rides, which all three of us mainly slept through, we discussed going for a little luxury. Even I, the most hardcore budget traveller, was tempted. But then our consciences overcame our desires and we ended up here. And it's fine – the reception is hung with gaudy holograms of dancing Hindu goddesses, there's a creaky old elevator and the rooms are very clean, if basic. Mine even has a balcony overlooking the bustling bazaar below.

Sue suggested we share a triple, but after what happened between her and me, I felt a little weird about that. Sure, we were in a communal room in Kanha, and she and I even made love in that room while her brother was sleeping, but that was an accident of sorts, a moment of blind passion. If it's going to happen between us again, I want to have more of a say in the matter, and more privacy. There's a seedy edge to having done it in the same room in which Dean slept that taints, at least a little, the memory of my first time.

In my rare waking moments on the bus journey down to Bangalore, I looked over at my sleeping would-be lover and wondered about what had happened between us. She had come to me, under cover of dark, and though I had more than submitted to her embraces, had reciprocated until they became a full-on fuck, the whole thing did sort of occur under false pretences. Or rather, even if Sue wasn't pretending to be Dean, or implying that she might be, I let her seduce me, up to a certain point, in the hope that it was her brother whose hands were on me.

And so, beautiful as she is, as great as the shagging was, I can't help but ask if I'd have been up for it if I'd known from the start who I was dealing with. Although I've finally had the fuck that I needed to get out of my system in order to start living, I'm still not clear about my sexual proclivities. Sue is wonderful, and if it were just her and me, I'm sure I wouldn't say no if the chance arose again. But there's Dean in the equation too. And I still want him, no holds barred. Will doing it again with her jeopardise any chances I may have with him?

I'm musing on all this when there's a rap at my door and I realise that the others must be waiting for me. We've agreed to go to a club tonight, to experience the city's famous nightlife.

'Come in,' I call, still sitting on my bed. The door swings open and Sue appears, framed like a painting, a vision in slinky hipster jeans and a silver lamé top, which shows off her amazing boobs to full advantage. Her hands are on her hips, and the look on her face lets me know that she's all too aware how great she looks.

'Not ready yet?' she purrs, and my cunt melts. For all I was just thinking, if she came into the room now and sat beside me on my bed, I wouldn't be able to keep my hands off those gorgeous tits. I'd push her back on the cover, push her top up over them and, taking one in each hand, squeeze and kiss and lick them until she sloughed off those jeans and proffered me her pussy, all wet and glistening.

'What are you thinking about?' she says, still in the doorway, still smirking.

I look down at my hands in my lap. 'Of fucking you,' I feel like saying. But I don't, of course, and luckily so, for a moment later Dean appears in the doorway behind, rests his chin on his sister's shoulder and flashes me a heart-melting smile.

'Not ready yet?' he echoes her.

I stand up and reach for my unpacked rucksack. 'I've not really got anything clubby to wear,' I say, peering inside. I hadn't really counted on going clubbing – not even, or perhaps especially not, in Goa – and my bag is full of practical, easily washable garments with lots of Lycra, which don't need ironing. I pull out a nondescript black T-shirt. It will have to do. I look over at Dean and Sue. 'Be with you in a min,' I say.

We're at Spinn, a disco-lounge in an old colonial house, recommended to us by a fellow-traveller at the guest house. Part of the lounge is outside, and Dean and I are sipping cocktails under the stars. Sue is on the dance floor, head thrown back, already lost to the progressive house music that's being spun by the DJ.

'Is she on something, your sister?' I say to Dean above the music.

He smiles, shakes his head. 'Nah,' he says. 'Sue's just high on life. She loves going out, showing herself off.' He looks at me. 'She's gorgeous, isn't she? An amazing creature.'

For a moment I can't reply, I'm so taken aback. It seems such a weird thing for a brother to say of his sister. And then the paranoia sets in. Does Dean know about me and Sue, about what happened in the park lodge? Did he wake up and hear us going at each other in the dark? Is this his way of telling me that he knows and, if so, are my chances with him blown?

'She's ... she's very uninhibited,' I say at last.

He chuckles. 'Oh yes, that's Sue all right,' he says. 'Never happier than when all eyes are upon her. Ever since she was tiny she wanted to be the centre of attention.' He looks at me. 'Of course, it's a sort of control, isn't it?'

I don't answer, lost again for a reply. What he's telling me could be construed both positively or negatively, but in the light of what's happened it seems like a warning. Only there's no way of finding out if he does indeed know what's happened without asking him directly.

The dance floor is busier now and the pace hots up. Though there are quite a few Westerners here, most of the young crowd is Indian. They're all dressed up in Western-style clothes, however, with plenty of designer labels – fake or otherwise – on show, and to all intents and purposes we could be in London. As Dean and I watch, fallen silent now, an unusually tall Indian girl appears at one side of the dance floor, pauses for a moment, and then strides onto it. There's not a head that doesn't turn to look at her as she crosses the floor, seeking some space to stake out for herself – or only Sue's, which is still thrown back in abandon, her eyes closed.

'Uh-oh,' I hear Dean say next to me.

I turn my head. 'What's up?' I ask.

His eyes flash at me. 'Just watch,' he says.

I turn my gaze back to the dance floor and, sure enough, the ravishing Indian girl has planted herself close to Sue, and Sue, opening her eyes, does an obvious double-take, as if she can't believe her luck. The rest of the crowd has lost interest: the girl is beautiful, incredibly self-confident, but they are not here to ogle, after all. The place is no meat market. But Sue keeps looking and the girl looks back at her, brazenly, and little by little they move towards each other, like two planets broken free of their orbits and growing closer and closer, with the inexorability of fate.

As they approach and start to ape, perhaps unconsciously, each other's moves, their hips swaying ever-closer together, I can't tear my eyes away either. Partly, I'm plain jealous. I thought I had a prior claim on Sue, that there was something between us, no matter how much I also wondered whether that was something I wanted to continue. Partly, however, I'm simply fascinated, and also more turned-on than I'd like to admit, by the spectacle of these two beautiful girls dancing together, clearly hot for each other, acting out on the dance floor the fuck they'd like to be having.

Finally they touch, and I let out a little cry, almost as if I've come. Sue lays one hand over the girl's shoulder, the girl places her hands on Sue's hips, still gyrating her own. Their torsos come together, and a thrill jags through me. My cunt aches. I want Sue, I want the Indian girl, so hard it hurts.

'Told you,' comes Dean's voice and, as I turn my head to him, I feel him take my hand. 'Had Sue told you she's gay?' he asks, and I shake my head. So he didn't hear anything – what a relief.

'What about you?' he says.

'What about me?'

'Which way do you swing?'

I'm not going to spoil my chances – if I have any – by telling him that I don't know, or that I swing both ways, so I shrug my shoulders, say, 'I'm straight, of course.' I can't look at him, my heart is racing so fast.

'Thank God for that,' he says, and then I do look at him and he jerks his head towards the exit. 'Shall we go?' he asks, and I nod, my cunt throbbing, shooting only the briefest of glances back towards the dance floor. Sue and the girl have their fingers in each other's hair, look as if they're going to kiss, but I don't care, no longer wish I was part of it.

Outside Dean and I jump into the first in a line of waiting rickshaws. My whole body is in a state of high alert now, adrenaline coursing through my veins like a potent drug. I'm afraid to even look at Dean, scared I will stop breathing. My desire for him is choking me. But almost immediately after telling the driver where we are heading, he turns to me, takes my chin between his fingers, and eases my head around so that we're looking into each other's eyes.

'I've wanted you since the minute we met,' he says, and I think, Why the hell did you wait so long to give me a sign? Why did you let your sister get in first? Sue might be showing all the signs of not giving a fuck about how I feel as she writhes on the dance floor with the Indian girl, but I'm not sure that sharing a lover with her brother comes into her plans. Of course, Dean doesn't know the whole story, so why should he have hurried? Some people like to bide their time, to savour the build-up. It's all part of the fun.

When he brings his lips to mine, it's as if I'm being engulfed not only by physical pleasure but by a tide of emotions, some of them contradictory. The thought that I am kissing this man for whom I feel a desire more forceful than any I have felt before is foremost. His lips and his tongue are so sweet: sweet-tasting, but also a little shy, making little advances and retreats as if testing the terrain, seeing how far I want to go. Unlike Sue, Dean doesn't ride roughshod, assume that I want to go the way he does. He tests the waters first, then takes things further.

Although my legs have parted automatically, almost without

my even realising, he goes slow there too, pressing his fingers into the tops of my thighs, through my jeans, inching them towards my groin, but without any kind of forcefulness. It's as if he's saying, through his gestures and body language: *We can do this, but only if you want to. Or we can do this, if you prefer.*

I unloop one arm from around his neck and reach down to unbutton my jeans. I'm not wearing knickers, to avoid VPL, and already my nectar has soaked through the gusset. He moves his head away from mine, looks down at my drizzling cunt and lets out a little moan. With my foot I locate the crotch of his jeans; he's as hard as bone. Reaching down between my legs, I slide my fingers between my lips, rub a little, then bring them to Dean's mouth. He takes them inside, deeply, sucks at them as if he can't get his fill of the honeyed liquid. Then, backing away a little more, as much as the restricted space in the rickshaw will allow, he slides my jeans down to my ankles and then off over my feet, lifts my thighs from behind so that my legs loop over his shoulders and back, and goes down on me, lapping at me like a cat at a bowl of cream, with the same sounds of satisfaction.

For a while he concentrates on my clit, working at it with his lips and tongue, one hand full of each of my buttocks. My own arms are outstretched, a hand on the rail on each side of the rickshaw. If anyone were to look in, they'd get a real eyeful, but luckily the motorised machine is speeding along now, and the driver too seems oblivious: the noisy engine must be drowning out the sounds of our lovemaking.

For that's what it is – making love, creating love – with a slow measuredness, in spite of our surroundings, that's quite unlike the hurried desperation that I experienced with Sue. With her it seemed to be all about coming, coming fast and hard, as if it was a race to the finishing line. Or that's how I think of it now. It was all such a blur at the time, a chaos of girly limbs and soft, yielding parts.

I'm forcing images and thoughts of Sue out of my mind when Dean raises his head, as if summoned back to reality from a place far far away, and looks around him. His stubble glitters with pinpricks of my juice, like dew on blades of grass.

'I think we're nearly there,' he says. 'Shall I ask him to do another few blocks?'

I laugh, touched and flattered that he doesn't want this to end. Of course, I don't either, but I want him inside me, want Dean to be the first man to enter me and bring me to orgasm, and I don't think the rickshaw is private or comfortable enough for that. And so, as I suggest, he has the driver pull up outside our hotel, hands him a pile of uncounted notes that probably bears little relation to the sum requested and, taking my hand, rushes us inside and up the stairs.

My room is the most obvious choice, but as we're halfway along the corridor, a voice halts us in our tracks and I feel Dean whisk his hand away from mine before he turns to face it.

'I was wondering where you two had got to,' she's saying as she stalks along the landing, eyes narrowed.

'Oh, hi, Sue,' says Dean. 'Nadia had a headache so I thought I'd bring her back here. We didn't want to interrupt you, spoil your fun.'

Sue smiles ambiguously. 'Oh, you shouldn't worry about me,' she says, and I sense something icy to her voice all of a sudden.

'No, but ...'

She carries on to her room, unlocks the door. 'I'll find some aspirins for you, Nadia,' she says as it swings open. 'It's probably all the travelling. The best thing for it is to go straight to bed and get a good night's sleep. Actually, Dean, would you be an angel and have a look for them in my washbag while I give Nadia a hand? Thanks.'

I can't see in what way I might need a hand, given that I'm only supposed to have a headache, but nor can I think of a polite way of protesting, so Sue and I go into my room while Dean goes into theirs in search of aspirin. I'm more than miffed, of course, that Sue showed up and put a spanner in the works, but that could have been pure chance, ill luck. Now, however, it seems she's deliberately trying to come between us and I'm seething inside. What gives her the right? Sure, we fucked, her and I, and it was great, life changing even. It was my first time, after all. But we haven't discussed whether it is to be an ongoing thing, and as such she has no claim on me. Even if she had, she repudiated that claim by what she did in the nightclub, when she showed me that she was free to do whatever she wanted. Why, in that case, am I not? And why is Dean not?

'Come on,' I hear her saying through the cauldron of my thoughts. 'Let's get you into something comfortable.'

Despite my anger, I give in to her, let her lift my arms and pull up my T-shirt, then reach round and unclasp my bra. As it falls away, she looks down at my breasts, smiles, tongue poised on her upper lip.

'You have fucking gorgeous tits,' she whispers, reaching for them.

I'm paralysed, and not only because I don't want to make a fuss and alert Dean. The feel of her cool flesh on my nipples makes them harden and sets my brain on fire, in spite of myself. Her eyes are on mine, as if she's searching my soul, and I have to close mine to escape her scrutiny. She knows I love this, that I'm hers if she wants to take me, in spite of Dean. The pleasure is too strong; I'm putty in her hands.

She's undone the top button of my fly now and one finger

is creeping over my mons, slipping through my wet lips and into my cunt. Head still back, I look anxiously towards the door, but even as I do so I understand that there's no danger that Dean will show up with the aspirin. I don't know how I know that he'll keep away, but I do.

As the knowledge hits me, I fall back against the bed and Sue yanks down my jeans and brings her mouth to me, to the place where her brother had his not half an hour ago. I try to resist now, thinking of Dean, but the orgasm that I didn't have time to reach with him surges up and, while Sue's expert tongue flickers on my clit and three fingers push in and out of me, I arch my back and feel my whole body go rigid as I abandon myself to it. When I actually come I feel super-tense and warm and light inside, simultaneously.

Afterwards, as we lie in each other's arms, I look into the dark and ask, 'So what about the Indian girl?'

'What about her?' says Sue.

'I . . . I don't know. What was happening there?'

She laughs, but there's a hollow, joyless ring to it. 'Just a bit of sport,' she says. 'I see a beautiful girl, I wonder if she's up for it. It's like a challenge. But once I know that I can have her, most of the time I just lose interest.'

'You lost interest? But she was amazing!'

'There are lots of amazing girls. It doesn't mean I have to fuck them.'

'And will you lose interest in me?'

She sighs and for a few moments there's silence. 'Who can say what's going to happen?' she answers at last. 'Nothing is ever certain. I make no promises.'

I frown, but she can't see me. 'I'm not asking for promises,' I say. 'It would just be nice to . . . to – oh, I don't know . . . to get where you're coming from.'

I feel her shoulders twitch as she shrugs. 'Where I'm coming from,' she muses. 'Now there's a question. The thing is Nadia, I'm twenty years old, not that much older than you, and I'm trying not to think too hard about anything. Maybe ... I don't know you well enough by now, but maybe you think too much, about the consequences of things and how they're going to turn out. Me? For the moment, I guess I'm just in it for the ride.'

And with that, as if she doesn't expect me to answer or actually wants to discourage me from continuing the conversation, she takes my hand and places it on her muff. 'My turn now,' she says, opening her legs, and as I slip my fingers between her sweet, moist labia, her cunt appears to me as black hole, devouring, treacherous, all-consuming. The kind of place from which you might not escape intact. The thought, as I push inside her, my mouth on her clit, both terrifies and excites me.

'Next time,' she's saying, 'we'll use a dildo. I'll fuck you to high heaven.'

She's leaning over me in my bed, brushing my hair back from my forehead with one hand, twisting one of my nipples with the other. I can feel the sparse hair of her bush against my hip bone. I'm wondering what Dean will say when he wakes up, when he realises that I've spent the night with his sister. Will he feel hurt and rejected? Will I get the chance to explain to him that I didn't choose her over him, that it was coercion of sorts? Will he believe me, and even if he does, will he be appalled by my spinelessness, my lack of willpower? Surely I don't stand a chance with him after this?

A knock on the door makes me gasp.

'Quick,' I say, sitting up and pushing her away from me. 'Hide somewhere.'

But Sue ignores me, and even calls, 'Come in,' and of course in all the confusion of last night we forgot to lock the door and the handle is pressed down from outside and Dean walks right in. Sue doesn't even bother to cover herself up, just sits there in all her glorious nudity smiling up at her brother. I lie beside her, under the sheet, feeling like I'm dying inside. There's no doubting what we've been up to together, but as if she wants to make it super-clear, Sue now stands up, and in doing so accidentally on purpose takes half the sheet with her, so that I too am exposed to Dean, under circumstances so different to those I had imagined as we sped home in the rickshaw last night.

I can't look him in the eye. I'm mortified. But he doesn't react in any way that I expect, either by laughing – incredulously, bitterly or in genuine mirth – or by getting mad. He just bids us good morning and then starts talking about the train that we have booked tickets on later that day, taking us overnight to Kerala.

I want to scream, lash out, tell them that I can't do this any more, that I'm too confused to go on with them. Why, after what we did together in the rickshaw, after his sister showed up and spoilt our fun, is Dean not mad at me, and at her too? He's obviously not in love with me, but isn't his male pride wounded, at the very least? Doesn't his sister not only denying him his shag but stealing it from him merit at least a few harsh words on his part? He should be livid at both of us, but here he is calmly talking about train times.

He leaves, at last, and Sue looks at me. She places her hand on my belly, smiles kindly. 'You're not thinking of bottling out, are you?' she says, and her eyes probe mine. When I don't answer she says, 'Please don't, Nadia. It would be a big mistake. Especially now that things are about to get interesting.'

I sit up, stare at her. 'What do you mean?' I ask, but she's already up and halfway out of the room before I've got the words out. Her only response is to half turn in the door and wink at me, one finger over her lips.

24

'Vajrayana,' Chris is saying, 'is partly based on Tantric techniques, as a way of achieving Buddhahood.' He's reclining on the chaise-longue, looking out into the courtyard. 'You can only see the superficial aspects,' he goes on musingly. 'Even talking about them to the uninitiated is harmful.'

I roll over on his bed, exposing my naked breasts and pussy to him, hoping to tempt him back, though it's only five minutes since I climaxed, and I thought I was sated for a while.

'But I still don't understand why, say, Jasmine can be your acolyte and I can't,' I say. 'Is it that I'm too old?'

'Don't be silly. Age has nothing to do with it. Age is a state of mind.'

There it is, that dismissive tone again, the platitude ... Last night I thought I'd achieved nirvana, fucking a blindfolded Chris on the chaise-longue, drawing out both our orgasms so that when they did finally arrive, it was with unbelievable intensity, both physical and mental, leaving us both shattered, like shipwrecks washed up onto a strange shore. This morning, although I'd slept over again, he flatly refused to go to the beach with me, insisting that I make it seem as if I was arriving at the meditation session from my room. He's been unavailable all day, as usual, and I had to accost him at dinner again, virtually force an invitation to his room out of him when it didn't seem one was to be forthcoming.

I love the sex, can't live without it. I love how he's made me see the value of holding off on one's pleasure, how that can deepen it, make the whole thing more fulfilling. But I hate the secrecy aspect of things. Chris plain avoids many of my questions with either outright dismissal or obfuscation, and that makes me feel small. It devalues the sex, ultimately, however good it feels at the time. What's the point of striving to achieve this rare intimacy only to tear it asunder again with an uncaring attitude, harsh words?

Perhaps I'm being too touchy. I guess I'm missing Nadia too, not least as someone to confide in. But what help would she be, having felt the way she did about Chris? She'd only tell me to leave him, and that's not something I feel I can do. Charles – that was easy, once I'd realised I'd have to share him. With Chris it's less straightforward.

There was another woman in his room this afternoon; I saw her arrive and sneaked to his room to listen again – only for a minute. This time I did care if he caught me snooping, because last night showed me how much I want to be with him. I just wanted to reassure myself that she was indeed another acolyte, like Jasmine, but I couldn't hear enough or stay long enough to glean much information. Yet assuming that she was another acolyte, then I knew at least that Chris could be a guru to more than one person at a time, which meant that I could ask to become one of the initiates too, and enter fully into his world. Only then, I thought, would I feel secure in this relationship.

The sex, tonight, blew my mind. This time, rather than holding off from penetration or using a cock ring to delay his orgasm, Chris used a technique he called ajna chakra focus.

'The ajna chakra,' he told me, as we sat cross-legged, facing each other after harmonising our breathing, 'is an energy point in the forehead, in-between the eyes. If you focus on this point, both physically and mentally, you can stave off orgasm.'

'How do you focus on it, either physically or mentally?'

'It's not easy, but once you have it, you can do it again at will. Basically, after you've spent a few minutes meditating to clear your mind of all thoughts and rid your consciousness of external stimuli, you picture two paths leading from your eyes and meeting at a midpoint about five centimetres above your eyes and two centimetres into your skull. Then you try to pull your eyes inwards towards this point.'

'Sounds painful.'

'It's not, but it is strange to start with.'

'Then what?'

'Well, now you've located the ajna chakra, or third eye. What you have to do at this point is meditate, and as you're meditating focus on drawing up all the energy from every limb, muscle and organ in your body to this point you've found inside your head. The energy is then directed out through this tiny point.'

'Where does it go?'

'Nowhere. Or into the void. You have to imagine that outside the ajna chakra is a vast – an infinite – black space devoid of words, sounds, images or thoughts.'

'And this stops you from coming?'

Chris smiled. 'For a while, yes. I am only human, after all.'

I smiled too, but there was an acrid taste to it. Part of me just wished he'd get on with it, and I was also suspicious of his role as a guru. Talking about his 'tutorial' with Jasmine, he'd referred to himself as a deity. The assurance that first attracted me to him was starting to look a little like arrogance, or at least the conviction that he knew better than anyone else. But perhaps that was an attitude necessary to those who choose to make their living by instructing others.

He placed two fingers on my pussy lips but kept them still. 'Clittage,' he said. 'Ever heard of it?'

I shook my head.

'It's where *you* take control, where you masturbate with

your clitoris against my fingers or against my penis, dictating the speed and intensity. Want to try?'

I nodded.

'Then kneel up.'

I obeyed and, while he supported me with one arm wrapped round my waist, frotted myself against the two fingers he held still against my lips. I was surprised by just how good it felt to be in charge of both speed and pressure. Then Chris arched back and away from me, and I found myself able to straddle him and continue the same technique against his cock, as he'd suggested. This too gave us both an enormous amount of pleasure – a pleasure I knew derived as much from the effort involved in resisting the natural urge of his cock to enter me and for my pussy to be entered, as from anything else. Again, the smoothness of his cock and balls, where he had shaved or at least pruned, added to the intensity; there was little hair to soak up my juices, meaning he was as wet and slippery as me. Peeling back my lips and holding myself open heightened the sensation even more.

We kept this up for a long time. Despite the temptation to start fucking each other's brains out, it was so amazing in itself that it was hard to stop. After a while, we turned over so that I was in the standard missionary position, but Chris didn't enter me even then. We continued to rub ourselves against one another and we found that, strangely, the more slowly we did it the better it was. We kept gasping and looking into each other's eyes with wonder, and then looking down at our bodies as they pressed together, gently but firmly, massively wet. I really thought then: this is it, I've found it, the place I want to spend the rest of my life. This was heaven, or nirvana as Chris would say.

He placed his cock inside me but held it still. The very fact that he could do that excited me so much that I brought my hand to my clitoris, began strumming at myself, my fingers sliding over myself, I was so sodden by now. I looked up at Chris in panic; there was no holding this off any longer, I was going to come. He just nodded, then a blankness stole over him and I knew he was looking inwards, locating the ajna chakra. It felt odd, eerie even, when my orgasm blasted through me a moment later, to be contracting and relaxing around his motionless cock, but it felt good too. It allowed me to concentrate purely on the sensations that threatened to rip me apart, rather than on what was happening to him.

As the pleasure subsided, like the aftershocks of an earthquake, I started to cry and, as I put my head back, I looked up at Chris in time to see him open his eyes, releasing the ajna focus. He came, then, like a train.

I'm remembering what Chris said before, about the inevitable sadness that comes after sex – 'the reckoning', as he called it. Looking at him across the room, reclining on the chaise-longue, and both wanting him again and feeling like more sex is really the last thing I need – that I've had more sex in the last week than in the previous five years and that that might not necessarily be a good thing – I wonder if that's why I feel so empty. Or is it purely his disengagement, the way we can seem so close during the sex and so apart afterwards?

I'll probably stay the night again. I suspect that Chris knows that I'll throw a complete wobbly if he sends me back to my room, having let me stay over on previous nights. But already I dread tomorrow: the time spent without him, despite being in his company. Having to put up with the way other women look at him, despite knowing that he's mine. Or do they do it *because* they know we're sleeping together, to prove to me that he's *not* mine? How often does Chris engage in affairs with students? His classes are weekly, so there's fresh blood every seven days. And then there are his ongoing students, such as the lovely Jasmine. Can I really be the only one who's caught his eye?

I turn away from him, extinguish the lamp by my side and pull the cover up over me. Chris doesn't look like he has any intention of coming back to bed, not for a while at least. I close my eyes, as much to stop myself crying as because I think I will get any sleep.

25

As we board the train tonight, Sue's words are still playing in my mind; in fact, they haven't left me all day. Things were just starting to get interesting, she'd claimed, but what did she mean? Things between me and her? I don't see how they might get more interesting, rather than be just more of the same, unless she was referring to the dildo she mentioned this morning too. In fact, that is my whole problem with being a lesbian: once you've worked through the limited repertoire, isn't it all just repetition?

Of course, the same can be said of sex with men. Only it seems to me, with my albeit limited experience, that there is more variety with men, a greater number of possibilities to explore. And then, it isn't all about sex. There is a progression in a relationship with a man, the question of children and creating a family together. Again, this isn't something that couldn't happen with a woman, by one means or another, but my future, as I see it, involves child-bearing and child-rearing, and being part of a traditional family. I know it isn't the only path, and not necessarily the right path for everyone, but it is the path I envisage taking myself. Perhaps that's why I can't reconcile myself with my taste for girls.

In any case, I have the funny feeling that Sue was talking about more than the dildo. Something about the relish with which she spoke makes me think that she was talking about something much bigger, more far-reaching. And as she'd intended, although her words frightened me, in some ways they also intrigued me enough to tip the balance. I will travel on to Kerala with them and see what happens. Otherwise I'll always be wondering. But if Sue thinks she can mess with my head, I'll be off like a shot. I love how she makes me feel, but I don't love her. I can cut free at any time.

I look at Dean as he bends over the lower bunk in our compartment, rooting around for something in his rucksack. Is he the reason I am still here? Do I really think I'm still in with a chance after what he saw this morning? Nothing has been said, by anybody, about the incident; nor has there been any mention of what happened, and what nearly happened, between him and me last night. There have been no recriminations, no bitterness. Dean continues to look at me kindly, in a friendly way. Perhaps if I dared to hold his gaze I might see something more there, the truth about what he thinks of me, of my 'betrayal'. But I can't look him in the eye longer than I strictly have to when we exchange a sentence or two, so I don't know. Yet even if I don't expect anything to happen, there's the possibility I may still be here just to *be* with him, in however restricted a capacity. If I can't have him, at least I can see him, look at him, hold on to what might have been.

We have dinner on the train. We ordered food in advance and, at the second stop of many, a man climbs aboard from the platform and hands us each a paper bag. To our delight, each contains little pots of curry and *dhal*, to be scooped up with rice pancakes, which arrive wrapped in banana leaves, or soaked up by sticky lumps of coconut-scented rice. As we eat, we talk little, content to watch the sunset over the stunning scenery beyond our window – of plains, at first, but later of forested areas too, rich green and full of wildlife and wild noises. As it begins to get dark, Sue takes out a scented candle – fig and cardamom, she says – lights it, and we all sit and observe the light die fully outside, the blackness punctured only by the odd speck of light in the distance, its source unguessable.

It's only as we're thinking of settling onto our bunks for the night, when Dean has gone to pee, that our conversation is anything more than small talk. Checking, or so it seems, that he is out of earshot, Sue turns to me, and in the candlelight her eyes gleam dangerously.

'What do you think of him?' she says.

'Of your brother?'

'Of course.'

'Why do you ask?'

'I can't imagine you don't fancy him. I can't imagine there's a woman alive – bar lesbians, and I know you're not really a lesbian – who doesn't fancy him.'

'I . . . er, well, yes, I guess he's pretty good-looking.'

'"Pretty good-looking"?!' she parrots, incredulous. 'He's a god! You won't meet many more fuckable men in your lifetime, I guarantee it.' She peers round her seat again, checking he's not on his way back, and I wonder again at this curiously sexual way in which they speak of each other, this sexual appreciation they seem to have of each other. It seems to go beyond the objective recognition of beauty and perhaps even beyond sibling pride.

'I mean,' she says, looking me full-on in the eyes. 'Who'd turn that down? I know I wouldn't.'

She holds my gaze, freezes me with it, and there's something provocative to it all, something she's trying to tell me.

'My God!' I exclaim. 'You haven't? Sue, tell me –'

She's nodding even before I've got the words out, and my heart and belly flutter. This is beyond any complication I could have imagined, beyond 'interesting'. I shouldn't be here. I want out.

But then Sue bursts into laughter. 'I've had him,' she said, 'but of course he's not my brother. Did we really have you fooled?'

I wrinkle up my face. Suddenly it all makes sense and I feel such a fool for having been taken in by their charade. Of course Sue didn't want me to sleep with him, but not out of possessiveness over me so much as possessiveness over him, her lover, her boyfriend. Her boyfriend who, on the other hand, doesn't seem to mind sharing her with other girls. But then isn't that every man's fantasy?

I don't have time to react in any coherent way before Dean returns and his face tells me, as soon as he sees us, that he knows that I know. Undoubtedly it's inscribed on my features. I'm probably as pale as I feel, washed out and exhausted by all of this, and my eyes probably give away the shock from which I'm still reeling. But I suspect, in any case, that this was all orchestrated, that he was instructed by Sue to disappear for a few minutes while she let me in on their little secret.

For the moment, I'm trapped, sharing this tiny compartment midway between stations, on a train otherwise full. I don't want to move places, to sleep among strangers, in any case, and I don't want to get off in an unknown town in the dead of night. I have no choice but to stay here, with these people who've been messing with my mind.

I turn away from them, start rustling through my wash bag for my toothbrush and toothpaste. As I turn back, about to head for the loo, a hand falls on my shoulder. I look round and it's Dean, smiling at me. 'Stay,' he says, and I melt. It's a word that I resisted once before, on Juhu Beach, and I regret having done so.

'Why should I?' I say, and the hurt in my voice can't be mistaken.

'Because,' he says, bringing his other hand to my other

shoulder, eyes fixed on mine, 'Sue and I are going to take you to places you've never been before.'

Sue steps up to me, places one hand on the side of my head and runs her long fingers over my hair, smiling at me. 'How can you resist?' she says, and she's right – already I'm crumbling inside, like an old wall whose foundations have failed. I swoon back as Dean brings his head to my neck, starts brushing his lips over the flesh of my shoulders. There's nothing I wouldn't do to keep hold of this moment; it must never end.

Meanwhile, Sue has come behind me, is reaching round me, slipping one hand down the front of my combats. 'Mmmmm,' she says, as her fingers meet my clit, standing proud for her, for him, for them – I no longer know where this desire is directed. On my belly I feel the solid mass of Dean in the crotch of his trousers and knowing now that I will have him inside me after all unleashes a sort of fit of anticipation in me. I can hardly bear it. I'm crying, tears coursing down my face, beset by a terrible feeling that I am losing myself even as I'm finding out who I really am. Or is the first a precondition of the second?

By some unspoken accord, Dean and Sue stop what they're doing and guide me over to my bunk. There Sue lays me down and asks if I'm warm and comfortable. I nod dumbly, too stunned by what is happening to speak. Standing up, she turns to Dean, steps up to him and gives him a long kiss while fondling his prick through his trousers. He closes his eyes, grabs one of her buttocks and pulls her towards him. I moan too, clutch my snatch, pressing my clit with my thumb. I could bring myself to orgasm in a trice, just watching them. Is that what they have in mind? Are they the kind of people you hear about, who get their kicks from shagging in front of others?

But Sue pulls herself away from Dean, gestures back at me.

'Strip her,' she says authoritatively, and he steps towards me, pulls down my jeans from where they were bunched around my lower hips, then reaches up and pulls my top up over my head. For a moment he stands back to look at me, perhaps even to admire me. I spread my legs to show him how ready I am for him, if that's part of the plan. I'm feeling more brazen now I know that I am to be fully involved and not a bystander. Already I sense that if I'm not to feel used, doll-like, after this encounter, I must assert my own needs and desires too.

'Her bra,' says Sue, and Dean leans over me and reaches round me to unhook me. My breasts spill out; he takes one in each hand, starts licking and sucking at them alternately. Even through the noise, I can hear Sue's breathing behind him growing heavy and irregular. It's clear she's enormously aroused, on the verge of losing it. I turn my head and watch as she undresses quickly, then, after a moment during which she stands fingering herself, climbs onto my bed behind Dean, encircles him with her arms and with agile fingers undoes the fly of his jeans. When she's done that, she slides them down over his hips, along with his boxers, and his cock springs forth. I strain up with my hips, desperate to have the beautiful golden rod inside me, but Sue's hand is on it first, shuttling it back and forth. I'm not left bereft, though: with her other hand she seeks me out between my legs, shoots bunched fingers up into my hole. I snake my hips on the bed, so horny I could pass out.

Not taking his face from my breasts, Dean now reaches down, takes my clit between two fingers and gives it a little tug, before massaging it vigorously with his fingertips. With my major erogenous zones all being pleasured at once like this, it's impossible not to come, and I do, loudly, yelling out in surprise and awe at what these people are doing to me, at their generosity. I don't know why Sue is prepared to share her lover like this with me, but I'm immensely grateful.

I decide to show her how grateful I am by sitting up, reaching for her, and pulling her down so that now it's her who's recumbent on the bed. Bringing my mouth to hers, I kiss her passionately. 'Thank you,' I whisper when we come apart, and she reaches between my legs to where I'm still numb from my climax. For a moment I let her tease at my clit, then I back away down the bed, plant my mouth on her cute little snatch. It's sopping, of course – how could it not be? I lap at her juices, revelling in her fruit and honey sweetness, at the hint of musk. For a moment, I forget about Dean, but he's still there behind me, and he reminds me of his presence by parting my bum cheeks with his hands and seeking my own hole with his mouth. After coating it with his saliva – unnecessarily, since I'm still wet – he kneels back up and with his fist guides his prick inside me. I cry out in triumph as I feel myself impaled, thrust myself back harder onto him, even as I continue working at Sue's snatch with my mouth. Sue now places her fingers flat against my clit and lips and presses hard while moving them from side to side. I feel myself on the verge of a second orgasm. I tell myself that it's not fair, that it's someone else's turn, but it's too late, it's bowling towards me, and I take it greedily.

Afterwards, I fall down onto Sue and we kiss avidly again. Dean withdraws from me. As our tongues are still curling around each other, I feel the pressure of Dean on my lower back and realise, from his position and from Sue's cry, that he's entered her where she lies beneath me. I remain sandwiched between them as he fucks her, harder and harder, and it's my hips that he's clutching as he comes inside her, my back he falls onto, gasping like a fish on the shore. Her orgasm comes a split second after his, and I feel her nipples harden where they touch mine.

We all fall apart, the force of our separate orgasms sending us spinning off into our separate worlds, and when I wake, at dawn's light, at our penultimate stop, Sue and Dean are curled up together on the bottom bunk opposite mine. Brushing my hair out of my eyes, I sit up and for while watch them sleep, trying to decide if they look more like co-conspirators or, bizarrely, what they created the illusion of being – brother and sister. Yes, for a moment, in the dim light of early morning, they look young, childlike even, innocent in their dreams. But after last night I doubt their dreams are ever pure.

We arrive in Kochi, from which it's quite a long bus ride down to Kovalam in the far south of the state, where we've agreed to stay. Nothing is said of last night during the journey, but I feel a sort of new complicity between us all, that I have become part of something, albeit something I don't necessarily understand. That makes me a little uneasy too, I have to confess, but the physical exhilaration of the experience overrides any niggles. Sue's generosity, Dean's cock inside me at last, after the disappointment of the previous night – these things put any thoughts of fleeing out of my mind. I'm in for the ride, for the time being. I just can't wait to have Dean to myself, for a while at least. Weirdly, I'm already reconciled to the fact that he's Sue's boyfriend. Perhaps I'm growing up a little.

There are three crescent-shaped beaches here, and we rent a traditional thatched hut close to the main one. There's only one double bedroom inside, albeit one with a king-sized bed, and at first I'm surprised that Dean and Sue seem happy with this arrangement. But then I tell myself I should be flattered that they intend to share their bed with me, that we have become a bona fide threesome. Especially as it makes it more likely that I will get Dean to myself at some point, in that big comfy bed, when Sue goes off to take more of her pictures.

Already she's talking about wandering round to investigate the lighthouse perched at the end of the bay, red and white striped like a stick of Blackpool rock.

But it's late, now – the light will be no good, she says – and we decide to walk along the seafront and perhaps take a swim in the calm sea before choosing a place for dinner from the array of seafood restaurants. Shouldering towels, we head out, and I feel as light-hearted as Dean and Sue look.

We're too hungry, after all, and the beach is still too crowded for us to want to swim. Sitting on the terrace of one of the restaurants, watching the sun slot down behind the horizon like a giant orange coin, we chat idly, about nothing in particular. There's a commotion at one point as a fishing boat is hauled ashore and six men struggle up the beach with its catch – an enormous swordfish. We're in luck – it's to our restaurant that they heave it, and we order swordfish and lemon rice in the sure knowledge that the main ingredient couldn't be any fresher.

As we eat, I study Dean and Sue, their body language with each other, the looks they exchange, the things they talk about. I notice that they have a habit of finishing each other's sentences, and wonder for the first time how long they were together before coming to India. It's curious how little I know about them as a couple, but then I have only just found out that they *are* a couple. Yet something stops me from asking them any questions about their relationship – perhaps I'm afraid of what I might find out – and our conversation remains relatively superficial.

I suppose my first and main question would be whether they are in love. Sitting here chatting in the waning light, they seem much as they did before I knew they weren't brother and sister – affectionate but not overly so. Of course, they may be holding back on physical affection to spare my feelings.

Also, I know enough about couples to understand that public displays of affection might serve to mask private problems, and that the converse is equally true – couples who are restrained in public may be demons with each other in the bedroom.

At last, having lingered over coffees and shots of the local spirit – toddy, fermented from coconut and palm saps – we pay our bill and step down onto the sand. The moon is a thin sliver above us, like the tip of a fingernail. The sea glints darkly, almost menacingly. I hold my breath, wondering what is about to happen, what the night has in store.

Sue strips off first, as you'd expect of the exhibitionist in the party. In the pale moon she's barely visible. She approaches me as stealthy as a panther, pulls my top up over my head and inclines slightly to lap at my breasts with her tongue. I scoop them up, thrust them more fully into her face, little gurgling noises of pleasure bubbling up in my throat. My head is cast back; I turn it and look at Dean. He too has undressed. A sound escapes from my throat, something animal, as I watch him stride out into the water and plunge in. For a moment there's no sign of him, and then he reappears, farther out, just a dark shape above the water, which you might mistake for a seal's head if you didn't know it was a man.

Sue pulls her head back, turns and looks out over the ocean, then starts to follow him. Not wanting to be left out of anything, I pull off the rest of my clothes and, leaving them heaped on the sand, run after her. I catch up just as she's located Dean, is winding her arms around his neck, mouth already open to meet his. For a moment they kiss, and I feel a twinge in my belly as I see how they eat at each other's faces, as if they were new lovers. Then each of them holds out one arm, opening the circle to include me, and I step into it.

I'm not sure whose hand it is that enters me first, but it

doesn't seem to matter – what matters is the sensation, as the fingers go round and round inside me, deeper and deeper. Then I realise that it's Dean's hand, from the way his shoulder is gyrating. Pretty soon he releases his other arm from around Sue's bare shoulder and that shoulder starts to follow the same motions. Sue's face confirms that he has his other hand inside her, is pleasuring her in exactly the same way. Looking back at me, she sends me a complicitous smile and leans forwards a little to kiss me, open-mouthed, giving herself fully, one hand back on my breast. I hold hers too, and feel her nipple bullet hard on the flat of my palm. I groan; my orgasm is coming, coming too soon. There's an ache for it not only in my cunt but in my arse too. I keep kissing Sue as Dean's hand increases speed inside me, and presumably inside her too, and, perhaps pulled along in the wake of my excitement, Sue comes at the same moment as me. Our mouths are still locked onto each other, our cries half stifled by each other's tongues.

Taking charge now, but wordlessly, Dean turns me around in the thigh-high water, so that I have my back to him. Sue places herself in front of me, back to me too. When Dean puts one arm around my waist and pushes me forwards over it, she bends forwards in front of me, and I put one arm around her waist obligingly. Having given me barely a minute to recover from my climax, Dean spits into his palm and, as if he's read my mind, felt my urges in some telepathic way, massages it into my anus. Then, checking me for readiness, he eases a finger into my sphincter. I gasp, in pain but also in delight. He adds another finger, then another, and then he murmurs something, takes his hand away and I feel his cock at my entrance. I'm still a little high from the toddy, and I guess that maybe this makes the first time easier. Despite his having prepared the way with his fingers, though, it's still tight, and he has to make his way in gradually, like an animal forging its burrow. Muscle by muscle, however, I open up to him, until my arse is full of him and he's free to start thrusting.

Not forgetting Sue, who's looking over her shoulder at proceedings, going at her clit with her fingers, I pull her hand away and start massaging her clit in her place, occasionally letting my fingers wander down over her soft lips to her hole, lingering there and then returning to their starting point. I put the fingers of my other hand into my mouth then bring them to her arse and replicate Dean's actions with me of just a few moments ago. They go in easily, from which I deduce that she's no first-timer like me, that this is a regular part of their love-making. I wonder what else is in their repertoire. One thing's for sure: this week is going to be an education for me. A virgin only a couple of days ago, I sense that over the course of the coming week I'm going to be taken to places few people ever visit.

The waves splash around my thighs as Dean continues to move in and out of me and I in turn duplicate his rhythm with Sue. Then, abruptly pulling out of me, he lifts me up with the arm that's still around me, causing my hand to slip out of Sue, and lifts Sue under the other arm. Surging out of the sea with one of us under each arm, he lowers us to the sand.

We are by some rocks at one end of the beach, where it curves around to the lighthouse, and are not on view to those still dining at the restaurants. A ramshackle fishing boat beside us conceals us too. Sue and I are looking up at Dean. It's clear that he's in charge this time and we await his instructions or directions.

He looks at Sue, nods, and she knows from that simple gesture what he wants. Lying back on the sand, legs open, she reaches over and pulls me back down against her. I feel her boobs against my back, the wetness of her snatch against the very tip of my tail bone. She has her arms round me, one hand playing with one of my nipples, the other fingering my clit. Already I feel so hot I could come.

But Dean is kneeling between my legs, fist around his prick, jerking it backwards and forwards towards my cunt. I let out a moan of frustration; I need him inside me now, and with one hand I try to reach for him. But with Sue pinning me back against her, it's impossible to reach. I have to wait, wait until he is ready to bestow his gorgeous dick on me again. My mouth is dry with anticipation.

He lowers himself, and I close my eyes, but when his skin touches me it's not his prick but the swell of flesh and bone above it, and I realise with wonderment that it's Sue he's entered beneath me. Her body goes rigid against my back, and her grip tightens on my breast. Despite my weight on her – Dean is supported on his arms above us – she arches her back. I press my clit into her fingers and despite her rapture she responds immediately with increased pressure from them, then a frenzied side-to-side motion. I feel the tide swell inside her, and I know that though she's struggling to fend it off, it's proving irresistible. This time it's her excitement that goads me and, as I feel her lose it beneath me, I too start to come, legs spread as wide as can be. Unable, inevitably, to hold back given that two women are screaming their heads off in orgasm beneath him, Dean yields too, face tautening in a grimace as his hips twitch and he spills his seed inside his girlfriend.

We all collapse on the sand, laughing. 'Fuck me,' says Dean, and Sue says, 'We just have, haven't we?'

'I think you'll find it was me fucking you,' he says. 'But anyway, who cares? Coming together takes on a whole new dimension when three of us manage it, don't you think?'

I can barely speak, I'm so overcome. For a few minutes I just lie there, panting, and then I sit up, my back to them, and look out over the sea. The moon has moved across the sky and the sea looks like a magical silver carpet which might take off and carry you away into the sky. For a moment, thinking these thoughts, I feel a sort of grief, and my first pang of homesickness too. It comes from nowhere, or seems to.

'Come on, Nadia,' I hear Sue say. Her voice is strident, an imposition in the quiet of the night. She's like a schoolteacher, bossy, chiding, and the teenager that I still am, after all, rises up instinctively in rebellion.

'Do you want to come back to the cottage,' comes Dean's voice, softer, as if sensing my feelings, 'or are you staying out here for a while?'

I nod, grateful to him for understanding that I need to be alone. 'I'll catch you up,' I say.

'OK,' he says, bending to touch me lightly on the shoulder. 'We won't lock the door then.'

I continue to gaze out over the water, but before they're long gone I can't help but turn around and watch as they make their way back down the beach, still naked, clothes tucked under their arms. My heart clenches like a fist when I see that they are holding hands. I haven't known them to do that before, and it's a cold hard reminder of the fact that they are a couple, a couple who pre-date me and exist beyond me, without me. Whereas without them, everything that I now have, my whole world, is gone. I fold in on myself, arms around my knees, suddenly chilled. Am I any less lonely than before, despite this attachment? I look back at them, Sue's head is now on Dean's shoulder. I wish I'd never looked. The three-way sex we had seems to have brought them closer, where you might expect it to drive a wedge between them. Dean was, after all, inside me, exploring my most intimate realms. Does that not loosen the bond between them?

I sit out for a long time. I have a strong feeling that the night is not over for Sue and Dean, that they have more in store for each other when they get back to the room, and I don't want to walk in on that, no matter how intimate our bodies have been tonight. The sky is already paling when I finally make up my mind to return, bundling up my clothes in my arms and walking naked along the beach, as they did.

In the room I find them sprawled across the bed, Sue's head on Dean's belly, her hand wrapped around his cock, even in sleep, almost proprietorially. As I climb in one side, claiming the narrow space left for me, I look at them and bring myself to yet another orgasm with my hand. But it's one that leaves a sour taste in my mouth.

Sleep eludes me, despite the advanced stage of the night, and I'm too tired to get up when Dean and Sue do. In the kitchenette I hear them making coffee, but I can't make out anything from the murmur of their talk. Drifting in and out of sleep, I'm beset by visions of the night before, of Dean bearing down on me as he comes inside Sue, as Sue comes beneath me and I come to the pressure of her fingers on my nipple and my clit. It was amazing. So why am I feeling so down?

I sleep some more, and when I wake it's almost as if I can see the steaminess of the heat outside in the air itself, though the fan above my head – Sue or Dean must have switched it on before leaving – is keeping the room surprisingly cool. Still oddly depressed, and no doubt exhausted from what we all did together in the sea, on the sand, I close my eyes and seek sleep again. I'm just drifting off when the door squeaks. I keep my eyes closed but feel my legs part, almost automatically. I bring my hands down and am stunned by my wetness.

Of course, I want it to be Dean: this could be my big chance, the moment I've been waiting for. But I know that in spite of what my head is telling me, in spite of my pique last night at

Sue's bossiness, the juices are not for Dean alone but for his lover too. No matter which one of them it is, I'm ready.

My eyes are closed, deferring the revelation, my throat tight. The bed sheets have been thrown off while I slept – or perhaps Sue or Dean removed them when they switched on the fan, either out of thoughtfulness or to admire my body against my knowledge, or perhaps both – and I am exposed. I part my legs further, allowing whichever one of them it is to see that I am awake and ready for them. The message is received: fingers alight on me, softly as a butterfly might, and then slip inside me, easily, naturally. Equally lightly, the pad of a thumb brushes my clit, gradually growing in speed.

I've unfurled myself over the width of the bed and my head hangs down, my hair trailing to the floor, fully abandoned. I feel a mouth on my breast, teeth on my nipple, and I shout out, not a word but a sort of guttural cry, only half-human even to my own ears. It's as if I've become some primordial being, slave to the body's urges, without reason or the power of speech.

My eyes burst open, and it *is* him. I knew it was, in my heart, in my blood and in my bones. He has a tenderness that Sue doesn't, that butterfly touch. It's unmistakeable, now that I know him. He's kneeling there, prick in his hand, and the way he's holding it, tending it towards me, makes me feel like my birthday's come round early, and I'm receiving a gift that I have longed for for so long, without ever really believing that I'd get it. As he moves towards me I wonder if I'm going to faint. But I don't, and I even act, reaching between my legs and holding myself open for him.

He plunges right inside, as if aware that time isn't on our side, and I wonder exactly where Sue is and how long we've got. I hate to rush, but on the other hand the thrill of having Dean inside me without her watching or being involved is huge, and I know my climax won't be long in coming. I'm wailing beneath him, thrashing my head from side to side, my fingers still pinning back my lips. His smooth balls bash against my perineum and sphincter as he moves in and out of me.

A movement in the doorway stills my head. Sue is standing there, smiling strangely, eyes flashing. It's a smile that's not quite sure of itself but that refuses to go away. I sense that beneath it lies anger: this was not part of the plan.

Still, she's going to make the most of her little discovery. This is not the type of woman not to turn everything to her advantage. She walks towards us, pulling off her bikini bottoms, smile triumphant now. When she's nearly at the bed, she stops, turns, reaches into her rucksack propped against one wall. Then she turns back, climbs onto the bed, and places one hand on Dean's hip. He's still moving in and out of me, only more slowly this time. His eyes are closed.

I stretch my neck and peer around him. Sue is tightening some kind of halter around her hips. As if foretasting what she has in store for him, Dean's jaw flexes, his whole face tenses. He groans heavily, and I know she's parting his cheeks, pressing the tip of the dildo against his arsehole. I didn't see her apply any lube and I guess this can't be the first time.

He plunges hard into me as she thrusts into him, and from this moment on the cadence of his cock in me is an echo of her movements inside him. I feel that she's taken control and, trying to wrest back what limited power I might have had, I grope around and take Dean's balls in my hand, give them a good squeeze. He opens his eyes, smiles at me gratefully, kindly. It's a smile in which I think I read, although this may of course be wishful thinking, an apology. *I tried*, he seems to be saying, *but she wouldn't have it*.

I smile back, keeping one hand furled around his balls but bringing the other to his strong, reassuring jawline. Certain that she can't see what I'm doing from the position she is in behind him, pumping in and out of his arse, I lift my head towards his face. He brings his down for a moment, and we exchange a brief and somehow chaste kiss that speaks of so much more than it is. That speaks of lost hopes and wishes that will never be fulfilled.

Then I close my eyes, let myself be rocked into oblivion by these movements of his that are really her movements, and for a moment I find I can forget that she is there at all, and forget, too, that I will never have Dean to myself.

26

It's at breakfast the next morning that I realise that something is very wrong. There's a woman in the yoga class – Kat, she calls herself, although I suspect her name is really Kate, as in Katherine, and she's truncated it even more to make herself seem more interesting. But her name is irrelevant – it's just something else that annoys me about her, that gives me a clue as to who she really is, or thinks she is.

Kat and Chris exchanged a look this morning, as the session was about to begin, that made me almost certain that something had happened between them. She's fit, this woman, cheery in a nauseatingly wholesome American way, and has a good fifteen years on me. Her skin glows as though she's constantly just finished exercising – or fucking. She has the latest yoga gear, the designer stuff. A pierced nose, a pierced belly button, and a pierced clitoris in all likelihood. I wonder if Chris knows for sure about the latter.

The look, a sizzling one, made me very uneasy, and I wasn't concentrating as much as I ought to have on my postures. Kat had chosen to sit at the back, which I thought was unusual for her – not that I took too much notice of these things, but I seemed to remember she was normally in front of me. In fact, I was sure of it, since in addition to her piercings she had a butterfly tattoo on one of her shoulder blades, and I often used that as a point of focus to stabilise myself during difficult positions, such as one-legged balances.

But this morning, this morning she was at the back and that

made me suspicious too. So whenever Chris walked to the rear of the studio I pretended to do something, such as adjust my hair-tie, which allowed me to turn my head a little and sneak a look at them. It wasn't long before my unease was justified. I heard her ask for help going into shoulder-balance, and when I looked round I saw Chris not only tweak her into place by putting his hand on her hips and adjusting them slightly, but then, so quickly that afterwards I told myself I could have been mistaken, put his hands between her legs and run his fingertips over her pussy in her clingy Lycra bottoms.

I spun my head forwards, in denial, not wanting to admit what I had seen into the realm of possibility. But my intuition was normally strong, and I'd known, from the moment Kat entered the room and electricity flew between them in the form of a glance, that something must have happened between them yesterday.

I think back to last night, to the intimacy of what I thought was our love-making and turns out to have probably been just another fuck for Chris to add to his collection. All that crap about closeness, and taking things slowly to achieve it, when at some point in the day he'd already taken his fill of one of his other students. I wonder when it was: there's no way of knowing, but now I understand, at least, why he never has time for me in daylight hours. Who's to say Kat is the only other one besides me? What about Jasmine, and the other acolyte I overheard him 'instructing' in his room? What about the other students? I stand in front of my mirror, in my room, looking at my naked body, and I resolve to find out.

Most of the other women head to the beach in the afternoons, no further. For all their talk of higher planes of consciousness and spiritual awakenings, they seem more concerned about getting a good all-over tan than experiencing any local culture. Like a row of sardines frying in a pan, they lie naked on the beach, slick with oil, indifferent to the stares – and sometimes more – of the Indian boys who come to stand on the rocks at the end of the bay just to catch a glimpse of them. Indifferent to having their photos taken for the boys' private delectation. Do they have no pride, or cultural sensitivity?

Today I join them, although I know that I won't be terribly welcome, given how I've been with Chris. Now, knowing what I do, I feel a little sheepish, a little stupid. There I was, feeling superior, lording it over them, thinking they were all green with envy, when they were in all likelihood laughing behind my back at my idiocy, my gullibility.

I lie down at one end of the row, beside Marigold, who is one of the oldest of the group. A hippie who never left the 1960s behind, hair hennaed bright red, she is a quiet soul and strikes me as one of the more amenable of the group. She turns her head to look at me as I spread my towel beside her.

'You don't mind, do you?'

'Go right ahead,' she crackles, voice wrecked by too much weed over the course of decades.

'Thanks.' I pause, casting around for a conversational gambit. 'So,' I say at last, 'are you enjoying the classes?'

She nods. 'They're not bad,' she replies.

'But you've had better?'

'Oh yes. I've been doing yoga for thirty years, so I've encountered some of the world's finest teachers in that time, as you can imagine.'

'Of course. But you obviously rate Christopher, to be here on this course.'

She looks at me, one hand shielding her face from the sunlight. 'He's fine,' she says. 'But let's face it, no one's really here for the yoga, are they?'

I eye her nervously. 'Then what are they here for?'

'What are *you* here for?'

'The yoga.'

'And the rest.'

I blush.

'It's all right,' she says, placing one hand on my forearm. 'You don't need to be coy about it.'

'I . . . I didn't come here for that,' I say.

'You didn't? Then you're the exception.'

'You mean . . . ?' I can't finish my sentence.

She nods, eyebrows raised a little in provocation.

'How many?' I say, voice faltering.

She looks round at the line of tanned naked bodies stretching away from her along the sand, and I sit up and peer around her. It's like a line of doll parts. All shapes and sizes are here, a variety of ages. None are unappealing – these women all look after themselves, and all have good firm boobs. Pussies come in different guises – wholly shaven, bushy and proud of it, dyed, pruned into little tufts. From some glint piercings. It's easy to see why Chris can't keep his hands off them. But why take the trouble to keep it a secret from me: that he works his way through them, that he's a sexaholic? Why pretend fidelity when losing me would barely impinge on his sexual intake?

'Pretty much everyone,' says Marigold.

'But when?'

'Afternoons, mainly. Sometimes early evening. He's got a special touch, in class – a signal – that lets you know to turn up at his room. That you've been chosen.'

'But . . . but how does he do it all? I mean, logistically? Time-wise?'

'Two by two, sometimes more,' she says. I think I see a flare of *schadenfreude* in her face as she tells me all this, watching me for my reaction.

'Have . . . have you?'

'Just once,' she says, a little ruefully. 'Me, Daphne and Roberta – we got the summons a few days ago.'

I pull a face. 'The summons'. The same as me, when he tells me at dinner what time I am permitted to visit him later that night. In some ways I suppose I should feel honoured to have him to myself at these times, given what I've just found out. But it's scant consolation that I am, for whatever reason. Knowing that he has a parade of women through his room every day – and that's not even counting his acolytes, whatever he gets up to with them – makes me feel cheap and used.

I rest my head back on the sand and imagine him in his room, cross-legged on his bed, coming out with his spiel about sacred breath and the third eye and god knows what else. It made me laugh, all that spiritual stuff, but part of me wanted to buy into it. And in terms of sex, it did translate into some of the most amazing experiences I've ever had. But now I imagine him doing the same things with all the other students, spouting the same lines about intimacy, and I feel sick.

At dinner, I'm unsurprisingly subdued. The last thing I want is to talk to him. I just want to leave. But of course he can tell something's wrong, and in an apposite moment he approaches and asks me to call by at eleven o'clock, the same as yesterday.

I look at him, as if seeing him properly for the first time. His long lean face has something wolfish to it. 'I'm tired,' I say. 'Can I come earlier?'

'I'm sorry,' he says. 'I have some urgent admin to do.'

'What exactly?' I feel as taken aback by my own cheek as he looks.

'What do you mean?'

'What is it you have to do?'

Thunder steals across his face, and I'm intrigued by this

evidence of a bad temper lurking below the surface. But he immediately recovers himself. 'It's the website,' he says. 'It's not working right and I need to fix it straightaway.'

'OK,' I say, faux breezily. 'I'll just have to last. Did you have a nice afternoon, by the way?'

He frowns. 'Yes, thanks.'

'Why the frown?'

'I don't know. Just – why the sudden interest?'

'Oh nothing. Just showing a polite interest in your life.' I stand up and head for the dessert buffet with my plate, trying to control the feeling of being a kettle about to boil. I have to control myself till later; this is not the place to confront him.

I look back over my shoulder and he's staring at me, a perplexed look on his face. When he catches my glance, he looks away, down at his hands in his lap, and for a moment or two he's lost in thought. Then, seemingly resolute and focused again, he gets up and strides purposefully from the room.

Going back to my room and twiddling my thumbs until 11 p.m. is not an option; I'll go crazy if I do that. I decide instead to go the internet station in the reception area and email Nadia, see how she is getting on, find out where she is and if she has any plans to come back to Goa. Her anger must have died down by now, and even if she hasn't got over Chris, she can stay nearby. She doesn't have to see him.

As I log on, I wonder what is going to happen tonight when I confront Chris with my knowledge of his philandering. I'll rage at him, of course; I'll ask him what the hell he thinks he's playing at. But I'd be a liar if I denied that there is some part of me that thinks I might talk him round. I'm curious to know why I was singled out for special treatment, why I could have him to myself while the others had to share. And our nights together, three in a row, must count for something. Is it too much to let myself hope that he has feelings for me despite his dealings with the others? Feelings that might mean I can persuade him to stop fooling around and commit himself to me.

There are no emails from Nadia and I have a panic feeling when I think that I have no idea where my little girl is, who she's with, what she's doing. Of course, at eighteen she makes her own decisions in life, goes her own way. She's capable of looking after herself. But lately I've sensed a fragility to her, perceived something lost to her – a look in her eyes, a confusion and vulnerability. Nadia, for all her beauty, or perhaps because of her beauty, doesn't yet know who she is. I'm hoping India will help her to find out. I send a short email to her, telling her that I love her and hope all is well, that I'm sorry and that I hope to hear from her soon, and then I read one from Ravi – a practical one about the cats needing to go to the vet – and finally I log off. For a moment I remain seated, unsure what to do with myself. I look at my watch. It's still only nine. And then I can't stop myself – I stand up, head out of the reception and along the corridor that will take me to Chris's room.

I halt outside his room, and immediately I hear a woman's voice inside, two women's voices, and from time to time Chris's too. Like before, it's hard to make out anything that's actually being said, and I realise that they are consciously speaking in hushed tones. I press my ear against the door, hold my breath.

'Hello,' says an amused voice beside me. In all my concentration I hadn't heard anyone approach, and Jasmine is right beside me, clad in a long kaftan-like robe made of such thin fabric that it's plain to see that she has nothing on beneath.

'I –' I stop at once. Any attempt at justification is pointless, there's nothing else I could have been doing but spying.

She smiles, a little archly, smugly. 'You might as well come in,' she says. She reaches past me and gives three little raps on the door. 'Chris won't mind.'

I stand, frozen, terrorised. There's no time to get away now, and Chris will know that I've been eavesdropping, and will despise me for it. There's no chance our affair will withstand this. Although I'm not going to try to flee, I recoil from the door, wondering what I'm going to say.

The door opens, and for a moment Chris does look a little stunned to see me there with Jasmine. Then his face relaxes into a restrained smile and he pulls the door back further. 'Well, you might as well both come in,' he says.

Jasmine's hand on the small of my back urges me into the room ahead of her. Chris still stands with one hand on the door, beckoning us in and waiting to close it after us. I avoid his gaze as I walk past him, and I almost flinch when I feel his hand on my arm, gentle, trying to reassure me. My breath catches in my throat when I see the two women on his bed, each of them secured, with bound wrists, to one of Chris's bedposts.

I turn, ready to plead with Jasmine to let me go, but already she has pulled up her kaftan and is strutting naked across the room. She has the most beautiful body I've ever seen: pale as milk, with creamy-beige nipples, everything in perfect proportion. Clambering onto and over the bed, she places her face between one of the women's legs. I hear deep sighs escaping from the woman in question and, as she starts writhing on the bed, pulling Jasmine's face into her, ever closer, ever harder, her shoulders turn and I catch sight of the telltale butterfly tattoo. It's Kat. I can't see who the other woman is, though I hear her cry out too as Jasmine reaches out, her mouth still on Kat's pussy, and slips her fingers inside her.

I spin around, straight into Chris's waiting arms. 'You're not thinking of going, are you?' he says, and I burst into tears. He pulls me in closer. 'Don't cry,' he says, running one hand over my hair. 'I hate to see you cry.' He catches my tears on his thumb, brings it to his lips. 'This is supposed to be a joyful time,' he says. 'We are here to share joy.'

'Joy,' I almost spit, pulling back from him. 'I...I...you let me bloody well fall in love with you, and then I find out you're shagging just about all of your students. That this –' I wave my arm back at the three women making out on his bed '– is how you live.' I ball my fists up, start pummelling his chest. 'You dirty, dirty fucker. How do you think I feel?'

I'm crying again now, but he stops trying to quench my tears, steps back from me, arms raised. 'Whoa,' he says. 'Take a deep breath and calm down, Val. We never once talked about love, about this being an exclusive thing.'

'No, but all that crap about intimacy, building trust, taking things slow. You...you misled me. You're just a sex maniac who can't keep his hands off anybody.'

He smiles, and again I see the wolf in him. 'Why should I?' he says. 'Why should I resist all the lovely creatures who parade themselves in front of me everyday? Who present themselves to me? Why deny myself all the pleasure that is offered to me on a plate? That would be like turning away a plate of lush tropical fruits, ripe and ready to eat. What a waste that would be. All that trouble and effort they took to grow, only to be rejected.'

'But what about love, commitment?'

He shrugs. 'Commitment to earthly things is a no-no for us,' he says. 'That's what the meditation is all about – loosening oneself from the here and now, renouncing all the bonds that tie us to the Earth and to earthly pleasures.' He makes a tsk-tsking sound. 'Haven't you learnt that by now?'

I point at the women on the bed. 'And are they not earthly pleasures?' I say. 'You're full of shit, Chris. You're a walking mass of contradictions.'

He shrugs, sits back on the chaise-longue behind him. 'Maybe so,' he says. 'I am only human. But let me just say this, Val – don't knock something till you've tried it.'

'What do you mean?'

He jerks his head over towards the bed but doesn't say anything. I look at the women, at Jasmine's beautiful bare rump raised in the air, pink and proud.

'Sex is sacred,' I hear Chris murmur, his voice hypnotically slow and low.

'You don't mean for me ...'

I turn back to find him naked now on the chaise-longue, cock in his fist, massaging it slowly with one oily hand. He looks at me intently, then back at it. 'The lingam,' he says, 'or wand of light is an instrument of energy and pleasure. And as such it is my duty to fulfil its honourable destiny.'

'But why not just give pleasure to me? Why do you have to sleep around?' I realise that I've stepped closer to him, as if his cock is exerting some kind of force over me. I don't take my eyes off it. The knowledge of the pleasure that it has given me so far is causing me to froth between my legs. I step closer, let myself fall to my knees. He is right: his cock is a holy thing, and as such it must be worshipped. I place my hand over his own, assume the rhythm he has set up – slow, measured. I put my other hand beneath his cock, to where some of the oil has pooled, and begin rubbing his balls and perineum.

Chris places his free hand on my head, puts his own head back as if in surrender. The sounds that escape from him are echoed by those of the women on the bed, and I look over and see that all eyes are on us. Jasmine, who is sitting up now, loosens the ties and Kat and the other woman, who turns out to be her room-mate Dionne, rise. After studying us for a minute, Kat rolls over and climbs on top of Dionne. She begins kissing her deeply, all the while mashing her groin into hers. For a moment Jasmine watches them, smiling, her hand running up and down Kat's leg. Then she looks back at us, lets her hand drop between her legs and, opening them wide, starts bringing herself off on the edge of the bed, eyes still trained on us.

I'm caught in her gaze, a rabbit in her headlights. I feel exposed, and yet I find that a curiously pleasant sensation. Realising suddenly, however, that I'm the only one who's still clothed in the room, I let go of Chris for a moment, letting him continue to massage his sacred lingam, and strip off. My nakedness spurs me on. These girls are beautiful, I realise, but I am too, otherwise why would Chris have fucked me in the first place? I may exceed them in years but I can still hold my own.

Jasmine stands up, fingers still moving up and down between her lips, and walks towards us, slowly, resolutely. 'Look into her eyes,' she says in a commanding voice, and Chris opens his eyes as if awaking from a dream and does as she says. He lets goes of his cock and I take it in my hand, continue the slow but firm massage. I meet his gaze and I feel all anger, all resentment burn away like smoke. Perhaps he's right, I tell myself: why try to hold onto things, when everything, ultimately, turns to dust? Why not embrace change, surrender to the chaos of the universe instead of trying to impose order?

Jasmine is kneeling beside me now and I feel the soft skin of her upper arm against mine. Reaching out, she places her hand over mine, falling into sync rather than contradicting my momentum, and we continue the massage. Then she lets go, reaches over for the oil and, kneeling before us, begins to massage Chris's chest and nipples, flat belly and thighs. When she's done that, she cups his balls and, coating them with the excess oil, massages them gently, followed by his perineum again.

'The shaft,' she says in a hushed voice, turning her head

slightly to me. 'Concentrate on the base of the lingam now and start to vary the speed and pressure. Squeeze it gently at the bottom, that's right, gently does it.'

Behind us I can hear Kat and Dionne rising to meet their orgasm, welcoming it with strident cries, but I focus on Chris's cock, edging the sounds out of my mind as if it's the only thing that exists in the world right now.

'Pull up now,' says Jasmine, 'and slide your hand right off and then do it with your other hand. That's right, well done. Now do the same again with the right hand, then the left, and carry on alternating.'

She rises to her knees, hangs over Chris and watches his face as I carry on these motions for several minutes. His eyes are closed, his breath almost imperceptible; he seems to have entered a state of relaxation so deep it resembles meditation, perhaps even death. For a moment I am actually afraid. Then Jasmine turns back to me.

'Change the direction,' she instructs me. 'Squeeze the head of the lingam, then slide your hand down and off, still swapping hands.' As I obey her, she explains to me: 'It's said that a lingam massage such as this can cure many ailments. It's a bit like reflexology – some of the nerve endings on the lingam are believed to correspond to points on the rest of the body, and problems there can hence be treated by massage here.' She smiles, showing small white regular teeth. 'See, it's not all about sex. Or should I say, there's a hell of a lot more to sex than most people think.'

As she talks, I notice that Chris's cock is softening then growing hard again, over and over, as if he is riding a wave. Sometimes he seems as if he is approaching orgasm, then he grows flaccid again. The changes don't seem to correspond to exactly what I am doing with my hand, and I know that, despite his profound relaxation, he is using the power of his mind and his breathing to control what is going on between his legs.

'Open your legs wider,' Jasmine whispers, and Chris does as she bids. 'Now,' she says to me, 'I'm going to show you the sacred spot. Here.' She takes my hand and guides it between his legs, to a spot roughly midway between his balls and arsehole. 'You feel that small indentation, about the size of a pea? Push it with your fingertip, ever so gently, while I carry on the lingam massage. When you feel him about to come, push in a little harder. The Taoists call this the Million Dollar Point. It has the same effect as when you stick a finger up a man's arse.'

I look at her, half embarrassed, half grateful that she is sharing this sexual wisdom with me. And more than a little shamefaced that a younger woman than me knows all this. I think of Ravi and all the things we didn't do together. What a waste. If only I had known all this back then, our life would have been so different. Perhaps we might even still be together.

'Beware,' Jasmine is saying. 'Chris, bless him, is used to all this.' Not taking her hand from around his shaft, she leans forwards and caresses his hair. 'Aren't you, honey?' she says to him. His facial expression remains unchanged, as if he is in some kind of trance. 'But if you're doing this to a novice, you have to go very slowly, be very gentle. It can hurt at first. And also, when you're accessing the sacred spot, it can open the man up to very powerful emotions, and even repressed memories. I've had men cry on me.'

'So then you have to stop?' I say.

'Not necessarily. You go with the flow, let yourself be guided by him. You are in a very important position of trust, in one of the most intimate roles that any human being can take on. You're a sort of healer, and healing means letting his emotions run their course. If they feel like crying, or screaming, or if they feel like stopping, you encourage that.'

She pauses. 'He's near,' she says. 'It won't be long now.' She leans over Chris again. 'Breathe deeply,' she says. There's affection in her tone when she speaks to him, genuine affection, and I feel warmth towards her. There's been nothing much in it for her so far; she's devoted herself to Chris's pleasure and also to furthering my knowledge. I'm grateful that she dragged me in here, when all I wanted was to run away and pack my bags.

'He's letting go,' she says. 'He's been on the edge at least six times, so this is guaranteed to blow his mind.' She looks at me. 'Make yourself come too,' she says, 'if you need to. But if you can hold off, watch him, study his face as he climaxes. There are good things in store for you too, if you can just wait a moment. Now, push in a little on the sacred spot.'

She's right. Chris's hips suddenly buck, his face contorts in what looks like agony and he comes with an amazing, almost frightening violence, which is one of the most magnificent things I have ever seen. As he does so, he grabs Jasmine and me by our upper arms and pulls us into him, and as his orgasm dies away we all lie close together, drifting for a while, in what feels like a state of bliss and perhaps even innocence.

I wake with my head still on Chris's chest. Jasmine is stroking my hair; behind her, the two other women are asleep on the bed, arms and legs still entwined from their love-making.

'Thank you,' I say.

'You're not finished yet,' she replies.

'Whatever next?' I say, laughing a little nervously.

Chris opens his eyes, and we all sit up.

'The yoni,' he says. 'The sacred space or temple.' He reaches down between my legs. 'Your beautiful little cunt.'

Jasmine nods approvingly. 'It is lovely,' she says, and I feel an instinctive urge to cover it with my hand. She's shared so much with me tonight, but suddenly her interest in my pussy makes me feel prudish, shy.

As if sensing this, she rises to her feet, crosses the room and seeks out a candle, which she lights. On the way back over to us she stops and turns out the light. Chris and I are still reclining on the chaise-longue, his fingers massaging my pussy lips, his gaze pinning me down. I swoon, open my legs wide, inviting him in, but he keeps up the outside pressure without slipping his fingers inside.

Beside us, Jasmine begins laying cushions on the floor. When she's done, she turns and switches on the CD player, slips a disc inside it. It's some kind of chanting, but very soft, very slow. Then she comes over to us, takes us both by the hand and, urging us to rise, guides us over to the cushions she has arranged. Before letting us sink down to them, she gives us both a long hug, as if we are setting off on an epic journey. For a moment our pussies touch, our breasts press against each other. I have never been so close to a woman before, either physically or mentally.

We lie down, Chris and I: me on my back on the cushions, him on his side beside me. There are two pillows at the end where I am directed to place my head, so that I can see my pussy. Kneeling beside us, Jasmine also places a pillow under my hips and eases my legs apart, bending my knees slightly. For the briefest moment, she pauses, looks at my pussy as if she wants to go down on me, to eat me all up. But she contents herself with a rapid, barely perceptible stroke of my lips before kneeling back and giving me over to Chris.

The latter assumes the lotus position between my legs and, breathing very slowly and deeply, locks his eyes with mine. For several minutes we just gaze into each other's eyes, and I feel again the profound connection for which we strived when we were alone together. Then he places his hands on my belly and begins sweeping them over me, down to my thighs and then back over my breasts. I close my eyes, relinquishing the visual connection. I feel as if I am sinking into a deep, dark, warm space, something akin to a womb, and that I am now alone, although far from lonely. Instead I feel a profound connection with everything around, as though my blood is flowing outwards through all the universe, as if my heartbeat is the engine that keeps everything in it alive.

'The yoni,' I hear Jasmine whisper, and it is as if I am hearing through water. 'Here.'

Oil glugs from a bottle, then Chris's hands make themselves felt on my pussy, massaging first my mound, then my outer lips, softly squeezing the latter between his thumb and finger. I start to get very aroused now, my hands flitting up to my nipples. Jasmine gently pulls them away.

'Breathe,' she soothes. 'Just breathe.'

With infinite slowness, Chris now eases one finger into my pussy and begins massaging me inside, moving upwards and downwards and from side to side, constantly varying the speed and pressure, and the depth. After a few minutes I feel him crook his finger backwards towards his palm and know he is looking for my G-spot. I've read about it in magazines, over the years – in *Cosmo* and such like – but have never known that it really existed. Chris shows me it does. There is a moment almost of pain, resembling an intense need to pee, and then, as he again moves his finger, this time in a circling motion, great waves of pleasure. At the same time I feel Chris's thumb on my clitoris. As he starts moving it up and down, he rests the remainder of this hand on my mound and massages it. With his free hand he begins massaging my breasts.

'Look into his eyes,' whispers Jasmine. I come up and out of the dark warm space and meet Chris's gaze. As soon as I do so, I burst into tears.

'Just hold her,' says Jasmine to Chris, and then to me: 'Don't be afraid. It's normal in yoni massage as in lingam massage to experience violent feelings. Just trust in him. Let him hold you and heal you.'

I am still crying as I come, and I carry on crying as Chris continues to massage my sacred spot, my clitoris and my breasts. The orgasms keep coming, each more intense than the last. I feel Jasmine's hands on my shoulders as my whole body spasms, hear her urging, 'Ride the wave, ride the wave,' in a low voice.

When finally I cease coming, both of them remove their hands and I let my head fall back on the cushion, close my eyes again, wanting to feel the afterglow for as long as possible. Chris still lies on one side of me; Jasmine comes round me and lies on the other side. She places one arm over my belly, snuggles up to me. I feel soothed, for a moment. And then the loneliness kicks in and all I feel is homesick. From out the blue I want to be home.

I open my eyes. Chris is still beside me, but Jasmine has withdrawn her arm and, legs parted, is bringing herself to orgasm on the cushion next to me. Her eyes are trained on my face. When she sees me looking, she brings her face towards me as if to kiss me. I turn my head away, then I quickly stand up. For a moment I feel so spent and used up that I consider just lying down beside Kat and Dionne on the bed, letting myself sleep awhile. But I fear what will happen when I wake up, or even before I wake up. Fear that I won't be able to say no, even though all of this is not part of me, not what I want. Not that I haven't had an amazing experience, but I want to draw the line here, before I get in too deep.

I gather my clothes together, dress and leave the room.

* * *

The week is coming to an end and it's decision time for me: do I stay or do I go? I know in advance that Chris will not consent to giving up the way of life he has created for himself here, but despite my twinge of homesickness, in the cold light of day, away from Jasmine and Kat and Dionne, I wonder if I can live without him. My life before him seems so arid, so devoid of meaning and of meaningful pleasure. He has taught me so much. So I have to decide if I am willing to live with him as he is, even though it will make me miserable. Perhaps a degree of misery is the price to pay for having been enlightened, for being with somebody interesting. Who knows?

I lie on my bed. I know, in my heart, that I can't live the kind of life Chris would expect me to here, tolerating the endless procession of women through his room, even if sometimes he shared them with me – or let them share me with him, or himself with me. That's not what I want, however grateful I am to Jasmine for passing on her not-inconsiderable wisdom to me. I want Chris and Chris alone. I'll never have that, so I must leave.

I eye my case in the corner. I feel a kind of paralysis, can't seem to bring myself to get up and start packing. And anyway, where would I go? I've no idea where Nadia is. I've no desire to go anywhere particular, see anything specific. None of it would mean anything without her or without Chris.

I close my eyes, pull the cover up over me. I'll decide another time. I'll give him another week. Who knows? Perhaps he won't want any of the women booked on the course next week. Perhaps he'll realise that he's in love with me and change his ways. Perhaps he'll even renounce Jasmine, renounce his role as a guru and understand that sharing pleasure with one person can be enough. Yes, that's it, I'll give him another week, see how I feel and how he feels then. I won't give up hope.

27

I kept a diary this past week, the week I have come to call 'the week from hell', the week when I thought I was losing my soul. Having realised that Sue would never leave me and Dean alone together again, that she was afraid of what might happen, I should have left immediately. But at that point I guess I was still mistaken about their motivations. It was only later that I stood on the abyss and, seeing no way out, wondered if it would be easier and ultimately less painful if I just hurled myself in.

Thursday: *Dean up and out early; I wondered if perhaps he was embarrassed about the previous night, about Sue fucking him with a dildo while he fucked me.*

I woke up to Sue's face between my legs. She was tender, to start with. I clutched the back of her head with my hand, pushed myself into her, needily. Her tongue was expert on my clit, circling it, and I felt like I was swooping up and down like a bird. I wasn't long from coming when she reached down and hunted around beside the bed, and before I could stop her she'd strapped on the dildo and was plunging into me doggy-style. She fucked me hard and fast, and I felt like the biggest slut, like filth, as I rubbed my clit and ground myself to an almost painfully intense orgasm, thinking of Dean. Then she fell away from me, wanked herself off on the bed, eyes closed. She got up and showered without even looking at me. I felt like I was being punished, punished for trying to have Dean to myself.

She went to meet him for lunch. I cried off, stayed in the room. To my disgust I found myself sniffing the knickers she'd left lying on the floor, then rubbing them against my clit and making myself come again. I started crying when I was done. I hated her, hated what she'd made of me, hated that I still let her at me despite everything that had happened.

I met them for dinner, but when we went back to the cottage I told them I wanted to read and sat up in the lounge, drinking toddy and feeling sorry for myself. I heard them fucking in the next room and touched myself between my legs and wanted to die.

Friday: Avoided them all day, taking a bus to Trivandrum and having a look at the market there. I bought a few souvenirs I didn't really want, more to take my mind off things than anything else. Having dinner together was unavoidable, though Sue barely acknowledged my presence, and I felt as if I might as well not be there. But when we went for a walk up the beach, she draped an arm around my shoulder, nibbled on it. When we got to one of the abandoned fishing boats that line the end of the beach, she stepped inside it and pulled me towards her. Sitting down on the vaguely intact wooden bench across the middle, she yanked her bikini bottoms to one side and gestured me for to kneel in front of her. In two inches of sea- or rain-water, I don't know which, I grazed my knees against old splintered wood as I licked and bit and fingered her to orgasm. Dean watched, smoking a joint. We walked back to the cottage in silence, and I sat up again, telling them I wasn't tired. When I woke up on the sofa in the morning, nobody said anything about me not coming to bed all night. Sue did mention, however, the possibility of my posing for some photos for her, as we spoke about at Kanha. I told her I'd think about it. The thought no longer turns me on, now that all trust is gone.

* * *

Saturday: *Couldn't help myself – when they went out for a morning swim, before the sun grew too hot, I looked through both their rucksacks. I didn't know what I was looking for, but I had a feeling that there was more to everything that was going on than met the eye. It had stopped being fun. There was a nasty undertone to everything Sue did, even her ostensible love-making. I realised I had overstepped the mark in trying to have Dean to myself, if only for an hour or so, but to be edged out like this, when it was her who invited me in, just didn't seem fair. Especially when I was now prepared to abide by the rules.*

Inside Sue's luggage was a notebook a little like this one. I thought I'd lucked out – that it was a day-by-day journal that would give me the key to her heart, explain her behaviour to me. But only the first page had writing on it, and it was a list without explanation, a list of girls' names: Emily, Sarah, Danuta, Kristina, Sophie, Gina, Sunita. Down the page, each on a new ruled line. As I leafed through the blank pages, a number of photographs fell out. Pictures of Sue and Dean with different girls, self-portraits taken with the camera on a tripod, I guessed. In greater or lesser degrees of undress, everyone mugged for the camera. Looking more closely, however, I noticed what looked like fear, or self-hatred, in some of the girls' eyes.

I replaced the pictures, not wanting to dwell on them, and put the notebook back in the rucksack. It seemed I wasn't the first to become ensnared in Sue's and Dean's web, and with that knowledge came the understanding of why I'd been feeling so cheap and sickened every time something happened between us – all three of us, or just me and Sue. I was a pawn, an interchangeable component in some kind of game between them. A power game perhaps, or perhaps just a game they'd invented to keep themselves interested. Sue, terrified of losing her Greek god of a lover, seemed the most obvious ringleader, sparking his jealousy and possessiveness by messing around with girls.

I recalled the girl she danced with in the nightclub in Bangalore. I'd thought she was doing it to make me jealous, and I couldn't understand why she felt she needed to do that. Now I understood that it had been Dean to whom she was relaying a message. But it wasn't only about making him jealous. We – by which I mean me and the other girls in the photos – also served as offerings to Dean, little titbits to keep him titillated. But there was only so far we were allowed to go with him, for fear that he would prefer one of us to her.

I stood in the bedroom, thinking all this through, thinking about Dean and feeling sad that I would have to leave him. He was clearly complicit in all this; Sue couldn't force him to live the way they did if he didn't consent to it in some way. And I reasoned that he must get a lot out of it – he'd be a fool to turn down the chance of fucking both his girlfriend and an endless parade of cute chicks who she lures into their trap. But I remembered the apology in his eyes, the chaste kiss, as he'd fucked me while being fucked from behind by Sue. It had seemed genuine and I suspected that part of him rebelled against what they did to people.

Whatever – it seemed clear that I must leave. The situation was undesirable and, although I'd never forget them and what they'd taught me, it was time to put an end to things. I resolved to do it after a good night's sleep.

Now it's Sunday and, appropriately enough for the holy day, I find that miracles do happen – Sue has actually left us alone, Dean and me. Not really alone, but alone enough to talk. She's gone to take some pictures on the shore, leaving us in one of the beachfront cafés, sharing some poppadums over a beer.

Remembering Dean's apologetic eyes, I decide to forewarn him of the announcement I am soon to make.

He looks genuinely disappointed, if not wholly surprised.

'You must have noticed how unhappy I've been,' I say, 'these last few days. This is just not me at all.'

Looking out at the beach on which Sue roams, he reaches for my hand under the table. 'Stay,' he says. 'Even if it's for just one more night.'

'One more night to fall even more in love with you,' I say. 'One more night to realise all the more completely that I'll never have you.'

'You'll have me,' he replies.

'What do you mean?'

'I'll sort it out.'

I look into his eyes, those eyes that I wanted to wake up to every morning, and I don't believe him. Which isn't to say that I think he's a liar. I think he believes it himself, that he can engineer the situation. Whereas I don't – I think Sue is far too clever and cunning for that. But in any case, tempting though the prospect is, what good would it do? I'd sleep with him once, and no matter how good it is, I'd never do it again. Not unless he fell in love with me and left Sue ...

'How long have you guys been together?' I ask, remembering how little I know about them.

He sighs, sits back and lights a cigarette. Then he returns his gaze to the beach. 'Forever,' he says as he exhales his first mouthful of smoke. 'Forever and a day.'

'You speak as if it's a prison sentence,' I venture.

His eyes are still on the beach. 'If it is, then it's one in which I acquiesced,' he says slowly. 'In which I still acquiesce.'

'You're her puppet,' I say gently. 'Does it really make you happy? I know all the fucking, all the other girls – it must be great. But ...'

He shrugs. 'To be honest, I don't need all that,' he says. 'I'd stay with her even if it wasn't for that. No, it's Sue who needs it all. She just doesn't realise.'

'So you go along with it for her sake?'

He nods. 'I love her. What can I do?'

I stand up. 'I'm going for a walk,' I say. As I descend the steps to the beach and march away in the opposite direction to where Sue is, I swear under my breath. Things are far, far worse than I imagined, and so much more complicated. I'm an idiot not to have seen how they were using me. And in spite of Dean's apology, I now see him to be as guilty as Sue, or perhaps even more so. She, it seems, is at least acting on her own desires, acting out her fantasies, realising some kind of need. He is only going along with her so he doesn't lose her, and that's cowardice. He should put his foot down, tell her to stop playing mind games with innocent bystanders.

Before I know it I'm around the headland and onto the next beach, where few tourists stray – it's rocky and uninviting. I pace up and down for a while, but there's nothing really to think about – it's over. I just need to tell Sue that, unless Dean does me a favour and gets there first. I don't imagine she'll be happy, but judging by the photos I can't imagine it will be long before they find another sacrificial victim to lay on the altar of their warped relationship.

I sit down on a rock and lose myself in the sight of the sea. Ancient yet changing every minute, it offers me a lesson in perspective. My problems are so silly, I realise; it's not as if I'm losing someone in my family or have discovered I have a terminal illness.

As I'm standing up to leave, a figure appears by the rock, and a hand is extended to help me down. I take it gratefully. It's a fisherman, and I trust in his friendly open face that he means me only good.

'Thank you,' I say as I reach terra firma again. 'That's very kind.'

'No problem, madam,' he says.

'A good catch today?' I ask.

'Not bad. Not bad.' He grins, and I see that several of his teeth are missing. I look back out at the sea.

'Do you see many dolphins when you go out?'

'Sure, every day. There are many colonies here.'

'Would you take me out to see some one day? I'll pay you, of course.'

'I take you out now, if you like.'

'I'd love that.'

The sun is setting when I get back to the cottage, refreshed from watching dolphins play alongside our boat, as well as from talking to someone sane. Communing with nature has cleared my head and I'm resolved to pack and leave now, without discussion and also without recriminations. I'd intended to have a go at Sue and Dean, to tell them how unfair it is to fuck with people's lives. But I know now that that will do no good; that nothing will change them. And so I'll simply walk away.

I won't go far, not least because Ajay, my new fisherman friend, has invited me to his house tomorrow evening, to meet his children – all seven of them. I'm flattered to be considered worthy of such an invitation, and intrigued at getting this chance to see at first-hand the home life of a Keralan family. So I will find my own cottage nearby, and stay for at least a few days more. In the meantime, I'll email Mum and apologise. I feel terrible about the things I said to her, the way I behaved. After all, what did I know about Chris and his feelings for her? For all I know, they're very happy together. And even if he's not squeaky clean, as I suspected, then that's fine too. She has to make her own mistakes.

I open the cottage door. Sue and Dean look up at me from the sofa. They're naked; Sue is kneeling with her buttocks up in the air and, while Dean fucks her in the arse, she's plunging a dildo between her legs. She smiles, gives me a come-hither look. For a moment I'm tempted, I'm sorely tempted. Watching their bodies thrill to each other turns me on more than I like to admit. But I remind myself of what's at stake, of how they have used me. I don't – I can't – regret having met them, for they have helped me to find myself. I'm scared, however, of getting snared once more in their net, in thrall to the sex, and I shake my head at Sue and head for the bedroom to pack.

28

Nadia's email comes at just the right time, at the height of my despair and self-loathing, when I'm desperate to break away from Chris but can't find a way. I fear I've become sexually dependent on him, can't imagine ever finding a man who can satisfy me in the way he does. The thought frightens me more than staying here and being unhappy does.

Responding to mine, she too apologises for the row, tells me she hopes things are working out for me in Goa. I bite my lip, frown at the screen. 'Things are not working out at all,' I mutter. Then I realise the idiocy of talking to myself and go back to my room and call her from my mobile.

'Mum!' She sounds thrilled to hear from me, and I'm over-whelmed with love at the sound of her voice.

'Where are you?' I ask.

'In Kerala. Kovalam Beach.'

'Is it nice?'

'It's gorgeous. I've ... oh, it's a long story. But I'm renting a cottage. I've made a friend, a fisherman who took me out to see dolphins. It was amazing.'

'A friend, or more than that?'

'Oh no, it's not like that. Ajay is way too old for me. He's just ... he's so nice. A widower. I'm going for dinner at his house tonight, to meet his kids.'

I must sigh then, for she stops, then asks, 'Mum, are you all right?'

'I . . . I . . . not really. No, I'm not all right.'

'What's happened? Is it Christopher?'

'Oh, Nadia, you were right about him all along. He is a philanderer, and worse – he dresses it all up as some kind of philosophical-stroke-spiritual quest. I . . . I thought if I gave him another week, things might improve, but . . .'

'Why don't you leave him?'

'It's not that easy.' I can't tell her that I feel psychologically trapped by Chris because I can't picture anyone ever satisfying me physically the way he does. Can't tell her I feel like a sex junkie, always going back for more. The highs are too high, the lows too low. I'm paying too high a price, yet I can't seem to break free of the cycle.

'Why not?'

'I . . . I didn't know where you are.'

'Well, you do now. Come to Trivandrum and I'll pick you up from there. Just make sure to charge your mobile, and if you or I are out of signal, find a public phone and call the Hermit Crab Café and leave a message for me there.'

There's nothing I can say to that, and in a way I'm grateful to her for being so bossy. However, part of me still fears what will happen to me if I leave Chris.

'I'll come for a few days,' I say.

She sighs. 'I thought you just said it wasn't getting any better, that he's still shagging around.'

'But . . .'

'OK, have it your way. Come for a few days and then see how you feel. It's your life.' She gives me directions to the cottage should there be some problem in getting in touch, then we hang up. For a moment I sit in the encroaching darkness of my room, wondering if I can go through with this. Then I give myself a metaphorical kick up the arse and start packing my things. When I'm done, I write a brief note to Chris that I will leave in reception on the way out. It's truthful enough: it says that I've gone to visit Nadia and will call to let him know when I'll be back. 'Thanks,' it ends, 'for everything.'

29

I'm sitting in Ajay's house, which is little more than a shack in a clearing in the midst of coconut palms. There are only three rooms, with floors of beaten earth, into which this family of nine – Ajay, his seven kids and his aged mother – cram. The latter sits in one corner all night, shaking and muttering in her rocking chair. I don't ask what her affliction is, assume Alzheimer's. Nor do I ask which illness claimed the mother of these children. If Ajay wants to tell me at any time, he will.

The children seem to range in age from about three to eighteen; the oldest, I learn upon arriving, is Hari, a beautiful ebony-skinned boy with a frank gaze reminiscent of his father's, but also a certain feminity to him that charms me. At first I see tantalisingly little of him; it's Hari, mainly, who cooks, as his dad introduces the other members of the family and proudly takes me outside to show me how even the youngest are capable of shinning the tallest coconut palms to shake loose the fruit. Before we eat, one of the oldest boys is even persuaded to sing for us, and I sit enraptured as sweet notes pour out of him. I don't understand the words, but it sounds like some kind of prayer, or a thanksgiving, and while he sings I find myself saying a little thank you to the powers that be that I have escaped Sue and Dean. Looking around at this contented little family makes me realise what I want in life, and it's not what Sue and Dean were offering me.

Hari comes in to lay the table with countless little metal dishes loaded with curries and *dhal*, with pancakes and pickles and *avial*. I watch him; he's confident, used to bearing the responsibility for his siblings while his dad earns a living out on the sea. His matter-of-fact assurance endears me to him just as much as his good looks. I'm not broody – far from it – but I know he'll make a wonderful father and for some reason that thought turns me on.

The one area where Hari seems not to be so sure of himself, in fact, is in regard to me. He keeps shooting me glances across the table, tentative smiles, but he never addresses me directly except when I ask him specific questions about the dishes he's served. And even then his answers are perfunctory, modest. At first I think he's just not interested in me, but before the meal is out I begin to entertain hopes that he might be attracted to me as I am to him.

Walking back along the beach, I think about Hari, and then I think about Ajay. He'd be perfect, I think, for Mum, and I resolve to introduce them when she arrives. Perhaps a little bit of matchmaking is exactly what is needed to stop her returning to Goa and falling back under Christopher's spell.

The following morning, not knowing how long Mum is going to take to get here – unsure whether she will be able to fly or will be catching the train – I take a stroll up to Ajay's shack to thank him again for the meal. If I'm truthful, I'm hoping I might also see Hari again while I'm there. I've been thinking a lot about him since last night.

Hari's not there, alas, and I'm shocked to find Ajay sitting alone at his kitchen table, head in his hands. 'What's wrong?' I ask from the open doorway. From behind me I hear kids playing and giggling in the coconut grove.

He glances up, cheeks wet with tears, and I rush to him and place my hands on his shoulders, kneeling beside him.

'Ajay, what's happened?'

He tells me, in faltering English, that he's just found out that planning permission has gone through for two five-star hotels in the immediate vicinity and that the family stands to lose their home. Not only that, but local water shortages will be exacerbated, threatening the south Keralan ecology as a whole.

I sit and listen to him talk, ashamed more than ever before to be a tourist, unsure what to say to make him feel better. I feel disgusted but impotent, unable to reassure him that things will be OK, because I know they won't. I know that the forces of global capitalism will win out, and that stands by individual travellers will have little impact.

When he's calmed down, I tell him about my mum's visit and ask him if we can come to see him. He's flatttered to be asked and agrees. Then I head off back to my cottage.

As I'm halfway back along the beach, I hear a voice behind me. I turn and am surprised to see Hari there, the sun flashing in his eyes.

'Have you heard the news?' he says, and there's a furious edge to his voice. Anger has driven away all traces of shyness.

'I'm so sorry,' I say. 'I tried to console your dad, but it's difficult, knowing there's no hope.'

'Who says there's no hope?' He's combative now, and so sexy with it, I feel faint. I'm just about to start my spiel about market capitalism and tourism's insatiable growth when he halts me with an authoritative motion of his hand, which only serves to heighten my ardour.

'I'm actually on my way to Kochi now,' he says, 'to meet some people about getting a petition going about the development.' He pauses, scrutinises my face. His own is alive with passion and righteousness and, although it doesn't have the

Greek god perfection of Dean's, I think to myself that it's the most beautiful face I have ever seen – both boyish and a little womanly at the same time. It's all I can do to stop myself from reaching out and placing my palms on his satinesque cheeks.

'I'm taking the backwaters,' he says. 'Borrowing a friend's father's motorboat. Would you like to come? It's very – what's the word – picturesome?'

'Picturesque. Yes, I've heard about the backwaters. I'd love to come, if you're sure I won't be in the way.'

An hour later, we're chugging up part of the network of rivers, lagoons, canals and lakes that lie just within Kerala's coastline. Although we're not moving as slowly as the boats punted by long bamboo poles, we're hardly speeding along, and I trail my hand in the water and surrender to the slow passage of time, admiring the surroundings – tall palms reflected in the water, cantilevered fishing nets, small settlements on skinny spits of land reclaimed from the water, with tiny vegetable plots. I watch as cashew nuts are loaded onto boats, as shellfish are dredged by hand, and as people tend to their pigs, cows, chickens and ducks. Occasionally we pass a group of children and, when they see a Westerner, they wave and shout, 'Pen, missus, pen, missus.' I feel guilty; if I'd have known, I'd have brought a whole stash of writing implements. It's so refreshing that it's those they are calling for and not money.

The journey takes hours, but Hari has already warned me that we will have to stay overnight in Kochi, and in fact I'm pleased that I will have some time to explore the former spice trading port and Portuguese capital of India. Of course, I'm hoping that Hari and his friends might let me be involved in their petition meeting – not that I think I can be of any help, but it's a unique opportunity to see the whole issue from the insiders' perspective. If they don't want me around, however, I won't take offence.

Mid-afternoon, Hari steers the boat to a shady spot on one of the banks and removes three or four little foil containers from his rucksack – a late lunch, leftovers from last night. We sit and eat, and he tells me a little more about his concerns for the Kerala coastline in the wake of five-star tourism. His family will have to move, he says. It's an upheaval but not a tragedy. What he fears most is the impact of luxury tourism on the local environment.

I want to help him, I think, watching his lovely animated face as he talks. But I also just plain want him. The two are intertwined. I feel myself falling in love with him for his ardour, for his morals, which are part of who he is. Chris, for all his talk, turned out to be phoney, from what Mum said. Hari is the real deal.

Feeling brave, I make up my mind to declare myself. What's there to lose? I'm sick of dissembling, of play-acting, of slippery things lurking below the surface. I want nothing but honesty with Hari. It's what someone like him deserves. But before I can say anything, I realise he's stopped talking and is staring at me.

'What? What is it?' I say, worried.

He smiles, a smile made up at least partly of sadness. 'You're so beautiful,' he says.

'Then why do you look so upset?'

'I'm not upset. I would just like to hold this moment forever. Look at your lovely face for the rest of my life.'

'I was just thinking the same about you.'

He leans forwards slowly, places his hand on my by now deeply tanned thigh. Our eyes are fast on each other. His are questioning, but I know that they already know the answer. His hand moves further up, and I slide myself beneath him, tugging at the zip on my shorts. I know this is moving fast, that I risk losing the romance to my need, but on the other hand it feels so right. It feels as if Hari is my missing piece and I must have him inside me in order to be complete.

He hangs over me for a minute, embracing first my mouth, then peppering my neck and cleavage with light little kisses that have me moaning with longing.

When I've pushed my shorts down with my hands and shrugged them down over my knees and off, I wrap my legs around his waist. I wasn't wearing any knickers and my snatch presses against his lower belly, already wide for him.

He pauses, raises his head from my breasts and looks into my eyes. 'Are you sure?' he asks gently.

I say, 'I've never been more sure of anything in my life.'

At that he slides backwards, so that my legs are looped up over his shoulders and, holding my buttocks up with his hands, brings his face to my cunt. He jabs out his tongue, teases me for a few minutes. It's like a bee darting at a flower, seeking the nectar. I can smell myself and I'm almost cloyingly sweet. I groan. This is what sex should be like. An exploration, a giving.

He lowers my bum to the seat in the middle of the boat, kneels in front of it and, taking his prick in his hand, feeds it into me, but not before I've had chance to angle my head and gasp in awe. It's like a baton of glossy dark wood, neither too large nor too small, sturdy and perfectly proportioned. It almost shines in the sunlight, as does the pool of my pussy. I clutch silken buttocks as he drives into me, cry out. It's like coming home.

He thrusts in and out of me, slowly to start with, and I raise and lower my hips in counterpoint, meeting each of his forays, which seem to get deeper and deeper. Then I wrap my legs around him again, squeeze hard, and my clitoris is crushed against his lower belly, where his pubic hair ends, and I feel the fizzing start – the onset of orgasm. I clench the walls of my cunt, sucking them in as far as I can, feeling that I fit Hari like a glove of flesh. His movements become more irregular as he too begins to lose control. The boat beneath us rocks precariously, beating a ragged pulse against the shore that echoes Hari's movements. His hands are full of my breasts and I feel my nipples harden beneath his palms as I begin to be engulfed by my climax.

'Oh God, Hari,' I hear myself say. 'Oh God.' And indeed it is as if something religious is overcoming me, something mystical. I close my eyes and behind them there is a burning white light as my brain catches fire, sparked off by the explosion inside me. For a moment I go numb, and floppy, but Hari keeps moving within me, slowly, and after a few minutes I am amazed to feel myself on the verge of climax again. I dig my nails into the flesh of his buttocks and he arches up away from me, teeth gritted in his own ecstasy, as I come again.

For a time we just lie there. Then Hari kisses me fully on the mouth and says, 'We have to be going now. It'll be dark soon and I don't have a light.'

'And your friends are waiting for you.'

'Right.'

We travel the rest of the way in near silence, but it's a companionable silence. I sit behind Hari as he steers us through the narrow waterways, watching the muscles of his strong, shapely back shift according to what he is doing, and I think that I trust him wholly with my heart.

Mooring at Kochi, we head straight for Hari's friend Pandit's apartment, where we sit up until late, drinking toddy and talking about the proposed new development and ways of opposing it. I don't contribute much, but I listen intently and think a lot about how I might help the cause.

After a late dinner in a nearby restaurant, we go back to the flat, where Pandit makes up his sofabed for us. Bloated by curry, I don't feel up to making love again, though I want Hari even more than I did earlier; his presence intoxicates me. I compromise by giving him a long slow blow job, looking into his eyes, which glitter in this room lit only by the streetlamps outside. He threads his fingers through my hair as he comes in my mouth, whispers my name as if uttering an invocation to the gods. Afterwards we hold each other for a long time.

At dawn, still sleepless, we creep out and borrow Hari's friend's scooter to take us to the beach. For a while we just walk, talking about our families, and then Hari says he wants to rest so we sit down.

I stare at him in the soft blue light of dawn, and I want to tell him that I love him. But he stops me, just nods, and I know that he knows. We kiss, as if we'll never come apart again. When we do, he lies back against the sand, eyes closed, and my breath catches in my throat at the beauty of his skin, mahogany dark in the moonlight, aglow like a swathe of silk. Pulse throbbing in my ears as if competing with the plash of the waves on the shore, I arch one leg and straddle him. For a moment I look down and survey my prize, already peeling my bikini bottoms down towards my knees, though part of me wants to freeze the moment, to hold onto it for a lifetime. Then he opens his eyes and smiles up at me, and I lose control all over again.

30

I arrive in Kerala without advance warning. I haven't been able to get hold of Nadia on her mobile and I forgot the name of the café that she wanted me to call and leave a message at. But it doesn't matter: I've made quicker time than she'll have anticipated, having found space on a flight from Goa directly to Kochi, and from there I splashed out on a taxi all the way to Kovalam.

Arriving at her cottage, I find that she's not here. That's no problem, I think; I'll just relax and read at a nearby café. Already I'm feeling more relaxed, more myself again. I thought it would be such a wrench to leave Chris, but now that I have, I feel only relief. Pleasure, after all, is transient. What he gave me couldn't be held onto. The pain, however, went on.

Or yes, he did give me something that I could hold onto. He gave me a greater knowledge of my own body and of how to please it, together with a deeper understanding of sex not just as passion and climax but as something that can be drawn out, savoured, experienced at a much deeper level than most people think, than I ever thought possible. These are things that I can use in the future, wherever my future may take me.

I'm reading my book when the café owner strikes up conversation with me and, realising that I'm Nadia's mum, tells me she left for Kochi yesterday, with a local fisherman's son. I'm taken aback, but I remind myself that she wouldn't have expected me so soon.

'Is that Ajay, the fisherman?' I ask.

'Yes,' says the owner.

'You don't happen to know where he lives?'

He nods, fetches a pencil and a scrap of paper and draws me a little map. It's not far away, and when I've finished my *lassi* I pick up my bag and walk along the narrow track that leads there. I'm greeted by a gaggle of incredibly cute chocolate-brown children, who gather round me and ask if I'm really Nadia's mum.

Ajay himself stands in the doorway. Despite his grin full of gaps where teeth have given up the ghost, he's a handsome man, with a roguish twinkle in his eyes.

'Greetings,' he says. 'You must be Val.'

We shake hands and I meet his gaze. There's something between us, I know it at once, but I don't entirely welcome the instant rapport. I'm exhausted by all that has happened – first Charles, then the camel driver and most latterly Chris. The last thing I need is another romantic entanglement. I'm erotically burnt out, and emotionally too.

Ajay confirms that Hari has gone to Kochi on what he describes as 'political matters' and that he has taken Nadia with him. I don't ask if his son is involved with my daughter; I'll find out soon enough. He suggests a boat trip out to see dolphins, to kill time until their return, which he estimates will be later this afternoon or early evening. First, though, he offers to cook me some fish for lunch. He goes inside and I hear him rattling pans. I sit down on the ground, smile, so glad to be here.

31

I arrive back at Kovalam exhausted but happier than I've ever felt in my life. To my surprise, as Hari and I approach the shack, hand in hand, I see Mum sitting outside it with Ajay, chatting and laughing with him as she drinks fresh coconut milk from a shell. She sees us coming and waves merrily, and suddenly I feel a bit sheepish. I'd have preferred to tell her about Hari first, rather than have her catch us unawares like this.

'I arrived super-fast,' she says, standing up to hug me, 'and came to find Ajay. He's been taking good care of me.'

I squint at her in the sunlight, wondering quite what kind of care he's been administering.

Hari lets go of my hand and approaches his dad, and I suggest to Mum that we go for a stroll and leave the men in peace to catch up on what's been discussed in Kochi.

'Sure,' she says, and as we walk towards the beach she tells me about her trip out to see dolphins, and about how she spent the late afternoon getting to know Ajay's kids.

Shading my eyes, I smile wryly. 'It sounds like you two having been getting on like a house on fire,' I say.

She chuckles throatily. 'He's a lovely man,' she says. 'And maybe if it hadn't been for the others – I don't know, maybe I'd have been tempted. In fact, I am tempted. But I've actually decided to go back to the UK early. I have things to sort out. And I don't want to play games with Ajay in the way that people have played games with me.'

'What kind of things?' I say suspiciously, half wondering if she's not actually going to sneak back to Chris rather than head back to the UK.

'Your father,' she says softly.

I stop and turn to her on the sand, mouth open. 'Dad?' I say unnecessarily.

She nods, and she can hardly bring herself to look at me, though there's a joyful radiance to her face I've never seen before.

'I'm not sure a mother should talk to her daughter in this way,' she says, 'but to hell with it. You see, if there's anything I've learnt during this trip, it's how to please myself. I've discovered myself, well, how shall I put it ... discovered myself sexually at last. That all sounds very selfish. But I've realised that learning about how to please oneself is the first step in learning how to please others. And I truly believe that I can use what I have found out about myself – about my body – to bring my relationship with your dad back to life.'

'You're getting back with Dad?'

'I hope so.'

I burst into tears, let myself fall into the arms she holds open for me. 'Oh, Mum,' I say, but I don't know how to go on. I don't need to: she's aware how happy she's made me.

'I'm sorry to leave you in the lurch,' she says. 'I don't want to abandon you here, without a travelling companion, but ...'

'I'm not going anywhere,' I say.

'You're staying here?'

'Yes, with Hari. I love him.'

'Oh.' She looks stunned. 'I mean,' she says when she's recovered herself, 'he seems like a lovely boy, from the two minutes I saw him, and as Ajay's son I can't imagine he'd be anything but. But ... but what will you do here?'

'I'm going to write, become a journalist specialising in

environmental issues in India, particularly Kerala. Raise the world's awareness of the tragedies that are going to unfurl here if the West doesn't change its ways.'

'And you will make a living that way?'

'Yes, and perhaps by also doing some PR work for ecologically friendly hotels and places like that.'

'And you don't think you'll regret not going to uni?'

'I realised as soon as I got to India that I wasn't really into that, that I needed something more solid to believe in. Something to dedicate my life to. And besides, if it all turns out to be a huge mistake, there's nothing to stop me coming back and getting a degree when I'm older.'

'Seems like I'm not the only one who discovered myself in India,' says Mum, stroking my hair.

I look back up the beach, see Ajay and Hari walking towards us. We turn in their direction, set out to meet them. My eyes, as I move over the sand, are full of Hari.

Visit the Black Lace website at
www.black-lace-books.com

LOOK OUT FOR THE ALL-NEW BLACK LACE BOOKS – AVAILABLE NOW!

All books priced £7.99 in the UK. Please note publication dates apply to the UK only. For other territories, please contact your retailer.

MAGIC AND DESIRE
Portia Da Costa, Janine Ashbless, Olivia Knight
ISBN 978 0 352 34183 9

The third Black Lace paranormal novella collection. Three top authors writing three otherwordly short novels of fantasy and sorcery.

Ill Met By Moonlight: Can it be possible that a handsome stranger met by moonlight is a mischievous fairy set out to sample a taste of human love and passion? But what will happen when the magic witching month of May is over? When he loses his human form will he lose his memories of her as well?

The House Of Dust: The king is dead. But the queen cannot grieve until she's had vengeance. Ishara must descend into the Underworld and brave its challenges in order to bring her lover back from the dead.

The Dragon Lord: In the misty marshlands of Navarone, the princess is being married. Her parents desperately hope this will cure her 'problem', which they have fought to keep secret for years. Her 'problem' has always been her tendency to play with fire – she lights fires in the grate with her eyes when no-one is looking and she is lustful in a land of rigid morality.

BLACK ORCHID
Roxanne Carr
ISBN 978 0 352 34188 4

At the Black Orchid Club, adventurous women who yearn for the pleasures of exotic, even kinky sex can quench their desires in discreet and luxurious surroundings. Having tasted the fulfilment of unique and powerful lusts, one such adventurous woman learns what happens when the need for limitless indulgence becomes an addiction.

To be published in June 2008

SOUTHERN SPIRITS
Edie Bingham
ISBN 978 0 352 34180 8

When hot-tempered Federal agent Catalina 'Cat' Montoya is partnered with her former lover Nathan Ames on her first undercover investigation, she is determined not to let feelings get in the way of work. But the investigation into charismatic criminal Jack Wheeler's latest enterprise – Southern Spirits Tours, an exclusive members club on a supposedly haunted luxury train, the Silver Belle – soon envelops her in a passionate love triangle. As she travels through the most haunted areas of the Deep South, where sex mixes with the supernatural, Cat surrenders to the extremes of erotic experience and is finally forced to solve a fifty-year-old murder mystery.

FORBIDDEN FRUIT
Susie Raymond
ISBN 978 0 352 34189 1

The last thing sexy thirty-something Beth expected was to get involved with a
much younger man. But when she finds him spying on her in the dressing room
at work she embarks on an erotic journey with the straining youth, teaching him
and teasing him as she leads him through myriad sensuous exercises at her stylish
modern home. As their lascivious games become more and more intense, Beth soon
begins to realise that she is the one being awakened to a new world of desire – and
that hers is the mind quickly becoming consumed with lust.

To be published in July 2008

JULIET RISING
Cleo Cordell
ISBN 978 0 352 34192 1

Nothing is more important to Reynard than winning the favours of the bright and
wilful Juliet, a pupil at Madame Nicol's exclusive but strict 18th century ladies'
academy. Her captivating beauty tinged with a hint of cruelty soon has Reynard
willing to do anything to win her approval. But Juliet's methods have little effect
on Andreas, the real object of her lustful obsessions. Unable to bend him to her
will, she is forced to watch him lavish his manly talents on her fellow pupils. That is,
until she agrees to change her stuck-up, stubborn ways and become an eager erotic
participant.

AMANDA'S YOUNG MEN
Madeline Moore
ISBN 978 0 352 34191 4

When her husband dies under mysterious circumstances in a by-the-hour motel,
Amanda inherits a chain of shoe shops that bleeds money. But luckily for Amanda,
the staff are bright and beautiful young people, ambitious to succeed and eager
to give her total satisfaction. As she sets out to save the chain, and track down the
woman involved in her husband's death, Amanda also finds time to amuse herself
with lovers – young ones, and lots of them. Heels, hose, and *haute couture* have
always been parts of Amanda's life, but now she's up to her dimples in duplicity,
desire and decadence.

Black Lace Booklist

Information is correct at time of printing. To avoid disappointment, check availability before ordering. Go to www.black-lace-books.com.
All books are priced £7.99 unless another price is given.

BLACK LACE BOOKS WITH A CONTEMPORARY SETTING

- [ ] THE ANGELS' SHARE Maya Hess   ISBN 978 0 352 34043 6
- [ ] ASKING FOR TROUBLE Kristina Lloyd   ISBN 978 0 352 33362 9
- [ ] BLACK LIPSTICK KISSES Monica Belle   ISBN 978 0 352 33885 3   £6.99
- [ ] THE BLUE GUIDE Carrie Williams   ISBN 978 0 352 34132 7
- [ ] THE BOSS Monica Belle   ISBN 978 0 352 34088 7
- [ ] BOUND IN BLUE Monica Belle   ISBN 978 0 352 34012 2
- [ ] CAMPAIGN HEAT Gabrielle Marcola   ISBN 978 0 352 33941 6
- [ ] CAT SCRATCH FEVER Sophie Mouette   ISBN 978 0 352 34021 4
- [ ] CIRCUS EXCITE Nikki Magennis   ISBN 978 0 352 34033 7
- [ ] CLUB CRÈME Primula Bond   ISBN 978 0 352 33907 2   £6.99
- [ ] CONFESSIONAL Judith Roycroft   ISBN 978 0 352 33421 3
- [ ] CONTINUUM Portia Da Costa   ISBN 978 0 352 33120 5
- [ ] DANGEROUS CONSEQUENCES Pamela Rochford   ISBN 978 0 352 33185 4
- [ ] DARK DESIGNS Madelynne Ellis   ISBN 978 0 352 34075 7
- [ ] THE DEVIL INSIDE Portia Da Costa   ISBN 978 0 352 32993 6
- [ ] EQUAL OPPORTUNITIES Mathilde Madden   ISBN 978 0 352 34070 2
- [ ] FIRE AND ICE Laura Hamilton   ISBN 978 0 352 33486 2
- [ ] GONE WILD Maria Eppie   ISBN 978 0 352 33670 5
- [ ] HOTBED Portia Da Costa   ISBN 978 0 352 33614 9
- [ ] IN PURSUIT OF ANNA Natasha Rostova   ISBN 978 0 352 34060 3
- [ ] IN THE FLESH Emma Holly   ISBN 978 0 352 34117 4
- [ ] LEARNING TO LOVE IT Alison Tyler   ISBN 978 0 352 33535 7
- [ ] MAD ABOUT THE BOY Mathilde Madden   ISBN 978 0 352 34001 6
- [ ] MAKE YOU A MAN Anna Clare   ISBN 978 0 352 34006 1
- [ ] MAN HUNT Cathleen Ross   ISBN 978 0 352 33583 8
- [ ] THE MASTER OF SHILDEN Lucinda Carrington   ISBN 978 0 352 33140 3
- [ ] MIXED DOUBLES Zoe le Verdier   ISBN 978 0 352 33312 4   £6.99
- [ ] MIXED SIGNALS Anna Clare   ISBN 978 0 352 33889 1   £6.99
- [ ] MS BEHAVIOUR Mini Lee   ISBN 978 0 352 33962 1

BLACK LACE BOOKS WITH AN HISTORICAL SETTING

BLACK LACE BOOKS WITH A PARANORMAL THEME

- BRIGHT FIRE Maya Hess — ISBN 978 0 352 34104 4
- BURNING BRIGHT Janine Ashbless — ISBN 978 0 352 34085 6
- CRUEL ENCHANTMENT Janine Ashbless — ISBN 978 0 352 33483 1
- FLOOD Anna Clare — ISBN 978 0 352 34094 8
- GOTHIC BLUE Portia Da Costa — ISBN 978 0 352 33075 8
- THE PRIDE Edie Bingham — ISBN 978 0 352 33997 3
- THE SILVER COLLAR Mathilde Madden — ISBN 978 0 352 34141 9
- THE TEN VISIONS Olivia Knight — ISBN 978 0 352 34119 8

BLACK LACE ANTHOLOGIES

- BLACK LACE QUICKIES 1 Various — ISBN 978 0 352 34126 6 — £2.99
- BLACK LACE QUICKIES 2 Various — ISBN 978 0 352 34127 3 — £2.99
- BLACK LACE QUICKIES 3 Various — ISBN 978 0 352 34128 0 — £2.99
- BLACK LACE QUICKIES 4 Various — ISBN 978 0 352 34129 7 — £2.99
- BLACK LACE QUICKIES 5 Various — ISBN 978 0 352 34130 3 — £2.99
- BLACK LACE QUICKIES 6 Various — ISBN 978 0 352 34133 4 — £2.99
- BLACK LACE QUICKIES 7 Various — ISBN 978 0 352 34146 4 — £2.99
- BLACK LACE QUICKIES 8 Various — ISBN 978 0 352 34147 1 — £2.99
- BLACK LACE QUICKIES 9 Various — ISBN 978 0 352 34155 6 — £2.99
- MORE WICKED WORDS Various — ISBN 978 0 352 33487 9 — £6.99
- WICKED WORDS 3 Various — ISBN 978 0 352 33522 7 — £6.99
- WICKED WORDS 4 Various — ISBN 978 0 352 33603 3 — £6.99
- WICKED WORDS 5 Various — ISBN 978 0 352 33642 2 — £6.99
- WICKED WORDS 6 Various — ISBN 978 0 352 33690 3 — £6.99
- WICKED WORDS 7 Various — ISBN 978 0 352 33743 6 — £6.99
- WICKED WORDS 8 Various — ISBN 978 0 352 33787 0 — £6.99
- WICKED WORDS 9 Various — ISBN 978 0 352 33860 0
- WICKED WORDS 10 Various — ISBN 978 0 352 33893 8
- THE BEST OF BLACK LACE 2 Various — ISBN 978 0 352 33718 4
- WICKED WORDS: SEX IN THE OFFICE Various — ISBN 978 0 352 33944 7
- WICKED WORDS: SEX AT THE SPORTS CLUB Various — ISBN 978 0 352 33991 1
- WICKED WORDS: SEX ON HOLIDAY Various — ISBN 978 0 352 33961 4
- WICKED WORDS: SEX IN UNIFORM Various — ISBN 978 0 352 34002 3
- WICKED WORDS: SEX IN THE KITCHEN Various — ISBN 978 0 352 34018 4
- WICKED WORDS: SEX ON THE MOVE Various — ISBN 978 0 352 34034 4
- WICKED WORDS: SEX AND MUSIC Various — ISBN 978 0 352 34061 0

Please send me the books I have ticked above.

Name ....

Address ....

....

....

....

Post Code ....

Send to: Virgin Books Cash Sales, Thames Wharf Studios, Rainville Road, London W6 9HA.

US customers: for prices and details of how to order books for delivery by mail, call 888-330-8477.

Please enclose a cheque or postal order, made payable to Virgin Books Ltd, to the value of the books you have ordered plus postage and packing costs as follows:

UK and BFPO – £1.00 for the first book, 50p for each subsequent book.

Overseas (including Republic of Ireland) – £2.00 for the first book, £1.00 for each subsequent book.

If you would prefer to pay by VISA, ACCESS/MASTERCARD, DINERS CLUB, AMEX or SWITCH, please write your card number and expiry date here: ....

M ....

Signature ....

Please allow up to 28 days for delivery.